BURNING NIGHT

~where the ashes of the past awaken the future~

NIKKI BROADWELL

AIRMID PUBLISHING
TUCSON, ARIZONA

This is a work of fiction. All names, characters, places and ideas presented here are the product of the author's imagination.

ISBN: 978-1-7326173-1-5

All that we see or seem is but a dream within a dream.
~Edgar Allan Poe

PROLOGUE

The truck let out a groan of protest as I inched forward along the loose gravel. The trailer behind lurched and slid sideways, pulling the steering wheel out of my hands. Maybe this 'Burning Night' thing was not such a good idea after all.

A wolf ran in front of my car, yellow eyes meeting mine for a split second before it disappeared into the brush and trees on the other side of the road. By that time I'd slammed on the brakes, tires skidding. I sat there dazed. Whatever telepathic communication had passed between us in that moment was too profound to ignore. It was only when I heard the honk of a horn and an angry voice yelling that I eased the truck to the side of the road.

"What the hell is wrong with you?"

I ignored the red-faced man as an awareness of the mystical floated through my brain. The wolf was a messenger. I was supposed to be here and my appearance at this *burning night* was required. After all, I had driven nearly two thousand miles to witness the longest day of the year and take part in the ceremony known as Burning Night. The travails of my trip slipped away as the message became clear. *This is the turning point.* A second later, the engine sputtered and died.

1

"Collie—where the hell are you?"

My stomach contracted at the sound of Dean's voice. "I'm in here," I called from the bedroom.

"Where's my dinner?" he yelled. He peered around the door to where I sat cross-legged in the dark room, his frown deepening. "What in hell are you doing? Is this some spiritual practice?"

"I...I didn't expect you back this early...usually you..."

His face turned red, anger spreading like a stain from one side to the other. "Usually...I what? You know I like to eat when I get home. What is *wrong* with you lately? And why are you still dressed in your nightgown? God, you look like shit. When did you stop combing your hair? Maybe you need to see a shrink."

He was right about my appearance. I hadn't felt up to combing my hair, taking a shower, or even dressing. I knew enough to recognize the signs of depression. My interest in life was as shallow as the dish I kept under the potted plant that had recently died. There were lots of things wrong with me, but admitting it to this man would not help.

I rose and slipped by him and headed for the kitchen. The

open refrigerator revealed very little in the way of food, but I managed to pull a meal together from the leftover pickings of fried chicken from the night before, adding a small salad. Blessedly I knew that dinner would be consumed in silence and that Dean would leave again, heading to the bar around the corner to drink himself into oblivion.

It hadn't always been like this. I'd thought it was Dean's affairs that had wrecked things for us. But now, after nearly twenty years, the truth had finally dawned, sending me into a tailspin as I realized how much time I'd wasted on a man who had no respect for me and never had. He'd promised to stop drinking and seeking out other women, but both had turned into addictions, his pecker leading him on and his drinking the lamp that showed the way. At forty I was finally ready to be free of him. Any love between us had long since burned out.

I was asleep when he got home, his drunken advances unwelcome. "No woman to pick up at the bar tonight?" I mumbled, regretting the words as soon as they were out of my mouth. Less had caused rages in the past and I had the bruises to prove it.

He didn't answer, his grunts loud in my ear as he held me down and fumbled with his zipper.

"Get off!" I yelled, wriggling out from under his heavy bulk.

I was poised to run for the bathroom, the only door with a lock, but a second later he was face down and snoring.

"Why do you stay?" Mary asked for the zillionth time, a frown marring the perfect porcelain skin of her forehead.

Mary had been my friend long before I met Dean, our paths crossing at the public school during eighth grade. A year later she went off to a private high school, but we still managed to stay friends.

Mary pursed her lips. "I guess I know the answer to that—you have no self-esteem. I told you a year ago I'd pay for a therapist. You need help, Collie. Why won't you listen to me?"

I turned, readjusting the heavy basket of work clothes on my hip ready to be shoved inside the coin operated washer. "You are not paying for me to see a therapist. And besides, they can't tell me anything I don't know."

Mary's eyes flashed. "Like when your husband cheats on you that you shouldn't put up with it? Stuff like that?"

Around me the whirring of washers and dryers filled the small space, hollow-eyed women trying to corral small children as they waited for their laundry to finish. Dean worked for a garage and his clothes always smelled of gas and oil, the dark stains nearly permanent. He'd refused to buy us a washer and dryer so that I could do his laundry in the privacy of my own house. But then again, at least these weekly trips got me out. Even though Mary's home was equipped with every possible modern convenience she often met me here, slumming it so we could catch up.

"I've been thinking about leaving, but how would I support myself? The job market is saturated with low-skilled workers like me. God—how did I get so old?" I tried to laugh, but the realization of my age pressed on my chest, making it hard to breathe for a second. "Why didn't I finish high school? If I had my GED I could have gone to the community college."

"Because that man literally charmed the pants off you, that's why. You could always go now. You're a smart woman. You've read a ton of books on a ton of different subjects. Half the time you know a lot more than I do, and I have a master's degree! If you won't take me up on my offer, get yourself a used copy of a self-help book geared toward women in your situation—god knows there's a lot of them," she added, looking around the Laundromat at the tired faces, some of which sported bruises.

The used copy remark made me feel even smaller than I already did. I was couldn't even afford a book. Most of my reading lately had been free and done on my computer using the kindle app. "I don't have the money for college, and as to self-help books—I've read them," I lied. "Dean didn't want me to work and now I'm too old to get a decent job."

Mary pursed her lips and let out an exasperated sigh. "Why do you let him dictate your choices? If you'd had a job these past years, and put some money aside, you'd be a free agent now. Instead you sit around your crummy house and fix his meals and do his laundry. You don't even have any kids. What kind of a life is that? Just leave him. You can get a job at Starbucks. Staying with Dean is why your self esteem never improves."

"Says the woman who's been happily married for twenty years and has two perfect children to prove it."

Mary scoffed. "I admit I lucked out. But I met Bill in college. If you hadn't met Mr. Charmer when you were too young to know any better your life would have turned out very differently."

"If I hadn't gotten pregnant, you mean. I was lucky he married me after what I was doing at the time. He could have told me he didn't believe the baby was his and walked away."

Mary's eyes clouded. "I have to admit he did the decent thing."

I thought about the accidental pregnancy, the miscarriage at nearly five months, and my utter depression that lasted nearly a year. By that time we'd married, and I thought Dean was the love of my life. That's what getting married at age nineteen will do for you. He *was* caring and loving during that terrible year, and even skipped work once in a while to keep me company. The loss of the baby had hit him hard too. But that was then.

Marrying him was what got me out of the stripping business.

But just recently I'd discovered that while I was recovering he kept going to the strip club. I hadn't known it because I drugged myself every night in order to get to sleep. "Dean was messing around right after I lost the baby," I whispered.

"Did you just figure that out?"

"You knew and you didn't say?"

Mary looked away. "I thought he'd get back into the marriage once you got over your grief. You were pretty unapproachable for a long time."

"So because we weren't having sex he's excused for seeking other partners?"

She blanched. "I didn't say that, but you have to admit that men are different than women in that regard. As I remember you walled yourself off. He probably needed comforting too."

I let out a huff and watched the clothes spinning as I scanned backward through the years. Maybe Mary was right—Dean needed a woman and I wasn't there for him. It was my fault he looked elsewhere back then, and probably my fault that he was looking elsewhere now. I hadn't exactly been a model wife, especially in the bedroom. I couldn't remember the last time we'd had sex.

"Bill went to the strip club recently—the one where you used to work? He told me he saw Dean with one of the gals."

I turned from the washing machine. "Which one?"

"How do I know? Anyone you once knew is long gone now—they're too old."

Which meant I was too old too. I thought about the years since my last stripping job and how I'd let myself go. I hadn't exercised, hadn't even walked much. Instead I'd holed up here feeling sorry for myself. No wonder Dean treated me the way he did. "And why was your faithful husband at a strip club?"

She pushed her shoulder-length blonde hair behind her ears. "He was doing undercover work for a client."

Bill was a private investigator with a law degree—in high demand and very well paid. Mary had never worked a day in her life. My mind drifted to one of the times I'd visited her parents' house with its Olympic size swimming pool and uniformed maids scurrying about. Her mother sat like a porcelain doll on the veranda smoking a cigarette with a drink on the table next to her. "What are you two gals up to?" she'd asked in dulcet tones when she happened to glance our way.

"Just heading up to my room to do homework," Mary told her. In

truth we were headed into the woods behind her house to smoke some dope she'd managed to snag from one of her many boyfriends.

"How did you find out about Dean's more recent extramarital activities?" Mary continued, lowering her voice as a woman came close to heave a bunch of nasty smelling sheets and towels into a washer.

"His Facebook friends and a box I found while I was cleaning out the garage. He saves love letters. And it's pretty clear when he comes home smelling like perfume."

"Have you said anything?"

"I can't, Mary. For one thing he'd fly into a rage, and for another it's my own fault. If I ever let him touch me he'd probably stay home."

Mary pursed her lips. "A normal married couple would seek help. But instead you say nothing and he continues with his obnoxious behavior. You really drive me crazy, Collie."

I frowned at her. "He's never really never respected me. I'm sure it's because when he met me I was stripping—what normal man would respect a woman who takes off her clothes for a living? I don't respect myself. I stripped because it was the easiest way to make quick money. You remember my family life. Half the time Dad was too ill to work and the other half he was getting fired." Dark times. "I didn't inherit money like you did," I muttered.

Mary's mauve lips pressed together in annoyance. "Why do you have to bring that up? It's not like I could help it. Yes, I had a happy childhood, yes my parents provided for me. I'm sorry your Mom died when you were thirteen and I'm sorry your Dad was an alcoholic. But you made your own choices. You could have finished high school and gone to college."

"If I'd taken your advice, you mean."

"An abortion would have freed you, Collie. Instead you tied yourself to a guy who treated you badly and diminished any self-esteem you ever had."

"He told me early on he was falling for me, and he came to see me dance four times a week. He was very handsome back then, and charming too. I was too young to resist him. As to the abortion, Dean wanted the baby. And I did too." My eyes welled with tears, remembering how heartbroken we both were after the miscarriage.

Mary watched me, a sad smile on her face. "I get it, sweetie. What I want to know is how a shy girl like you managed to stand up in front of a room full of men and take off her clothes? I could never do that."

"It was a persona I developed—like acting, I suppose. On stage I wasn't Collie, I was the sexy woman who wore skimpy white lace and danced around a pole. It was so easy—weird that in real life I can barely function. I sometimes miss that feeling of being in control. Men were so sweet and adoring, calling me ma'am and walking me to my car. They respected me." I glanced at her. "And I think Dean did too—at least at the beginning."

I heard the derisive sound Mary made in the back of her throat as I put coins in the washer. She had no understanding of what I was trying to tell her. The first time I met Dean was between sets when he bought me a drink. We were like magnets, the chemistry between us lighting up the room. He gave me a hundred dollar bill to dance on his table. After work he was at the club's back door waiting for me. "Will you come home with me tonight?" he'd asked with a winsome smile.

Mary's question came back—why *had* I stayed? I could have walked out a long time ago. My father's death played a part in my reluctance to leave Dean; once he was gone I had no place to live and not a penny to my name. Every cent from selling my father's run-down shack had gone into paying for his funeral.

My mind rushed backward to life before I met Dean. Even Mary didn't know about my trips down back alleys, the furtive groping that brought me a few extra bucks here and there. When I met Robbie, the owner of a more high-end club, he encouraged me to work for him. "No stripping," he promised.

But even with the sizable tips I got from pole dancing it wasn't enough to pay for Dad's growing bills—on top of food and house payments he needed doctors, medicine. And after my Mom's chemo our insurance ran out. I did the only thing I knew to do, which was lying on my back in one of the rooms behind the bar.

Dean had entered the picture not long after that. And then I got pregnant.

⚶

It was six years into our marriage when he lost his job. One night he approached me, asking if I'd mind stripping again. "Just until we get back on our feet."

I was horrified that he'd want me to enter that seedy life again. "Are you serious?"

"Six months, that's all I ask. You can do that for me, can't you?"

Of course I could. I loved him and would do anything to please him. And so at twenty-five I went back to work, finding another club that specialized in strippers who pole danced. It was different this time, knowing that I had a home and husband to come back to every night. But the competition with the other dancers got to me. They were unfriendly and cutting whenever they had the chance, snide about the ring on my finger and why I was even there.

"Your hubby know what you're doing?" a woman named Kate had asked me one night.

"He's the one who asked me to do it," I told her, turning away to apply thick kohl to my eyes.

"If I was married and my husband wanted me to strip, I'd fuckin' divorce him," she'd muttered.

I had propositions every night, some of them tempting because of the extra money, but I turned them all down. When I told Dean about it, he narrowed his eyes.

"I don't want you screwing other men," he said sharply. "You could get some disgusting venereal disease and pass it on to me."

I had stared at him in surprise. "Is that the only reason?"

As I remembered he'd covered over his lack of concern by laughing. "I didn't mean it like that, Collie."

Like hell he didn't. Meanwhile our own sex life was turning into a wasteland.

I was six months in when I began to question Dean's dependence on the money I was making. It was after his purchase of a Corvette that I finally confronted him. "I'm not doing this so you can spend my money!" I shouted one night. That was the first time he'd ever hit me. I had a black eye for nearly a month. I covered the bruise with pancake makeup when I was at the club, but the other dancers saw it, sneering at me when they went by.

Six months later I finally had the nerve to quit. "I refuse to do this anymore. The money I bring in is allowing you to flake off from your job, drive around in your shiny new car, and drink too much. You're like a pimp—and pimping out your wife is pretty disgusting, if you ask me. And besides, I want to try for another baby."

At least that time he'd listened without going into a rage. He'd huffed around for a couple of days, but in the end he liked the idea of a baby and did his best to make it happen. When I didn't conceive I thought God was punishing me for the life I'd led. Dean told me to go to a fertility clinic, but I was too despondent to bother. Dean got another job and we gave up trying.

When Dean began staying out late, citing client business, I gave him the benefit of the doubt. But after a few weeks of this I wondered—why would he need to meet clients? He was a mechanic in a garage.

Instead of talking to him about it I lost interest in life in general. I was depressed again, and this time I didn't have anything to blame it on. I spent hours reliving my miscarriage and my inability to produce a child. Mary was right about the self-esteem issue. I still felt like a loser. I'd tried hard to let go of the stripper persona, but it stubbornly remained, emblazoned on my psyche.

"I know you said no, but if it's the lack of money that's keeping you with him, I can certainly help."

Her voice interrupted my trip down memory lane. "I've been sticking some away. I guess I knew this day would come."

"Stealing, you mean?" Mary laughed.

The remark bothered me. I'd never mentioned it, but if it hadn't been for my income we would have lost our house. "I've been taking some of what Dean brings home and saving it for a rainy day. Must be nice to have all your needs met."

Mary frowned. "I'm sorry. You're right. I've been spoiled. But you made your bed."

"You have no idea what my life has been like. I hardly ever see you."

Mary's face reddened. "I would have invited you, but Bill…"

"But Bill's a prig with rich friends and thinks I'm a loser? Don't bother making excuses."

Mary let out a sigh. "Remember what your name means, Collie."

Before she died, Mom told me the meaning of the Columbine flower, citing my Welsh heritage. The Celts believed in dreams and visions, and that the Columbine represented a portal between worlds. Mom had told me to 'believe in what you can't see.' I was never quite sure what that meant, but what she said after stuck with me: "Columbine Adain Morgan is special." Adain was a Welsh name that meant *winged*.

I glanced at Mary, tears pricking my eyes.

"It's time you took control of your life," she said, placing her hand on my shoulder. "I don't recall the last time you seemed happy. Do you remember when we were kids and your mom called us the two butterflies? She even made us butterfly costumes for Halloween one year."

The winged sisters. "I'd forgotten all about that. I still miss her."

"Of course you do, sweetie. Now tell me what you plan to do about the rest of your life."

I shook my head, wondering why I'd never told my best friend about the year I went back to stripping or the book I was writing.

2

Dean entered the kitchen looking grumpy and tired. The screen door slammed crookedly behind him, one of the hinges giving way. I heard shouting from next door, kids crying, and the whine of a lawnmower.

"Hand me a beer."

I stopped chopping vegetables to pull a cold one from the refrigerator, wondering why he could never do this simple chore for himself. He glared at me when I handed it to him unopened. "What?" I asked. "I'm supposed to walk across the kitchen, retrieve the church key too? You're closer."

He frowned and moved the few steps to the drawer where we kept the bottle openers. I heard the cap hit the floor and then the bang as he pushed the drawer in too hard. Paint chips drifted toward the floor. I bent to the carrots and peppers, trying to stay calm. This constant reminder of a marriage gone sour plagued me every day. But neither one of us had the energy to do much about it. The house was heavily mortgaged and both our names were on the deed. The thought of sorting through the detritus of a twenty-year marriage was too tiring to contemplate. And yet we were both unhappy.

"Did you pay this bill?" Dean handed me an envelope

addressed to Columbine A. Winter.

It was from the mortgage company and I knew what it said. I ripped it open. "It isn't a bill, Dean, it's a foreclosure notice. I've been telling you about the possibility for months. We need to deal with this if we want to keep the house."

"I'd like to just sell the damn thing and go our separate ways," he muttered with his back to me.

"I agree. Too bad we're underwater." Inherited from Dean's father, we'd been living in this money pit for years without the ability to pay it off or fix it up.

Dean turned, his skin taking on a ruddy hue. "And whose fault is that?"

"Why is it my fault? Who was it who decided to quit his job and take a lower paying one, and who is it that loves to buy expensive toys he can't afford?"

"You liked the sports car. And I'm working now. If we're going to play the blame game, why aren't you working?"

I glared at him. "Stripping again? I'm a little old for that now. All I've ever heard from you is how you want me to be here when you get home with dinner in the oven. I'm writing a book."

"The book?" he asked, with air quotations. "No one makes money from writing these days, especially when they haven't gone to college."

"At least I read, Dean, which is more than I can say for you."

Dean scowled. "Your only skill is stripping. And the way you look now I doubt anyone would want to see you dance, much less take off your clothes." He laughed nastily. "What do you think will happen with this book? Do you honestly believe a publisher would be interested? You're a loser, Collie— uneducated and too stupid to know it."

Tears welled. "You bastard." He was right, though. Writing was a dumb idea and I should have given it up a long time ago, but some stubborn streak kept me going. "I do your laundry, I do the shopping, I pay the bills, I keep the garden weeded and the house clean. I cook your meals," I muttered.

He laughed again. "A good little housewife? I should have booted you out years ago. I looked at your book and it sucks."

"Stay off my computer!" I yelled. "I write as well as many published authors I've read."

"By whose standards? Have you shown the piece of shit to an editor?"

I was suddenly tired, my gaze drawn to the mullioned window over the sink. The glass panes were loose and the paint was peeling.

"I couldn't even tell what the storyline was," he continued.

"It's about a marriage gone bust." That was a lie, but the theme was similar. My female protagonist was trying to escape a suffocating family. I wanted her to work through the trauma of her early years and become wise. But the wise part hadn't presented itself yet. It was why I hadn't finished it.

"So it's about us."

I faced him. "It's more about a woman searching for herself."

He scoffed. "Some kind of new age shit, then?"

I turned away from Dean's mocking expression, trying to breathe. He always managed to hit a nerve, his accusations striking home and making me want to disappear. I heard a dog bark, and a shriek from another child just on the other side of our six-foot laurel hedge. The hedge made it seem private but there were people all around us.

I glanced up to see the gutter hanging, clogged with pine needles and leaves. The last rainstorm had nearly ripped it off the house. This house could have been a showplace if we had the money to sink into it. If we didn't do something soon it would be foreclosed and that would be the end of it. I turned back to my preparations, spooning the vegetables into the rest of the mixture.

If I left now what would happen? Dean never paid attention to the bills. He'd told me several times that if I was going to lie around the least I could do was fix his meals and pay the bills. If I'd kept stripping I could have socked away a ton of money. Now it was too late.

Guilt filled my stomach, making me feel sick for a second. Last I checked, the only job I qualified for was flipping burgers or serving coffee. "One of these days I may be gone when you come home smelling like another woman's perfume," I muttered before I could stop myself. I braced for his fist.

"Good," Dean said in a nasty tone.

I didn't answer as I slid the casserole into the oven.

Dean left as soon as he finished eating, a belch of dark smoke emerging from the tailpipe of his truck when he took off. It was falling apart just like everything else.

Now that he was out of the house I headed to my computer, the one thing I'd bought for myself with money I earned. I could add a few more pages while he was gone.

I wanted him to be wrong about my writing. I'd worked hard and accessed the Internet to read every article I could about grammar and style, as well as carefully researching my main plot line and where it took place. I'd read article after article about writing a book, studying for hours. I'd always been an avid reader, noticing the flow of sentences and why they worked or didn't work. My story had morphed into a sort of memoir, the main character more like me than I cared to admit. Would I ever finish the damn thing? Not if I let Dean get under my skin.

Writing was the only thing I cared about now. Without it I

felt depressed and empty. Mary was right—I'd been unhappy for a long time. My fingers went to the keyboard.

> *May watched the rivulets dance down the glass, her thoughts miles away. She was part of an upcoming competition, and her name, **May Flowers**, would finally be on the marquee. Of course there would be other names along with hers, but that was okay. She smiled, looking at her reflection in the mirror. She twisted to see her back, admiring the curve of her spine, the way her butt filled out her jeans. Pole dancing was the best exercise she'd ever found. Too bad it came with such a bad rap.*
>
> *Just yesterday a man had approached her about joining his dance troupe. Flattered, she'd told him she would think about it. Illinois was a long way off now, a place she wanted nothing more to do with. At eighteen her entire life lay in front of her, a feast to be enjoyed.*

I glanced at the clock and stopped typing. It was after midnight, time to go to sleep so I could wake up in time to fix Dean's breakfast and make his lunch to take along to the shop. No sign of him yet. Maybe he'd passed out, or maybe he was getting serious about his new girlfriend. I stood and rubbed my lower back.

It was one a.m. when I closed and locked the front door and threw the deadbolt across. Let him spend the night with his girlfriend. He was probably wrapped up in her arms right now. The thought of it made my stomach clench.

"And do you take this man to be your lawfully wedded husband to have and hold in sickness and health for richer for poorer till death you do part?"

"I do."

I woke with a scream on my lips, the dream still fresh in my mind. The fabric of the lacy dress was pulled tight over the bulge of my pregnant belly as I said the words, my eyes full of stars as I stared lovingly up at Dean. I turned on the light and checked the time. Three a.m. I curled into a ball and burst into tears.

I slept in the following morning, glad of Dean's absence. But when he banged on the door around nine I woke and groggily went to open it.

"Why did you lock me out?" he demanded angrily. "Now I'm late for work!"

"I locked up at one in the morning, Dean. I figured you were set for the night."

He grabbed me roughly and slammed me against the wall. "I tried to get in last night, you bitch. You locked me out of my own fucking house!"

"Sorry, Dean. I..."

He put his face close to mine, his breath a miasma of smoke and whiskey. "Don't ever do that again," he growled. "This is my house and I can come and go as I please." He released my arm and pushed me toward the kitchen. "Now fix me something to eat."

I rubbed my arm where an imprint of his fingers had appeared and stumbled toward the kitchen.

It took me another month and a half before I made up my mind to leave. And in that time he beat me up twice—once during a drunken rage and a second time when I refused to have sex with him. He raped me that night and left me with bruises on my arms and a black eye. And all I felt afterward was the sense that I deserved it.

When Mary saw my eye she let out a shriek. "You have to report him for abuse!"

"I can't, Mary. It's my fault. He wanted to make love and…"

"Make love? That man is incapable of making love. Did he rape you?"

When I nodded her face paled. "You have to get out of there before he kills you. Your passiveness is what enrages him, Collie. He's a bully. If you stood up to him he'd leave you alone."

"I can't. He's right about me. I have no backbone and no reason for…"

"For what? Living?"

"I was going to say, no real reason to leave him."

"No reason…" she let out an exasperated huff as she stared at me. "If you don't leave I'll contact the authorities. I'm really worried for your welfare now."

And then she told me about the truck and trailer sitting on the five acres behind her house. "Let me talk to Bill about it. It's the perfect solution. You can drive away from this town and away from that maniac."

I was still in the thinking stages the night Dean came home drunker than usual and stinking of sex. It was two a.m. and I'd been hard at work at my computer, the door unlocked just in case he decided to grace me with his presence.

"Nice evening?" I asked him in as sweet a tone as I could muster.

He stared at me out of red-rimmed eyes. "I met a looker who likes to dress nice," he slurred, his gaze taking in my tangled hair and faded sweats and stretched out T-shirt.

"She doesn't mind you being drunk?"

Dean narrowed his gaze. "I wasn't drunk when I took her to bed," he said defiantly. "This is all your fault, Collie. Have you looked in a mirror lately? You look like shit."

"I'm leaving you, Dean, so what you think of me is of no matter," I whispered.

"What did you say?"

"I said maybe I should move out. Seems like having me gone would simplify things. You could bring your women here instead of sneaking off to screw them."

But Dean didn't hear me as he staggered away. I heard the squeak of the bedsprings as he fell onto the bed. My life flashed in front of my eyes—the years of abuse, the lack of anything resembling love or even caring. I had to act soon or he *would* kill me. Maybe not on purpose, but his rages were getting more extreme and the alcohol didn't help.

He was snoring when I collected the stack of cash I'd hidden in a coffee can in the kitchen cabinet. After talking with Bill, Mary had insisted on giving me the old truck and utility trailer, telling me it was rusting out and going to waste. My friend had already signed it over to me and outfitted the trailer with a mattress, a camp toilet, and small propane stove. At least I could disappear for a while. She'd told me to call her anytime day or night, and so I did.

"It's about time," she said when I told her I was ready. I heard Bill's voice in the background, her muffled reply before she spoke into the phone again. "Pack up. I'll be there in forty-five minutes."

My hands were shaking as I tiptoed around the bedroom finding the clothes I needed and trying not to wake Dean. I shouldn't have worried. He was out cold.

It wasn't yet dawn when Mary arrived driving the truck, the utility trailer hooked on behind.

When I slipped out the door with my bulging suitcase and satchel full of my computer, books and cell phone, she slid out and waved me into the driver's side. "Just drop me back at the house."

"Does Bill know what you're doing?" I asked, climbing behind the wheel.

"Of course he does—we tell each other everything. He helped me hook the trailer on."

"Must be nice," I said wistfully. "I feel like a washed up hag with no life."

Mary pursed her lips together. "You are a gorgeous woman in the prime of life who thinks of herself as nothing. If you want to meet someone else, you will. But first you need to figure out who *you* are. Living with that man all these years has diminished you. It's time you took your power back." She turned to face me. "Take a look in the mirror there."

I had shunned my face for so long I was afraid to look, but I pulled down the sun visor and stared at the reflection, surprised to see the image that stared back. My skin was clear and rosy, maybe because I'd taken a shower earlier, and my hair was shiny and thick, gold brown waves hanging around my shoulders. My hazel eyes looked worried, but still there was brightness there, a look of anticipation. And despite not wearing any lipstick my lips were plump and the color of ripe strawberries. I laughed. "My shower tonight did wonders."

Mary scoffed. "You've always been like this, Collie—I remember when we were kids you always thought you weren't pretty enough, or smart enough, or whatever…that attitude has kept you back for too long."

I pushed the visor back up, suddenly aware of what I was about to do. I glanced at Mary. "I'm scared."

"Of course you are, sweetie. Take it slow. Time will heal you, and just being away from Dean will begin to open up your eyes. There's a great big world out there. Just think of this trip as going on walkabout. You know about walkabout, right?"

"Spiritual journey that young aborigines take? I've read about it."

"This is your spiritual journey, my friend. Time to leave the past behind and take the road less traveled."

"You are just full of clichés," I laughed.

She glanced at the shadowy house. "Put the truck in gear and let's go. I told Bill I'd be back in an hour."

"He'll miss me," I muttered, part of me sad. Time had stolen my dreams of a life with him.

"Damn straight he will. He doesn't deserve you and never has. Don't ever settle again. Didn't I tell you back when you…?"

"You told me I was marrying too quickly, but I was pregnant, and…"

"I know you once loved him, but how long has it been since anything has flared between you?"

I scoffed. "Years."

"He's been abusing you and having affairs all this time."

"But I was the one who let him, Mary. He treated me exactly how I expected to be treated."

"That's no excuse for beating you up. He should be in jail for what he's done."

We rolled up in front of Mary's house just as the first streaks of orange and mauve colored the sky in the east.

Mary climbed out and came around to the driver's side. "There are maps in the glove compartment, and I left you a couple of pamphlets of places I thought you might be interested in. For this first leg I suggest heading to the closest state or Federal park. You can spend a couple of nights and get your sea legs. But make sure you go far enough to feel like you're really away. I would hate to think of you coming back because of fear or guilt."

"I won't come back. And thanks for everything, Mary."

"Don't forget to text."

"I'll text every day," I answered. "Unless my cell phone gets repossessed."

"That's not funny. I mean it, Collie. I don't want to worry about you. How much money do you have?"

"Two thousand dollars and a debit card. But once Dean gets wind of it he'll close me out of that account."

Mary nodded, wiping at her eyes. "You better get going before I change my mind about the truck."

3

Night fell like a velvet curtain, enclosing everything in a cocoon of softness. I hugged my arms around my body, staring out the open door on the back of the trailer to see the campers here and there, and the line of dark trees that surrounded the RV park. I'd taken a walk earlier, sat next to a stream and listened to the burble of water rushing over stones. I couldn't remember the last time I'd done that. Just the birdsong and the sounds of nature had soothed the part of me that was always tied into knots; I could feel them loosening. It was late now and I'd finished my meal of cheese and bread and eaten an apple. I flexed my fingers and opened my computer, excitement rising up as I thought about my story and realized there would be no interruptions.

May glanced at the door, her excitement a wild thing that wouldn't be contained. It was him—the man who'd watched her for two hours the night before, his gaze riveted. She swung herself upside down on the pole, her legs going into splits as she arched her back. A round of applause whispered around the room, accompanied by drawn in breath. She swung back around the pole and came to standing, her back to the crowd as she bent deeply, touching her hands to the floor. One more moment and it would be time for her to leave the stage. She grabbed the pole firmly and hooked one leg around it as she arched into a deep backbend. The crowd applauded. She bowed before walking off the stage.

Once backstage her legs wobbled, her body slick with sweat. "That was quite the show," her friend, Sara, said as she walked by. "Thanks," May answered. She hurried to the shower, hoping to see the dark-haired man later on.

I read over what I'd written, surprised by how the words poured forth. This character, May, resembled me, but her attitude was guiltless and her ego was intact—the person I wished I'd been back then. I'd never dared to dream like May did. I had the sudden epiphany that I was rewriting my younger life. I smiled, hit save, and closed down my computer.

The campground was dark and quiet, the earlier noise of rumbling trucks and the sounds of conversations gone. I'd been on the road for a week, and so far I'd enjoyed every minute of it. I especially liked the fact that I hadn't given up on my writing, the chapters dancing forward under my fingers every night. I loved the snugness of the trailer, the feeling of being on my own with no one to take care of but myself. I snuggled under the covers, let out a contented sigh and closed my eyes.

I woke to rain drumming on the metal roof, opening my eyes to gray light sifting through the vent in the ceiling. I'd had a terrible dream—hands clutching, pain, and my stifled scream. I'd been violated in some way and knew it was wrong. As I made coffee the treacherous visions hit me full force. My father stood over me, his hands around his erect penis. His eyes were glazed, a coaxing smile on his face. "That's a good girl. You know Daddy won't hurt you."

I let out a scream that must have awakened the entire camp, my hand flying to my mouth. This was no dream; this was a memory. A minute later the floodgates opened, my mind reeling with what I'd endured. He'd been doing it since the year I turned six, his late night visits to my bedroom terrifying and painful. I saw myself curled up in the fetal position, tears tracking down my cheeks. If I whimpered or cried out his hand would come down over my mouth, making it hard to breathe. My heart went out to that younger version of myself as I began to sob.

I heard a knock on the door before a male voice called, "You all right in there?"

I wiped my face and pulled my T-shirt down before I unlocked the door and peeked out. "I'm fine."

The guy was in his early forties, brown hair curling over his ears. "You sure? That scream didn't sound fine to me."

"I had a bad dream, that's all."

He watched me, his eyes narrowing with concern. "You've been crying."

"That's my business. Please just go."

He nodded, looking down. "I'm only two spaces up if you need me." I watched him leave, his shoulders hunched against the rain. He was soaked. A moment later he disappeared into an older Volkswagen Euro van.

I closed the door and finished making coffee, trying hard to keep the onslaught of images at bay. They came nonetheless— a spider web of nightmarish memories, bringing with them the emotions of that abused child, and the fear that had kept me awake every night. I remembered dragging myself out of bed in the morning, the dark circles under my eyes in the mirror as I brushed my teeth and got ready for school, the inability to face my father in the kitchen, and the feeling of shame. No wonder I'd chosen the career I did, and no wonder my father hadn't much cared that I was prostituting myself to keep him out of debt. Oh my god. I poured coffee and slumped onto the bed.

It was two hours later that I finally roused myself to call Mary.

"Are you sure this isn't some story you made up?"

"I remembered it, Mary. It's all disgustingly clear in my mind. You met my Dad—did he seem...?"

"He seemed perfectly normal to me, sweetie. Although a couple of times when we were teenagers he seemed to be eyeing me in a way that felt uncomfortable."

"From what I remember he stopped the year I turned thirteen. Probably afraid I'd get pregnant. My Mom died that year, you know, but I swear she wanted to warn me. I remember now the way she looked at him, like he was the devil incarnate. Whenever he tried to touch her she'd pull away. But by then it was way too late. After she died the shock of it must have caused me to block all the memories."

"Your choice of partners is beginning to make more sense. From what I've read, abused children tend to pick men who are abusers. You poor thing!"

"What do I do now? I can't come home and I can't go on. I feel like a limp rag. I can't stop crying."

"I say keep going. Maybe find a bookstore and pick up a book or two about this. Or even seek out a therapist. Coming home would not be a good idea. Bill said he saw Dean with another woman."

"So? He's been doing that for a while."

"At your house, Collie. He was taking her into your house."

"I don't care. Dean and his conquests pale in comparison to this."

"Where are you?"

"I'm in a forest somewhere close to Wyoming. There's an ancient site of a medicine wheel on this route. You left a pamphlet about it."

"Go see it and then go to the nearest town and find a bookstore. You need support right now."

When we hung up I felt a tiny bit better. Just sharing it with a friend who cared about me helped. But the feeling of guilt and shame persisted, as though it was my fault somehow. How could that be? I was only a little girl at the time.

The Bighorn Medicine Wheel sat on top of a very steep mountain at 9,462 feet. As the engine labored up the incline I wondered whether I would make it at all, but somehow the old truck rallied. I parked and got out, shivering in the cold air that blew across the flat space. Tattered flags fluttered among the remnants of feathers and beads stuck here and there around the circle of white stones. The pamphlet I held said it had been built over ten thousand years ago. Apparently no indigenous tribes claimed it, although it stood within the Crow homeland. *Ancient beings known as the little people are said to come to those who fast and pray deep into the night on Medicine Mountain,* I read. *The little people are said to live in caves beneath the wheel.* I gazed across the mountaintop, the whistling wind like the wings of many birds. I put the pamphlet away and walked the circle, slowing my steps until I felt a certain rhythm that seemed in keeping with the place.

"You shouldn't be here."

I jumped and turned, surprised to see an older Native American man frowning at me. "Why not?"

"We have ceremony tomorrow. We prepare today."

"I had planned to spend the night here," I heard myself say. "You see I've just had a terrible shock. I was hoping the little people could help."

He smiled, revealing a broken tooth. "Are you fasting?"

I nodded. "All I've had is coffee."

He reached into his pocket and pulled out what looked like a bunch of nuts. "Chew these," he said, handing them over. "They will help with the cold." He glanced up at the clouds forming. "There will be a storm tonight. Lightning. If you call on the little people you must remain inside the circle for them to find you. You must brave the storm and pray. Can you do this?"

"I think I can. I want to."

"If you wish it, then it will be so."

I turned away as a gust of wind hit me in the face. "So, it's okay if I stay then?" I asked, swiveling back to where he'd been. There was no one there, and when I scanned across the windswept landscape there was no sign of him anywhere.

It was dark when I entered the circle with my sleeping bag. I wrapped it around my shoulders and sat cross-legged, as close to the middle as I could get. "Please help me," I pleaded. "I need to know what to do, where to go, how to stop this pain." My eyes filled with tears as I popped a nut into my mouth and listened to the whine of wind across the bare hill. I had never prayed in my life, had never meditated either. And here I was at nearly 10,000 feet, barely able to catch my breath and with a thunderstorm approaching. I chewed up the dense and bitter nut and swallowed, my stomach roiling. I wondered if I might be sick.

The air turned even colder, the wind whipping around me like something alive. Thunder rumbled in the distance. I should just go and sleep in my trailer, I thought to myself. *This is dangerous and foolhardy—there are no little people, and even if there were, why would they help me? I'm not Native American.* But instead of getting up I stayed put, my eyes closing against the streaks of lightning moving closer. The wind changed into a pack of wolves that circled, surrounding me. I could hear them growling but refused to open my eyes.

I popped another nut into my mouth and chewed, trying to ignore the bitterness and the feeling that something was closing in. I thought of the native man, the look in his eyes when he smiled and handed me the nuts. He'd told me to pray, and so I did, asking the universe to take away the pain of my past. But still the shame rolled over me, making me dizzy. A part of me wanted to die right here, right now. I ate another nut and swallowed the vile stuff down with a few sips of water.

The rain came soon after, a drenching downpour that left me shivering and wet. And still I stayed, wondering why. Maybe the lightning would kill me. But as the hours went by and the lightning struck all around, I realized that death didn't scare me. I would rather be dead than living like I'd been. I hated myself, hated my past, felt disgusted with who I'd become and ashamed of everything I'd done. My father's face appeared before me, his leering grin mocking me as he bent over my bed. I recoiled from the sight of him, the scream ripped from my mouth joining the screech of the wind.

A sudden vision appeared before my eyes, another memory that I recoiled from in agony—my mother's face peeking around the door to my room, her eyes going wide when she saw what was going on. But instead of saying something or coming inside, she retreated. "Don't go!" I screamed out, the words lost in the every-increasing storm. My arms reached for her, my body shaking with fear and loathing.

My father had seen her, turning away from me only long enough to close and lock the door. "Daddy won't hurt you," he'd muttered when he came back, his eyes glittering.

But he'd already hurt me, had already destroyed my life. My mother had seen and done nothing, too afraid of him to save her only child.

I was sick then, vomiting up my past, and all the horrible things I'd endured at the hands of my father. Each spasm brought with it images of things I'd done and things that had been done to me. My stomach emptied as the last of it poured out of me. I lay spent on the ground, cleansed of the past.

Sometime later I rose to my feet, my eyes opening on a scene so surreal I couldn't believe what I was seeing. Ghosts danced all around me, their faces as white as the stones that surrounded the circle. They wore costumes from ancient times, feathers in their hair, their eyes dark with kohl. Before I could run to the safety of my trailer they grabbed me, pulling me into their midst. I danced alongside them, a frenzy taking me over as I responded to the drumming that seemed to emanate from everywhere at once. I tried to find the source, but all I saw was bits of feathers and dust being picked up by the wind and flung here and there. My eyes burned from it, my skin on fire as the night wore on.

The wind was as alive as I was, vicious and soothing at the same time as it swirled around me. When lightning struck the mountaintop my body tingled and became even more alive. Electricity danced from my fingertips. When I waved my hands, tendrils of light, like snakes, waved with them. I was pure energy.

The ghosts closed in and lifted me into the air. I felt light and insubstantial as they let me go to float downward, through the earth into another world, one where I felt safe and pure, as though I'd never been hurt or violated or ever done anything to be ashamed of. There were women there, their expressions full of love as they dressed me in deerskin, and placed beads around my neck. They braided my hair, tying feathers into it. My fear drifted away as I became another person—one of them, whoever *they* were. They were as tall I was, their bodies as solid as mine. The term 'little people' didn't seem to fit. They were loving and kind, taking away the pain of my past as they worked their fingers through my hair. I wanted to stay with them forever.

I woke in my trailer, sun sifting through the skylight to warm my eyelids. When I rose from the bed and looked outside, I saw mud left from the rain, but other than that nothing had changed from the day before. The sky was cerulean, light glinting off the white stones that surrounded the wheel. Had it all been a dream? I staggered toward the coffee pot, surprised by my tired muscles and the ache in my lower back. And that's when I noticed the beads around my neck—turquoise and silver. I pulled them over my head to examine them more closely. They were green turquoise with striations of brown, tarnished silver beads dividing them into sections. They hummed with an energy all their own. When I touched my hair I found it was braided, a couple of bright feathers coming loose to fall softly to the floor. It hadn't been a dream after all.

I made coffee and left the trailer, sitting on a rock to watch a hawk circling, dark against the pale morning sky. The tangled threads of my past had been pulled apart, my body as light as the feathers that drifted down from my hair.

4

I held the phone on my lap, the speaker on as I navigated the hill in the blue light of early morning. "Nothing like this has ever happened to me before," I said excitedly.

"I'm sure you dreamed it. There's no way that..."

My fingers touched the necklace around my neck, tingling moving up my arm. "I have beads to prove it, and I think they might be magic."

There was a long silence before Mary answered. "You need help, Collie. Did you do what I suggested? Being molested is no small thing, especially at such a young age. You need to seek professional help, not decide that all your problems have been solved from hallucinating on a mountain. Maybe the altitude caused it all."

I listened to her rational advice, wondering why I wasn't taking it seriously. "I'll look for a bookstore when I get to Lovell, but I kind of got what I needed from the little people."

"Little people? You're scaring me now."

"I'm so much better. I know this probably won't last, but it certainly helped. And Mary, my mother knew—she knew what Dad was doing and she didn't stop him."

"Your Mom? No, Collie. She wouldn't let him abuse you

like that. Do I need to contact the Wyoming police? You don't sound like yourself."

"That's because I'm not myself. I'm not sure who I am, but I've definitely changed. All that horrible stuff happened to another person in another lifetime. I feel like I've been reborn."

"Collie, I…"

"I'm losing the signal. I'll talk to you later." I hit end and placed the phone on the seat beside me. I wasn't losing the signal, but the road was steep, with hairpin turns, and it took all my concentration to keep from burning my brakes out. And I also didn't want to hear what she had to say. Maybe I dreamed all of it, but if so, where did the beads come from? And what about the braids in my hair? Mary's skepticism was ruining my mood and making me question what I knew to be true.

Lovell was a small town in the valley with high mountains as a backdrop. Brick buildings lined the main street, and along the side streets older cottages had been fixed up and painted, their colorful facades cheerful. The roadway was lined with mature trees, bright green leaves shining in the early morning sunlight. I was so caught up with it all that I nearly missed the bookstore, pulling off to the right as soon as I noticed the sign for Venus Books. *Nice name*, I thought, smiling to myself.

The woman behind the desk looked up as I walked in. "Can I help you find anything?"

"Maybe a book on the medicine wheel? I spent last night up there, and…"

"You spent the night up there? I don't think that's allowed."

I shrugged. "I didn't see a sign. I had kind of a mystical experience."

She frowned and looked me over. "You don't look like the usual riffraff who claim these things. Where did you come from?"

"I live, or rather, *lived* in Virginia. I'm doing some traveling."

"I'd say you are," she said, her brows lifting. "The books on the Natives and the Bighorn Medicine Wheel are over there," she said, pointing to the back of the store. When she turned away to replace her close-up glasses and bent to the computer, I headed to the self-help books.

Do you have trouble finding friends, lovers, and acquaintances?

Once you find them, do they dump on you, take advantage of you, or leave?

Are you in a relationship you know isn't good for you?

Are you still trying to figure out what you want to do when you grow up?

Are you drinking too much, eating too much or trying to numb your pain with drugs of any kind?

I thought of my life and how reclusive I'd become since my dancing days; my only real friend was Mary. I'd never considered a legitimate career—had never dared to dream that I could have one. My relationship with Dean had grown more and more abusive, and yet I'd been unwilling to leave him. I lifted the paperback off the shelf and carried it with me to the Native American section.

I left the store a half hour later after purchasing *Outgrowing the Pain*, by Eliana Gil, and a book on the history of the medicine wheel. I felt happy to have found what I needed, my gaze going to the stores on either side of the street, bright colors catching my eye. Some looked inviting, especially the ones with gypsy skirts and Indian style tops hanging on racks outside.

I was unlocking the truck with the idea of stowing my books and heading across the street, when I realized it was already unlocked. I was sure I'd locked it. But when I saw the glove compartment hanging open, and the envelope containing the rest of my cash lying empty on the passenger seat, I gasped in horror. Someone had jimmied it or I'd been too scattered to lock it. Panic entered my belly, cramps taking my breath.

My purchases flew out of my hands as I groped inside the glove box, searching fruitlessly for my money. I still had my debit card, but as soon as Dean found out he'd take me off the account. I sat heavily on the seat, staring blindly through the windshield. What in hell was I going to do now? A mystical experience did not make up for this disaster.

A second later my past came crashing back, and with it the nuts I'd eaten the night before. I ran for the trailer and barely reached the camp toilet in time. I poured sawdust on top, closed the lid and lay on the bed. But instead of being able to rest, my mind raced, all the horrors of the past arriving in my mind at once. I was a terrible person. I should never have left Dean. I deserved everything that had happened to me, including my father's abuse. I was a slut who didn't deserve to live. I was sobbing now, my head buried in the pillow.

It was an hour before I finally dried my eyes and went to search for an ATM. But when I found one my card didn't work. I glanced up and down the street, hoping to spot the thief who had stolen all my money, but that person was long gone.

Lovell's downtown had a sleepy feel to it, with colorful shop marquees and customers heading in and out. The sidewalks had been decorated with hanging pots of flowers, and cobbles had replaced the asphalt. I barely took it in as my gaze went past it all toward the flashing lights in the distance. A bar that advertised dancing girls. That's where I belonged.

I walked toward Bighorn Bar, a feeling of inevitability washing over me. By the time I reached it I was numb inside, any dream of a decent future gone.

The woman behind the bar was somewhere in her late fifties, stocky with frizzy over-dyed hair. She stopped what she was doing when I asked her about work, her blue eyes assessing.

"We're lookin' for a pole dancer. Have you danced?"

I hesitated for only a moment. This was my life, my fate. This is what I deserved. "Yes. I've danced. But I'm older now. I haven't done it in a while."

Her head cocked to the side. "Your face looks young, but that doesn't mean your body's in the same shape. How many children have you had?"

"None. I had a mis…"

"No children?" Her eyebrows lifted just before she turned to the middle-aged man at the other end of the bar. "Bernie, can you take over for a few minutes? We have a possible contender." She turned to me, gesturing as she moved from behind the bar. "Follow me. I have some lingerie for you to try on."

The back room was filled with clothing and other accouterments of dancers, including 'the pole'. She pulled some skimpy lingerie off a hanger and handed it to me.

"This looks about your size. If I hire you, you do know that you'll get paid in tips, right? And you'll need to give me a cut for the privilege of dancing here. We can provide food, but other than that you'll have to get the boys to pony up." She winked. "Looker like you should do just fine. Our last gal left nearly a month ago and we've been hopin' to find a replacement ever since. Your timing is perfect."

"If it wasn't for all my money being stolen I wouldn't be here," I muttered, pulling off my jeans. I was still feeling shaky, my stomach roiling. I hoped I wouldn't have to run for the bathroom.

"Now don't look like that. This is a respectable place—no touching allowed, and the men know what happens if they disobey the rules."

I tried on the lace teddy and the panties that matched, glad that Nadine didn't throw me out once she noticed my lack of muscle tone.

"You don't look too bad," she said, fiddling with the flimsy material to show off more cleavage. "I'd hoped for a younger gal, but you'll do for now. Our business has been way off since Maizie left."

"I don't plan to be here long. Just long enough to make enough money to get me to Alaska."

She straightened from where she'd been adjusting the straps. "Alaska? Why there?"

I pictured one of the pamphlets in the truck. "There's something happening at the summer solstice—I think it's called Burning Night—a celebration of some kind?"

Nadine laughed, revealing stained teeth. "I know all about it. I was there a few years back. It was a hoot."

"What is it, exactly?"

"It's a place for aging hippies to gather and have a party. If it weren't for my old man I never would have gone. He fits the bill perfectly." She glanced at me sideways. "Be careful up there—there's lots of cave man types who would love to carry someone like you off."

"Cave man types? You mean abusers?"

"No. I mean men who live in the bush who want a woman to warm their beds. I've never seen an abuser in that lot. They're too busy hunting down their dinner and workin' to stay alive to be mean to anyone."

I turned to see the back of my outfit, my focus going to the flab on my upper thighs. "Doesn't sound too bad right now."

Nadine raised her eyebrows. "Aren't you the innocent one? Now show me some of your moves on that pole over there."

I did as well as I could, considering my empty and roiling stomach. My muscles screamed when I attempted to lift myself off the floor. "Sorry—it's been a while."

"Keep it simple until you get back into it. As long as it's sexy the boys won't notice. Now show me some stage moves."

"Stage moves?"

"You know—dance moves without the pole. You did dance without the pole, right?"

I nodded and went into one of my old sets, trying to remember it and not strain myself. I was breathing hard by the time I finished. "I guess I'm out of shape," I wheezed.

"No worries, honey. You look good to me. You move like you've stripped."

"I did strip for a while," I admitted. It was all coming back to haunt me, the smell of cigarette smoke and alcohol—the bright lights above the stage that made me sweat, and the dark room in back. I was exactly where'd I'd been when I was twenty-five, except this time I was out of shape, flabby, and too old. Dean was right—once a stripper always a stripper. Tears welled.

"That's a good thing, hon," she said, watching my expression. "Don't feel embarrassed about it. Didn't you feel powerful when you were doing it?"

"I guess so."

"Men are like putty in your hands when you strip. I did it years ago. I miss it, to tell you the truth. There's nothing else like it." She laughed and ran agitated fingers through her frizzy mop. "I'll put you on right at eight thirty when the crowd comes in. Be here at eight so I can fix your hair for you. I have just the color to cover up those gray strands." She smiled. "I'll have to do up some flyers this afternoon to announce your debut. Stand over by the pole," she said, pulling out her phone.

"But..."

"Take a pose for me, honey. And look like you mean it."

I grabbed the pole and twisted one leg around it, letting my hair hang across one cheek.

"Perfect," she said, snapping off a few shots. "I'll just print these out and hand 'em around. We'll have a good crowd tonight."

I changed back into my jeans as she went off to download the photos. She was in the front when I came out. "Thanks for taking a chance on me," I said, shaking her hand.

She laughed and turned toward Bernie. "We got ourselves a new dancer," she told him. "Maybe now we won't have to close up shop." He gave me the once over and raised his thumb. "As I mentioned earlier, you do understand I take a fee. You don't work for me—you're an independent contractor."

"It wasn't that way back when I was stripping. I worked for the man who owned the club."

"Time's have changed. But don't worry, honey—you'll make it up in tips—trust me."

Nadine and Bernie were discussing their good fortune when I walked out the door.

❦

I found the nearest campground and settled in for the day, trying hard to recreate the feeling I had after my night on the mountain. But the theft and being forced to dance again had laid me low. And if that wasn't bad enough, I was plagued by the knowledge that my mother had also betrayed me. I felt utterly lost, like a child in a dark forest trying to find her way home.

After I made a mug of stomach ease tea I opened Eliana Gil's book and turned to the foreword. *As a therapist I have seen problems with a drinking or abusive mate, depression, general dissatisfaction with life, or a feeling of "wandering" without clear direction or goals…*

I'd never known what I wanted. I only did what was expected of me in the moment, and I'd put up with Dean's abuse because I deserved it. I'd been depressed for over fifteen years. I read on.

5

"And now we have a special treat for you. Miss Columbine will demonstrate the art of flower arranging!"

I listened to Nadine, waiting for her signal as the men clapped their approval. She'd sprayed my hair blue and braided some of it, leaving several curls to hang down around my face. I wore a flower tiara held in place with bobby pins and she'd rubbed sweet smelling oil on my skin to make it glisten. I fidgeted, pulling up on the gossamer material to cover more of my cleavage, but it didn't help.

Lights had been set up above the stage, turning from green to blue to lilac, and casting rainbows across the wooden platform. The pole was set up in the middle and hooked into a socket in the ceiling to keep it steady. Music wafted from two speakers—a slow and sensual piece. The room was filled to overflowing with men, drinks on the tables in front of them. I was suddenly overcome with stage fright.

"Give a big hand for our flower of the night!" Nadine yelled, gesturing for me to come out. I stumbled onto the stage, nearly tripping as I headed to the center. As soon as I appeared the crowd went wild, wolf whistles and clapping filling my ears. I didn't pause to think about it, going immediately into a set I knew by heart. I bent and swayed, arching backward and forward in time to the music. "Take it off, baby!" someone yelled. I ignored him and moved to the pole, performing some simple moves that didn't require much strength. Sweat beaded on my forehead and dripped down between my breasts. My heavy hair hung in my face and I brushed it back.

I was breathing hard when I went to the floor to spin and do splits, my toes pointed like a ballerina. When men threw money I incorporated picking up the bills into my languid movements as I kept time to the music. As the music faded I bent low with my hands on the floor, and moved from there into a cartwheel, a maneuver I hadn't done in years. Cheering and whistles followed me off the stage where I collapsed onto the floor and mopped the sweat from my brow.

"Well done!" Nadine said, handing me a glass of water. "They loved you."

I gazed up at her blearily. "When do I have to do this again?"

"Friday."

This was Wednesday.

By the time I'd changed and headed out to the truck, exhaustion had kicked in. *That wasn't so bad now, was it? An easy way to earn a couple hundred bucks*, a voice in my head said. At this rate it wouldn't take long to make up the two thousand I'd lost. But my dark mood persisted. My face grew hot picturing what I'd just done. At least I'd kept the lingerie on.

I thought about the early days of stripping, remembering how it hadn't really bothered me. I'd felt separate from my body, even when I was doing things I could barely admit I'd done. That younger version of me had performed with impunity, not stopping to think about her actions. I had to admit that it was just as Nadine said—I'd felt powerful. It was only when I met Dean and became his wife that all that bravado I'd cultivated on stage disappeared.

When I went back to it in my twenties, my attitude was all about the tips. *Only to make a few bucks,* was the mantra I'd whispered as I danced across stage shedding lingerie. Back then I'd worn pasties and a thong, that covered practically nothing, under my lacy outfits. I was brazen and sexy for the hours I was there, reverting to my insecure self once I reached home.

Dean and I never spoke about it except when he counted out the money I'd made. "A good night," he'd say tucking the cash into a zippered bag, or "What in hell happened?" when there wasn't much. There was only the one time when his greed got the best of him and he'd broached the idea of me doing a bit more. "Just make sure they wear good protection," he'd said after explaining his reasons.

"You said you didn't want me screwing other men."

He gave me a sheepish smile. "You could make double what you're making now."

"And it's worth it to you to have your wife lying on her back while strange men paw at her and do god knows what?"

He'd grabbed my arm at that point, twisting it and hurting me. I'd wrenched away and grabbed the frying pan off the stove and hurled it at him, missing him by a mile but sending grease spattering across the walls and floor. It had taken me hours to clean it up, my tears dripping into the mess as I scrubbed.

But in this job I didn't have to strip. It would be easy compared to those days. *At least I'll get in shape,* I thought, trying to justify it as I drove back toward the campground. The dancing had stopped my mind for a while, my past slipping away as the music took me over.

It was Friday afternoon and I was taking a much-needed walk in the park when a guy who looked to be in his twenties struck up a conversation. When he asked what I did for a living I told him to come to Bighorn Bar. His eyes widened. "Are you a stripper?"

"No, I'm an exotic dancer," I said, not even skipping a beat.

His smile was wide. "My name's Tim. When do you dance?"

"Tonight. I start at eight-thirty, but if you want a good seat you should come early.

He grinned. "I'll be there."

"You're too young for me," I quipped, looking him over.

He laughed, his head going back to expose his tanned throat. "How old are you?"

"Never mind. You'd be shocked and might not show up."

"Wild horses couldn't keep me away."

He was handsome and had an easy smile, and it made me feel good to know he found me attractive. I began to perk up.

Tim was sitting at a table in the front when I came out on stage that night. He winked and tipped his cowboy hat when he saw me. I gave him a smile before heading to the pole, taking in a deep breath before grabbing the slick metal with one hand and upending my torso. Nadine had outfitted me in cowgirl attire, a short leather breakaway skirt with a snap to release when the time was right. On top I wore a low cut lacey blouse with spangles all over it. I had on gloves to keep from slipping.

I was well into my set when I decided to pull open the snap, letting the skirt drop away to reveal the satin boxers I wore underneath. I slid like a snake around the pole, my muscles screaming in protest, every part of me in agony. The crowd went wild. The music was Van Morrison, the sexiest album he'd ever recorded, and that, coupled with the encouragement from the crowd, allowed me to ignore the pain. I conjured my mystical experience at the medicine wheel, letting how I'd felt there dictate my moves. I danced with abandon, just as I'd done with the ghosts, swaying in rhythm to the jazzy saxophone.

When I pulled off the top to reveal the bustier beneath, the room erupted, deafening applause accompanying yells of, 'take it all off!' A few minutes later I heard the sound of breaking glass—shouting. A man jumped onto the stage, but before he reached me Tim had come to my rescue, wrestling him to the ground. A second later Nadine was there, her arm around my shoulders to lead me off the stage. Out of the corner of my eye I saw Bernie grab the guy and manhandle him toward the door.

"Sorry about that," the older woman whispered. "It happens sometimes with the drunker ones. Are you all right?"

"I think so. I was kind of in a zone when it happened."

Nadine handed me a wad of bills. "Anything of this nature increases tips, Columbine. I bet you doubled what you made the other night. I already took out my fee."

I counted it out—four hundred dollars on the nose, mostly in twenties, and I was sure there was at least one twenty from Tim.

As if reading my mind Nadine said, "That young admirer of yours sure did act fast. Not sure what that drunken idiot thought he was doing, but Tim had him by the collar before he'd gone two steps."

"I met Tim earlier when I was out walking. He's kinda cute."

Nadine narrowed her eyes. "He's all right as men go, but you need to be careful. And after tonight I would suggest leaving your clothes on. You nearly caused a riot. Do you have any idea how good you are? In the right place you could make a boatload of money."

"The right place?"

Nadine scoffed. "Not here, honey. This is a podunk town. I'm talkin' New York or L.A."

I stared at her open-mouthed. "I'm forty years old! I don't want to be a stripper."

"I'm not talkin' strippin', Columbine. You have the moves of a real good dancer. As far as your age—it doesn't matter when you can dance the way you can."

"I've always felt bad about doing this. I didn't even finish high school—I have no education."

Nadine laughed. "Who the hell cares about that? Dancing doesn't require a degree. If you want to perfect it you should go to dance school."

"There are schools for strippers?"

"Well, yes there are, but what I'm talking about is a legit place where you can learn jazz and so on and find an agent. That set you did to Van Morrison was something else."

"I made it up as I went."

"That's what I'm trying to tell you, girl. You have talent."

I lay in bed that night thinking about what Nadine had said. Nobody had ever told me I was anything but ordinary. I'd always felt terrible about my 'only' talent, my self-esteem in the toilet as I struggled to come to terms with what a low life I was. And with the memories of what my father had done to me I felt even worse about it. Now I was being told I was talented? *Think of the source,* a voice said. Nadine worked in a bar and stripped when she was younger—hardly a good judge.

As I drifted into sleep my book came into focus—May Flowers, my protagonist, moved across my consciousness, her round face suffused with happiness. For the first time in several days I didn't dream about my father or my mother. Maybe I'd put the past behind me where it belonged.

I woke up early with the ideas for my book still there. I turned on the lantern and fired up my computer and set to work.

May was in New York for her formal debut, her excitement at a fever pitch. This was her first legitimate job. The dark-haired man who had watched her pole dance was an agent and brought her with him to New York. He hadn't even propositioned her. And now she was in a play off Broadway. Her part was small and non-speaking, but she would be dancing in front of at least five hundred people. She'd auditioned months ago and to her surprise been picked out of twenty gals to come back a second time. And now she was in!

My story was moving along. May had escaped a horrible life and had taken up this man's offer. Maybe I could do the same. Once I made enough money I could make a plan. But what did I want to do? What *could* I do, was the better question to ask. And the answer to that was not much. I had to admit that I was having fun and enjoying the attention. And now there was no one to complain about the hours I spent on my computer, or not having dinner on the table. I was free. But somehow that word didn't quite fit my mood.

6

Mary called at 9:00 a.m., bringing me back from worrying about my future. I ran my finger across the screen. "Hi, Mary."

"Where are you?"

I told her the name of the town and launched into my latest troubles, including what I was doing about it.

There was a long silence before Mary said, "Working in a bar is the worst thing you could do for yourself. I thought you wanted to put your nasty past behind you."

"It's the quickest way to make money, and I want to go to that Burning Night celebration—you know the brochure you left in the glove compartment? If I was making minimum wage it would take me all summer to replace what was stolen."

I heard a heavy sigh. "Does it make you feel good about yourself to dance half naked in front of a room full of horny men?"

I thought of my revelation the night before. I did enjoy dancing. "I'm trying not to think too hard about that part. I've already made back a good chunk of the money."

"I hoped you'd find yourself on this trip. It's why I gave you the truck and trailer."

"I appreciate that, but how do you know I'm not?"

Mary made a sound in the back of her throat. "Pole dancing? I sincerely doubt it. I just hope you don't start stripping again, or something even worse."

Did she know what I'd done? I'd never told her. "I'm not planning to prostitute myself, if that's what you're worried about."

"You're already prostituting yourself," Mary muttered.

When I heard a knock on my door I took the opportunity to get off the phone. I was fuming when I undid the locks and swung the door open. Tim was standing there, his cowboy hat at a rakish angle, his lips curling up in a smile.

"Good morning, Columbine," he said, taking his hat off in a gesture of respect. "Thought you might like a little breakfast. I know a great place."

I took in his wide shoulders and dark hair, the way his jeans hung on his slim hips. He was a hunk. I had to sternly remind myself of how much older I was. "I'd love it. Just give me a second to get dressed."

I secured my hair in a ponytail and applied bright lipstick before pulling on a pair of clean jeans and a T-shirt with an artistic rendering of the Hindu elephant god, Ganesha, on the front. When I opened the door Tim was leaning against the side of my truck staring into space. It was the quintessential shot of the cowboy, with his pointed boots and hat, one leg bent at the knee. I grabbed my phone and snapped off a picture before he noticed I was there.

"Ready!" I called a few seconds later as I stuck my phone in my back pocket.

He turned and smiled, gesturing to where he'd left his truck.

I found out that Tim was only twenty-nine, but there was something about being with him that made me feel better about myself. For one thing he appreciated me and thought I was interesting. And it didn't have to do with exotic dancing. When I told him about my experience at the medicine wheel he didn't bat an eye. "I've heard a lot of stories," he told me. We ate pancakes and eggs and bacon and talked for an hour and a half before he suggested we take a ride into the country. And he paid for breakfast.

We parked his truck on a hill overlooking a stream lined with willows. It was a beautiful sunny day with birds twittering in the trees, the miasma of swampy water and algae adding to the sensory experience. We took a walk along its banks and checked out the fish and frogs and newts, and then I rolled up my jeans and waded in the shallows.

He offered his arm when I slipped on a moss-covered rock. "How long will you be here?" he asked, turning his brown eyes to mine.

I shrugged. "Depends on how long it takes me to make back the money I lost."

"Where will you go? Home?"

I shook my head. "Not home. My home's a bad place. I'm going to Alaska. I want to be there for the longest day."

"Burning Night?"

"You know about it?"

"Hell, yeah. I've been there every year for the past five years." He stared at me. "We could caravan."

His dark eyes drew me in, and when he leaned forward and placed his hand on the back of my head, I didn't stop him. His tongue ran along my lower lip before he pulled me close, exploring inside my mouth. I pulled away.

"I'm sorry," he said, a frown of worry on his face.

"Sorry for what? I enjoyed it."

"You said I was too young for you. I pushed myself on you."

I thought about that. So what if he was younger than me? It was only a kiss. "I'm trying out new things," I said, offering up my mouth.

He received my offer and upped the anti, his arms going tight around my back as he pulled me against him. When we kissed my knees nearly buckled. I chalked it up to no sex in a very long time, but I'd never felt like this, not even as a teenager.

His eyes met mine. "Holy shit, woman."

I gazed at him, trying to get my breathing under control. "I wish you were older."

He scoffed. "Can't help my age. All I know is, I'm smitten."

I let out a nervous laugh, noticing the look in his eyes. "I don't think we should go any further."

"Whatever you say. But I'm not going to leave you alone unless you tell me to fuck off."

When we drove back to the campground I was sorely tempted to invite him in, but my little voice told me not to rush things. I was only here for a short time and this man was not relationship material. But when he drove off I wanted to kick myself. I'd been celibate for far too many years.

In my trailer the shame of the past stole over me again, a voice asking me what in hell I thought I was doing. Why had he kissed me? The only reason I

could come up with was he wanted sex and I was an easy mark. He'd promised to keep at it until I said yes. Was that all I was—a women to be used and thrown away? Of course the answer was *yes*. When my father's leering face appeared in my mind I let out a shriek, my heart thumping against my chest. I'd chosen this path and given the impression that I was a slut. Why else would I be wearing lingerie and dancing in bars? Before I knew it I was crying, all my bravado disappearing in a rush of self-pity.

By the time I reached the bar that night I was ready to quit, but as soon as I came onto the stage and saw Tim sitting in the first row, all my good intentions disappeared. He tipped his hat and that's all I needed. When I danced that night I danced for Tim alone, my gaze straying to where he sat every time I had a chance. By the time my set was finished I'd drowned out my voice of reason and worked myself into a frenzy.

"Wow, girl," Nadine whispered. "That was quite the show. I think several of those men may be in distress." She laughed.

I hurried to change into street clothes, anxious to see Tim again. I could barely contain myself. But when I left the bar he wasn't there. I berated myself for even thinking he'd be interested in me. There was too much age difference, and now that he'd seen my flabby thighs he'd decided not to pursue it.

I climbed into my truck and drove slowly back to the trailer park, a feeling of shame stealing over me. I'd been reckless and wild tonight, unaware of anyone but Tim sitting in the audience. Had I gone seriously around the bend? I'd just met the guy. He was too young for me. And I was a married woman escaping a terrible relationship with no plans for my future, other than a festival on the longest day of the year. Mary was right—I definitely needed help.

I should probably leave tonight, I thought as I pulled up to my trailer. Getting involved with Tim was a bad mistake. But the money I'd made so far was not enough to get me to Alaska.

I opened *Outgrowing the Pain* and began to read, startled to find so many similarities between me and the other women the author had worked with. Just like so many of them, I'd been stuck in an abusive relationship, my life on hold. In the last fifteen years I hadn't once tried to figure out a future for myself, just going through the motions of keeping the house clean, cooking and doing laundry. Writing was the only bright light in a world of darkness, taking me into a reality different from the one I was in. Writing had given me hope.

It was sometime around midnight when I heard a tap on the door.

"Columbine?"

I jumped up and hurried to open it. Tim was standing there looking crestfallen. "Can I come in?"

I switched on my battery-powered lantern and stepped back to let him inside. "This is nice," he said, looking around. His gaze met mine. "I'm sorry I wasn't there when you came out. I had a kind of emergency."

"What happened?"

His gaze went to the floor. "My girlfriend...former girlfriend, Maggie, was waiting for me outside the bar. We had to hash some stuff out."

I knew it. He was taken. I sat on the bed watching him shuffle from foot to foot, his hat in his hands.

"She gave me back the stuff I left at her house. It's all in the bed of my truck."

"How long were you together?"

"Two years. She...she wanted to get married, but I wasn't ready."

He still loved Maggie who was close to his own age. They'd been together for two entire years. "You shouldn't be here, Tim. This thing between us isn't going anywhere. I'm way too old for you."

"You've already said that, but it didn't stop us this afternoon. I like you and I think you're something special. How you danced tonight totally blew my mind."

I stared at the floor. "I shouldn't have danced like that. It was irresponsible."

He placed his hat on the bed and sat next to me. "I couldn't take my eyes off you. You were..." He shook his head his eyes meeting mine. "Let's just say I wanted you badly."

"I was dancing for you, Tim. It was wrong of me."

He reached over to touch my face, his fingers tracing along my jaw. "I want you now."

I stared at him, unable to say yes or no.

"Please. I'm in a state of agony here."

His eyes were soft with longing, his head bent in a way that I found incredibly endearing. It was my fault he was feeling this way, my fault for dancing the way I had. What had I expected? Of course he'd want to have sex—I'd driven him to it. His fingers worked at my nightshirt, finally pulling it over my head. He drew back to stare at my body. "You're beautiful," he murmured.

I resisted the urge to cross my arms over my chest. "Didn't you see enough of me when I was dancing?"

He shook his head. "This isn't the same," he whispered, cupping my breasts with his big hands. He moved back to pull his shirt over his head and unzip his jeans.

My stomach did a flip-flop when I stared at his taut muscles, and the way his body formed a V. He was seriously gorgeous. "You look like Adonis."

"What's a donis?"

I laughed. "He's the Greek god of beauty and desire."

His eyebrows shot up. "Desire says it all." A moment later he was serious again. "Are you taking anything? I mean..."

"I'm on the pill." Why I was taking the pill I didn't know. I hadn't had sex in so long it was completely unnecessary, plus it made me feel sick. And I was sure I was no longer fertile. My periods had been erratic for years.

When he pulled me down on the bed I wanted to stop him, my mind twisting in confusion. I didn't want him to think of me like this, to see me as easy. I wanted something else, but I didn't know what it was. But instead of saying no, I let him go ahead, even though I was numb and unable to respond. When he finished I lay under him, afraid of something I couldn't name. I felt nothing but shame.

It was later that I had an epiphany—a raw and terrible understanding making its way into my brain. As evidenced by my father, my worth lay in what I could provide for a man. Sex was the only way I had to feel loved. I tried not to cry, realizing that I'd given myself over physically because I had nothing else to offer. I glanced at Tim lying beside me, his closed lashes dark against his coppery cheek. He'd gotten what he wanted—after tonight I would probably never see him again. There was terrible emptiness inside me that I didn't know how to fill. I fell into an uneasy slumber, dreams of my father waking me more than once.

"What's wrong?" Tim asked me the next morning when I pulled away from his kiss.

I looked up at him bleakly, awareness of who I really was filling my eyes with tears. I turned away so he wouldn't see, but he took hold of me and made me look at him.

"Collie? What's going on?"

Why didn't he just dress and leave? "I realized something last night," I finally muttered, looking down. When I glanced up again he was watching me with a frown. "I'm damaged goods, Tim. My father abused me when I was really young. And because of what he did, having sex is the only way I…" I wiped at my eyes, unable to go on.

His eyebrows drew together in confusion.

"I can't really feel anything. I never have."

"You're talking about last night. Did you like it?"

I shook my head, tears welling and running down my cheeks.

Tim stared into the distance. "I could tell you were far away last night, but I was so into it I couldn't seem to stop. I'm sorry I didn't take care of you." His soft eyes met mine. "A betrayal by the person who's supposed to protect you is the worst kind. And it's not an easy thing to get over."

I heard the words, hardly believing what he'd said. He was actually apologizing for being unaware of my needs? He was still watching me, his open expression allowing me to continue. "My mother knew what Dad was doing and didn't stop him."

His jaw dropped. "Jesus. That's even worse." He stared at me. "No wonder you're feeling like this—you were all alone."

"Would you be willing to just be together for a while without having sex?" As soon as the words were out of my mouth I regretted them, sure he would just walk away and that would be the end of things between us. I didn't want him to leave, but I couldn't do what was necessary to make him want to stay. I watched him worriedly, waiting for the look of disdain, the shake of his head to this ludicrous request. But what he said surprised me.

"How long are we talking?"

"I don't know."

He shrugged. "If you need this, I'm willing to try."

Relief flooded through me.

7

The next couple of weeks went by in a haze as I danced at the bar and spent time with Tim. In the day we went for walks, and at night he slept in my bed. I had nearly enough money for my trip by now, but I didn't want to leave, my increasing affection for Tim keeping me in Lovell. He didn't try to touch me again, only arriving at my trailer and holding me through the night. I could feel him sometimes, and knew he wanted me badly, but he never asked and never said a word. We spent hours talking, my ability to open up increasing as my trust grew. He rubbed my feet as we talked, his fingers working out the sore spots on my insteps.

As I talked about my father and what I'd experienced, his face would crumple, his eyes welling as my story poured forth. Details I'd forgotten emerged, terrible scenes of shame that still haunted me. Tim listened as I went through them all, his dark eyes focused on my face.

"How can you be so normal?"

I laughed. "Am I normal?"

"That may not be the right word—I meant able to live your life. Your father was a monster who hurt you. And your mother didn't do anything to help. You had no one to talk to, no one to trust."

"I feel scared and insecure and I have no idea what I want or where to go. I have no plan for my life."

"You don't have to figure anything out, Collie. Just live day by day."

As the days went by I read my book on abuse and also searched on the Internet for articles on abused children, beginning to understand what had really happened to me. I read that physical abuse sends a message to the child that they are deeply flawed, inferior, worthless and unlovable. Some of this I kept to myself, and some of it I shared with Tim, but mainly I tried to comprehend my past and what it meant in terms of my future. I'd met a good man, one who I was beginning to trust, but I wondered if I'd ever be able to enjoy intimacy. It stood to reason that I'd clamped down on all my feelings after what I'd been through. But would I ever recover, was the question.

❧

We were curled up together and sound asleep when I heard someone banging on my door. It was 6:30 in the morning.

"Columbine? Open this fucking door before I break it down!"

It was Dean.

"What's going on?" Tim whispered, rolling over.

"That's my husband out there."

"Your husband? I didn't know you were married."

"I don't consider it a marriage—he's..."

"Goddamn it, Collie—I mean it!" Dean yelled.

Tim reached for his shirt. "He's probably going to be pissed when he finds me here."

"He's been having affairs forever. We haven't slept together in

years. He doesn't have a leg to stand on."

"Well, that's good, I guess, but he's out there and he's angry. What should I do?"

"I don't know," I answered, pulling my jeans on. "But I'm not happy about him waking us up."

We were both fully dressed when I opened the door. Dean was red faced and furious, his eyes darting from me to Tim and back again. "Decided to go back in business, I see. Get this fucking john out of here!" he shouted. "We need to have a little talk."

I glanced at Tim who was watching Dean with his eyes narrowed. "Tim is not a john and you have no rights here. How did you find me?"

"Your friend Mary told her husband what you've been doing. He came by and relayed the news. I can't have my wife slutting it up all over the country. You're coming home."

When he grabbed for me Tim's hand came down on his arm. "Do you want to go with him?" he asked me.

"No. I'm not going anywhere."

"The hell you aren't," Dean said, jerking me forward. I fell to my knees just as Tim's fist made contact with Dean's cheek. Dean staggered backward out of the doorway, his eyes blazing with anger.

"You fucker!" He lunged at Tim who was now standing barefoot outside the trailer. When Tim sidestepped, Dean fell face down into the dirt. When he rose I saw the look on his face—the one I'd grown to fear. He stared at Tim. "You think you can fuck my wife and get away with it? You may be younger than I am, but I was a street fighter when you were still hiding behind your Mama's skirts."

"I never hide behind anyone," Tim said evenly. I admired his calmness in the face of the mess I'd created.

Dean was holding a knife and advancing on Tim when I heard the sirens, the sounds growing closer as the seconds ticked by. "The police are coming," I said, trying to distract Dean from what he planned to do.

Tim did some tricky movement with his hands and the knife flew through the air, landing on the roof of the trailer. A second later a cop car pulled up and two beefy policemen exited the vehicle. "What's going on here?" the first one asked, glancing from me to Tim and then to Dean.

"This man woke us up and started a fight," I said, pointing at Dean.

"*This man* is your fucking husband, you bitch!" Dean yelled.

"We're separated," I told the cop.

"She ran away from me and now she's working as a stripper at the local bar!" Dean yelled. "How many husbands wouldn't get ticked off by that?"

The two cops exchanged a glance. "The bar in town doesn't have strippers," the other one said. "Only dancers."

"I'm a dancer," I said.

The first cop, who I now recognized from the Bighorn, put cuffs on Dean before turning to me. "You're a free agent whether you're married to this man or not. He doesn't own you."

"The fuck I don't," Dean muttered.

"Thanks," I said, before turning to gaze at Tim, who stood quietly to one side, watching the proceedings.

I watched them push Dean into the back of the squad car, glad when they drove off. But Dean would be back—he was just that kind of guy. I was beyond furious with Mary.

"Are you okay?" Tim asked, his dark eyes full of worry.

"I am now. Who taught you that knife maneuver?"

Tim laughed. "I'm half Apache. We used to fool around with knives when we were kids."

I examined him for traces of Indian blood. I'd thought he was tan, but now that I remembered he was the same gorgeous color all over. "Why didn't you say?"

"Why does it matter?"

"I took you for a cowboy, not an Indian."

Tim let out a belly laugh, a certain look coming into his eyes. "And who are you—the pretty farmer's wife who the savage carries off?"

I stared at him, an odd sensation working through my lower belly. I had an idea it might be sexual, but since I'd never felt it before I wasn't sure. I was suddenly afraid, my pulse quickening as our eyes met.

He watched me for an instant, his eyes narrowing. "We'd better go back to sleep before lust gets the best of me."

When I woke an hour or two later, Tim was leaning over me examining the beads around my neck. "Where did you get these?"

"The medicine wheel."

"You found them?"

I shook my head. "They were given to me by the little people."

Tim frowned, looking closer. "They're Native beads and really old." His questioning eyes met mine.

"I told you about my experience, Tim. The man I met gave me some nuts to eat and the women gave me the beads."

"Nuts? You mean peyote."

I shrugged. "I don't know. They were round and brown and tasted awful."

"Peyote," Tim said, nodding. "Peyote's hallucinogenic."

"But I didn't imagine it—these beads prove it."

"I didn't say you did." He watched me for a long moment. "I didn't expect to meet your husband tonight," he said.

"I didn't expect him to come here." I glanced at him. "Dean's a bastard and an abuser."

"I kind of got that vibe from him. He thinks he owns you."
I nodded.

"How long have you been gone?"

I shrugged. "A month or so?"

"And he's just now coming after you now? If you were my woman I would have been on your trail the minute I found out you were gone."

"I'm very glad he didn't. I needed to be on my own."

"How long have you been married?"

"Twenty years."

"Shit. That's a long time. Do you love him?"

"No, Tim. I haven't loved him since the first time he beat me up and gave me a black eye."

His eyes narrowed into slits. "Are you kidding?"

"I drove him to it. I'm too passive."

He shook his head and frowned. "That's bullshit. A man who beats up a woman is not a man. He's a bully and should be in jail."

"That's what my friend told me. But it's her fault he's here—she told him where I was. I'm more angry with her than I am with Dean."

"Why would she do that?"

"Because she thinks my dancing is wrong and she thinks I'm losing it."

"That isn't her call to make, Collie. It's your life. And as far as I can tell you're as sane as I am." He chuckled. "Which isn't saying much."

I looked up and met his beautiful brown eyes. "I'm so glad you were here. I don't know what might have happened otherwise."

And that's when I told him the rest of my story, the part I'd never shared with anyone. When he heard about what I'd done in back rooms a look of pain came onto his face.

"My father was destitute, and…"

"Your dad knew?" he interrupted, shocked.

I nodded. "He needed the money I brought in."

He stared at me in disbelief. "And that's where you met Dean?"

"And then I got pregnant."

His eyebrows drew together. "Pregnant? Do you and Dean have a child?"

"No. I had a miscarriage."

He turned away, his eyes dark. "You've had a crappy life," he muttered. "No wonder you took off. You did what you had to do. I hope you don't feel guilty about it."

"I do feel guilty, but I also know now that being a prostitute was a way for me to feel validated. From what I've been reading about abused…"

Tim grabbed me and pulled me close, stroking my hair. "No more, Collie. I can't take it. What you just told me is the worst thing I've ever heard." He released me, his soft eyes meeting mine. "If you let me I can help. I won't hurt you, I promise."

My insides clenched. "I can't. Not yet. I'm sorry."

He leaned close and kissed me gently, his fingers on my chin. "I can wait."

⁂

Another two weeks went by before the night I realized that something had shifted. Tim was rubbing my back when I had the sensation again, and this time I was sure I knew what it was. I turned my head and reached to kiss his bare chest, my tongue tasting the salt of his skin.

"Collie? What…"

I rose to face him, taking in his confused expression. For weeks now he'd given me what I needed, his expert fingers on my shoulders, my neck, and my back, working on my sore muscles, and allowing me to relax fully. He'd held himself back and given me the intimacy I didn't know I yearned for—closeness that had nothing to do with sex. And because of the trust I'd gained my body had finally come alive—my desire so strong there was no denying it. I wanted him with every cell of my being. "I'm ready now. That is if you still want me."

He watched me for a long moment before he bent to kiss me, his fingers moving through my hair. He took it slow, asking me several times if I was okay. I was hot, so hot that I could barely breathe, feeling things I'd never felt before. I could barely speak for wanting him. The only man I'd ever been with, aside from back room groping, was Dean, who got his rocks off and turned over to go to sleep. Even in the early days he never spent any time on my pleasure. I had no understanding of what was possible until this moment. I was lost inside the feel of Tim's mouth on mine, the feathery touch of his hands and fingers sending shockwaves through my body. The ecstasy of what happened that night was overwhelming, my tears accompanying the frenzied and unexpected release.

When I told him he stared at me wide-eyed. "You've never...?"

I shook my head no.

"Have you been with anyone since Dean?"

"Only you."

"What about before?"

"Men who paid me money and couldn't have cared less? I dated when I was younger, but we never went very far. I was too scared."

"Jesus, Collie. I don't know what to say."

"You don't need to say anything."

After that conversation Tim took it upon himself to teach me everything I didn't know about the workings of my body.

"Do you like this?" he'd ask, trying out something new.

Most times whatever it was took my breath away so that I couldn't answer even if I wanted to. I was in a state of constant arousal, an ache low in my belly as I waited impatiently for the next time we were together. When we made love I went other places, as if the two of us had lived lives together in some distant past. Some seemed tribal, others seemed to take place in palaces in which we wore embroidered robes. I was crowned in one and he was crowned in another. Sometimes I was a fish swimming in a rushing stream, experiencing primordial life. But in all of them we loved and touched one another, desire being the driving force. When I told him about it afterwards, he laughed, saying he was right there with me.

But it wasn't only about the sex. We'd become close friends now, our connection growing stronger with each passing day. We spent hours talking, sharing our likes and dislikes, and things we mostly agreed on, like our love of being outside and the lure of water.

"You have to go camping with me next time I go," he said one night, rubbing my feet after he'd worked his special magic.

I didn't answer, my eyes drifting closed as I relaxed more and more.

Spending time with Tim took away the sting of my memories, replacing them with what was going on in the present. Talking about it no longer bothered me, as though it was a story I'd read in a book. I felt happy and satisfied for the first time in my life.

"Do you mind what I'm doing?" I asked him one night.

"The dancing?" He shrugged. "If I think about it too much, yeah, maybe. But I enjoy watching you."

"Even though other men are there?"

He laughed. "You're here with me, right?" He reached over

to prove his point, pulling me close. "I'm the only one who can do this," he whispered, his fingers tracing a meandering line along my inner thigh. I let out a gasp and reached for him.

My dancing was better than ever, my muscles growing stronger with each night I spent spinning around the pole. Because Tim was there for me I loved my life, even if it meant dancing in front of men. But when he wasn't with me I worried—afraid he would tire of me. It was probably too good to be true. And then I'd think about the age difference, berating myself for robbing the cradle. I didn't deserve to be this happy.

8

I hadn't seen Dean since the night he was taken away in cuffs. But I knew he was still around. We had a psychic link and I could feel him. He wanted to ruin my new life.

And one night he just showed up in the bar, settling himself in the front row to watch me dance. His frowning eyes followed me, making me so nervous that at one point I tripped and fell. I was suddenly clumsy and unable to keep up with the music. When it was over the applause was minimal, Dean's voice the only one I heard. "Bring it over here, baby! Give me a lap dance!"

Like hell I would.

"What happened?" Nadine whispered when I staggered into the back.

"My husband's out there."

"You have a husband?"

"We're separated. He followed me here and he wants me back."

"Good thing Tim didn't come tonight. He'd lay him low."

"What do you mean?"

"I mean that Tim isn't somebody to mess with. He's Apache and violence runs deep in their blood."

I glanced at my husband talking with another man. His chair was tipped back, a beer in his hand. I'd have to sneak out the back to get away from him. And what if he came by the trailer again? I knew Tim would be waiting for me when I got back. "Is Tim violent? I haven't seen it if he is."

"Only if he gets pushed too far."

"Does he have a gun?"

"I've never seen a gun, but he carries a knife. I suggest you be super careful—keep that man out there away from Tim or you'll be picking up the pieces. Tim has chosen you, and until you end it, he'll fight to keep it that way. I've seen him do it."

"With Maggie?"

"He told you about Maggie? That girl wasn't good enough for our Tim. She dumped him for some creep. Tim was pissed, but he held it in, figured it was her choice."

Tim had told me she wanted to get married. I 'd gotten the impression that he broke it off. Which story was true? I thought of the knife incident. Tim had admitted his prowess. Dean was Mr. Macho, especially when it came to me. I was suddenly very nervous.

"What happened tonight?" Tim asked me later in the trailer.

"What do you mean?"

Tim scoffed. "I mean you're jumpy, and so far you haven't ripped my clothes off."

I turned away. "Dean was there."

Tim made a growling sound. "That dude better leave you alone."

"I don't want you getting into it with him. He can be really mean."

"Yeah? Well, so can I."

"I mean it, Tim. Dean fights dirty, and now that you've humiliated him he'll have some other scheme up his sleeve."

"If he comes prowling around I'll have to do something to stop him."

"Maybe I should move the truck and trailer."

Tim frowned. "You're going to run away because of me?"

"Not *because* of you. I just don't want you to get hurt."

His dark eyes narrowed. "If anyone's going to get hurt, it's Dean."

When he began unbuttoning my blouse, I stopped him, wanting to find out the truth about Maggie. "Nadine said Maggie dumped you, but you told me…"

He looked up. "I told Nadine that because I didn't want to embarrass Maggie."

I stared at him. "You were saving Maggie's feelings even though you were breaking up with her?"

He shrugged, giving me a sheepish grin. "She wanted to get married, Collie. How would you feel if the man you loved didn't love you back enough to commit?"

All I could do was stare at him, amazed by the depth of his concern. He was one of the good ones—a rarity in the world of selfish men. I helped him with the buttons, my senses coming alive. I slanted a glance at the door—it was locked. I kissed him, respect for the man he was rising up in me. "Hurry," I whispered, my fingers working at his zipper.

He chuckled and did as I asked.

A thud reverberated through the trailer. I surfaced from the place Tim had taken me, fear snaking through my belly. Tim stopped what he was doing to listen. "Is that your fucker of a husband?"

I reached to turn on the lantern. "Probably."

Tim moved away from me and grabbed his belt, pulling a knife out of a leather holder. I stared at the hand carved bone handle—the blade had to be seven inches long. "What are you going to do?" I whispered, watching him pull on his jeans. When he turned, his straight dark hair swung across his cheek. He was bare-chested, the knife in his hand. All he needed was some war paint to complete the image. I sucked in my breath.

"I'm going to defend my woman," he muttered, turning toward the door.

My woman—the words reverberated inside my head, something I'd never felt before tingling through me. I heard the lock click open and then the door swung outward, Tim leaping out with it. A second later there was a mumbled shout and then a thud.

"Fuck you!" I heard Dean yell. "She's my wife!"

I jumped up and pulled on Tim's denim shirt and crawled to the door. It was pitch black outside, the glint of the blade the only thing I could see. Two dark shapes and the sound of scuffling and grunting accompanied the dance they were in. When a shot rang out I froze. Was Tim hit? But in the next few seconds I could make out who was who, and saw Tim lunge at Dean, the knife grazing Dean's arm. Dean's grip loosened and the gun flew into the air, landing in the dirt a few feet away. I ran to get it. In the meantime Tim and Dean were grappling. I could hear Dean's labored breath from years of smoking, and pictured his fat belly from all the beer drinking. Without the gun he didn't stand a chance.

When I fired the gun into the air both men turned. "If you don't want to be dragged off to jail I suggest you stop fighting," I hissed, pointing the gun at Dean.

"Come on, Collie. Give me the gun," Dean wheedled, stepping toward me.

Tim grabbed his arm. "Leave Collie alone," he said, his voice pitched low.

"Shut the fuck up," Dean said, shaking him off. A second later Dean lunged for me, and in my haste to move away I accidentally fired.

I heard a scream, saw Dean double up. "You shot me!" he yelled. His hands covered the wound in his side where blood poured out. Tim grabbed Dean, ripped his shirt up, and pushed him backward onto the ground. He covered the wound with his hands and began to chant.

"What the hell are you trying to do?" Dean asked weakly, his face turning ashen.

I stared at Tim, who seemed to be in trance, before I ran to the trailer for my phone. "I'm calling 911!" I shouted. I told the operator what had happened. "We need an ambulance at Big Wheel trailer park," I said, my hands shaking.

It seemed like forever before the ambulance arrived, sirens blaring. Tim was still kneeling next to Dean, his hands hovering above the wound. Dean's eyes were closed, his head turned to the side. I almost hoped he was dead.

When the paramedics jumped out and hurried over Tim rose and moved out of the way. When I walked closer I noticed that the bleeding had stopped. "Is he going to be okay?" I whispered.

"He's lost some blood, but his vitals are strong," the young paramedic replied. "We need to get him to the hospital."

"I'm going with you." I hurried inside to dress as they lifted Dean onto a cot and carted him over to the ambulance. Tim was still standing there watching me when I climbed into the back. They closed the doors and we sped away.

9

"He's going to be fine," The doctor told me two hours later. "Can you tell me how it happened?"

I glanced around the white hallway, the linoleum floor sparkling in the fluctuating fluorescent lights overhead. I felt a headache begin as a buzzing came to my ears. My nose picked up an antiseptic smell that made me feel slightly ill. When I turned back to the gray-haired doctor he was watching me with a frown. "I accidentally shot him," I said, looking down at my feet.

The doctor gazed at me. "The medics said there was someone else there. Are you sure it wasn't him who shot your husband?"

"How did you know he's my husband?"

"Because he told us. He also said he was trying to defend your honor."

"Dean and I are separated. He was not defending my honor. And if you want to know the truth, I think Tim saved his life."

"How is that? When your husband came in he had a bullet wound."

"Tim chanted over him for like a half hour before the ambulance showed up. He stopped the bleeding."

The doctor pursed his lips and shook his head. "Sorry, but that sounds like a bunch of hocus pocus. We got the bullet out and cleaned up the wound. Your husband will need some TLC the next few days." He glanced at me sharply before gesturing to the curtain that separated us from Dean. "I'll leave you to it."

When I drew the green curtain back Dean pushed himself up, a grimace on his face. "Hey, sweetheart. Thanks for saving my life. That fucking dude shot me."

I cringed with the endearment that he obviously wanted the doctor to hear. "No, Dean. I shot you."

Dean shook his head. "I saw the entire thing, Collie. Tim shot me. And he's going to jail for attempted murder. I already told the cops."

My heart skipped a beat. "You saw me with the gun. Why did you lie?"

Dean smiled. "Who says it's a lie—you? They'll think you're trying to save your new boyfriend. They're probably already hauling his ass to jail." He laughed until a look of pain crept over his face. "I need some fuckin' meds. Call that doc back, would you?"

"I'm not doing anything for you."

"The hell you're not. I need to stay with you until I'm healed. The doc said. And after that you're coming home."

I gazed at him, my mind reeling, and then I turned and left. I could hear him yelling for me until the moment I walked out the emergency room door. It was already light, the sun about to rise in the east. It had been a very long night.

I pulled out my phone and called the bar. When Nadine answered I began to cry. "I need a ride."

"Where are you?"

I told her what had happened. A half hour later I was in her car heading back to my trailer.

"We'll figure it all out, honey," Nadine said, patting my arm as I sobbed.

When we reached my trailer the door was wide open and there was no sign of Tim. "If I've been robbed again I don't know what I'll do," I said, jumping out of the car. I hurried inside, checking for anything missing, but it seemed that my belongings were where I'd left them. Except for Tim's things. He'd taken them all, including his toothbrush. Even the knife left on the trailer roof wasn't there now.

I turned to Nadine standing in the doorway. "Where's Tim?"

She shook her head. "He's a smart boy. I'm sure he's gone to ground."

"He took his stuff, Nadine."

Her face softened. "You love him, don't you?"

"I don't know what I feel, but I certainly don't want him going to jail for something he didn't do! Why would he disappear like this?"

"He may have thought you planned to get back with your husband. He doesn't own a cell phone, so there's nothing to be done until he shows up. Are you dancing tonight?"

"I think I should get out of here before Dean comes looking for me. I have plenty of money now. If I stay he'll force me to go home with him. The doctor expected me to take care of that bastard!"

Nadine let out a sigh. "I'll be sorry to see you go, but it's probably for the best. You said your friend alerted Dean to your whereabouts? Don't call her again."

"I'm not going to. But I'm worried about Tim. Do you know any of his friends you could ask?"

"Tim is what you might call a lone wolf. If I see him I'll tell him you moved on."

I gazed at the older woman who had become my friend. "I

wouldn't call what I'm doing, moving on, exactly. Please tell him why I left. He knows where I'm headed."

Nadine didn't answer.

I packed up and secured everything before I brought the truck around and hooked it up. By the time I left the campground the sun was midway up the sky, billowy clouds moving in from the west. I felt sick thinking about Tim. If the cops had him I had to tell them the truth. But I couldn't stick around and wait for Dean to come looking for me. And besides, I was sure Nadine would call me if Tim got arrested.

It wasn't until the next morning that I called Nadine. By then I'd made it as far as Whitefish, Montana.

"No, I haven't seen him," she told me. "And my cop friend, Jerry, told me he hasn't been arrested."

"He didn't come to see me dance?"

"You weren't here, Collie. Why would he come to the bar?"

"How did he know I wasn't there?"

I heard her sigh of frustration. "Your rig is gone."

"Did I tell you what he did after I shot Dean?"

"You did. Tim has some healing gifts that I've witnessed before. Must be his Injun' blood."

"I think he saved Dean's life. But all Dean wants to do is have him thrown in jail. I hate that man."

"You take care now, Columbine. I have to get on with my day. Call again when you get a moment."

"Will you call me if you see Tim?"

"Will do. Be careful out there."

When we hung up I had an empty feeling in my stomach. I realized that Nadine and I weren't really friends, and now that

I'd left town I had the sense that what little relationship we had was over.

The drive north was tedious and long, my mind plagued with worry. Every day I woke up thinking about Tim, my heart giving a lurch as I realized I would probably never see him again. Was he ok? I'd let him creep into my heart and now I couldn't get him out. I'd never felt like this before. My heart literally ached.

I thought about all the conversations about our past and Tim's tales of his brothers, one full Apache who lived with his dad, the other his half brother. His mother was white—an unhappy woman who'd divorced his father soon after Tim's birth. Tim's half brother, Jake, was two at the time. Jake had left home at fifteen.

"I asked Mom where he went but she didn't know," Tim had told me. "He was into some pretty nasty drugs, so I think she was glad to get rid of him. It's like he disappeared off the face of the earth."

Tim turned fifteen two years later, and left home to find his father, searching him out in the White Mountains Apache Reservation in Arizona. His full Apache brother, Mohin, a tall and gangly twelve-year-old, lived with Kuruk, their father.

Tim was misty-eyed as he told me how happy his father was to see him, how he'd despaired of ever having contact with his other son. He also told me about learning to hunt, and fishing with his father and brother in the deep river that flowed in the Salt River Canyon. He talked about the eagles that nested there. The pictures he painted with his words made me want to see it for myself—but not without him to show me.

I'd been on the road for over two weeks before I reached the Yukon and settled in for a day of rest. It was the beginning of June now, and I no longer worried that I wouldn't make it to the Burning Night ceremony by June twenty-first. I found a campground outside the town of Whitehorse and drove my rig along the bumpy road to find a parking spot. Not a problem, since there wasn't another soul there. The mosquitos found me as I was walking to place my money in the box set up at the entrance. I swatted at them and ran back to my trailer.

I made tea and called Nadine, watching the mosquitos gather on my skylight. It was hot inside, but I wasn't about to open the damn thing; there were too many holes in the screen.

"No, I haven't seen Tim," she said before I asked. "I think he took off. He has a habit of that."

"A habit of up and leaving?"

"He spends weeks in the woods when he's hunting. I figured with the cops after him he probably decided to get outta dodge."

"Have you heard anything about Dean?"

"He came in here about a week ago, got drunk and yelled about his wife and what a whore she was. Bernie had to throw him out."

I could see the entire scenario in my mind's eye. "Has he gone home now?"

"Haven't seen him since. The boys certainly miss you, Collie. I've been looking for a replacement, but haven't found the right gal. I hope you take my advice and think about going legit."

I laughed. "Right now I'm battling mosquitos on my way to Alaska. My future is up in the air."

"Good luck with it all. I wish I had better news about Tim. I was kind of surprised he didn't go after you."

"It's probably for the best. I'm way too old for him."

That night I cried myself to sleep, aching for Tim. My blithe comment about being too old had no meaning in the world we created together.

I was wandering through a thicket, thorns scratching my arms as I struggled forward. "Tim? Are you there?"

I couldn't see him anymore, and when I reached the other side of the thick prickly bushes he'd disappeared. I looked down at my tunic where new life pressed against the fabric. I was going to have his baby. I gazed out over the valley that lay before me. It was desolate. No trees, no bushes—nothing but dust and rocks. I woke with a gasp. Tim was gone. My future was a desert. Being pregnant was a symbol of how he'd permeated my soul, his absence like a wound that wouldn't heal. I turned my face into the pillow and sobbed.

Morning brought more sadness, my restless night leaving me exhausted and empty. My phone rang as I was blearily making coffee.

"Hi, Collie. Thought you'd like to know that Dean's back," Mary said.

"Why would I want to know that?"

"He told us what happened. All about that guy shooting him and you leaving him sick and helpless in the hospital? I thought you were nicer than that. What's going on with you?"

"And you believed every word that came out of that liar's mouth? I thought you knew me, Mary. And I thought you were my friend. Wasn't it you who encouraged me to leave him?"

"I am your friend. And yes, I did encourage you. But I didn't know what trouble you'd get yourself into. Friends don't let friends behave badly."

"For your information, I was the one who shot Dean. Tim performed some Native American voodoo and saved the bastard's life. I should have told him not to."

"That isn't the story Dean tells. Where are you?"

"Do you think I'd tell you after that last crap you pulled? Leave me alone, Mary. I appreciate the gift of the truck and trailer, but I no longer consider you my friend."

"At least tell me if that guy's with…"

If I could have slammed the phone down I would have. As it was all I could do was hit end and throw it against the wall. I was furious, my body shaking in anger. How did Dean do it? One minute he was persona non grata and in the next he had Mary and Bill eating out of his hand. Some friends they were.

I had to brave the black flies to get from the trailer to the truck, but it was early and still too cool for the mosquitos. I noticed a hiccup when I started the engine, but I ignored it as I drove out of the campground, heading west and north toward Alaska.

10

I was on the Alcan Highway when a herd of caribou appeared out of nowhere and ran in front of the truck. I slammed on the brakes and sat there shaking for several long minutes. When I inched up the road fifteen minutes later a mother bear and her cub meandered across the road ahead of me. I pulled off and waited, my gaze caught by a moose standing on a hill to my left. I was suddenly overcome, my eyes filling. There was so much wildlife here—animals I'd only ever seen in zoos lived in these forests. I cut the engine and gazed out the window as I drank the rest of my thermos of coffee.

I was still sitting there when I heard an engine laboring up the road behind me. The RV stopped next to me and a woman rolled down her window. "Are you all right?" she called.

"I'm fine. Just needed another cup of coffee."

She smiled. "Just checking. Out here in the boonies we need to look out for each other. Where are you headed?"

"Fairbanks."

"That's a long way. If you have car trouble there's a place about forty miles up called Sam's Garage. He sells gas and diesel too. If you stop, tell him Lisa and Keith said hello."

"I will. Thanks for the tip. I'll probably need gas by then."

She smiled and waved before she and Keith drove away. I realized then what a remote area this really was. I knew nothing about engines, had never changed a tire in my life. I only hoped the truck would hang on until I reached my destination. But when I turned the key all I heard was a click. The engine didn't even attempt to start, and now Lisa and Keith were long gone. Crap.

It was a good two hours before another car came along. The man who stopped was nice enough, but there was something about him I didn't trust. "I think I need to get my truck towed," I told him.

He got out of his dark blue Subaru and opened the truck's hood. "You're low on oil," he told me, coming around to where I still sat behind the wheel. "Move over and let me give her a try."

I slid over to the passenger side, nervously watching him climb in. When he turned the key there was still nothing but a click. "You have a bad battery, lady. I suggest you hop in with me. I'll drop you off at Sam's Garage. He has a tow truck."

I pulled out my phone, weighing my options, but when there was no signal I decided I'd better take him up on his offer.

"I'm Lance," he said once we were in his car. "Long way from anything for a pretty lady like you. Where ya headed?"

I glanced at his profile, startled by the scar that ran from his eyebrow to his chin. "Fairbanks."

"Wish I was going with you. Unfortunately the wife wants me home."

At least he was married, but I didn't like the look in his eye when he glanced at me.

We'd gone barely two miles when he suddenly pulled off the road and reached for me. I grabbed the door handle, hurled myself out of the car and ran for the woods. A second later he was out and running after me. He was probably in his mid thirties, and looked in good shape, his legs pumping. I was heading up a steep hill when I had to stop to catch my breath. I hadn't seen him approach when he attacked me from behind and threw me to the ground. I screamed and clawed at him as he pawed at my pants, one hand holding me down.

"It'll be over faster if you stop fighting," he hissed.

He was heavy, his weight on top of me making it hard to breathe. He'd managed to pull my sweatpants down when I saw a pack of wolves appear from under the heavy bushes. They eyed us, and when I let out a muffled scream one of them stopped, his tawny eyes trained on me. He growled low in his throat and moved closer.

"What the fuck?" Lance yelled, rolling off me. "Get out of here!" he yelled at the wolf, doing up his pants. But the wolf stood his ground. Lance's face turned a peculiar pale shade just before he took off running. The wolf loped after him.

I rose to my knees, shaking from head to toe. While I was adjusting my clothing I heard a bloodcurdling scream that sent chills up my spine. But the silence that descended a minute later was even worse. I tore down the hill, twisting my ankle on rocks and ripping my T-shirt on a wild rose bush, in my haste to find his car. Once I reached it I jumped inside, sitting there for a long moment as my heart beat an erratic rhythm against my ribcage. After a few deep breaths I turned the keys he'd thankfully left behind, and put the car in gear. A minute later I was speeding up the highway in the direction of Sam's Garage.

Sam was a decent older man with a large belly and kind eyes. I was still shaking when I reached the garage, the tale pouring from my mouth before I could stop myself.

"You're telling me that Lance tried to rape you and a pack of wolves stopped him? I've heard all kinds of wild stories up here, but this one takes the cake. I'll admit that Lance isn't what you'd call a stand-up guy, but the wolf part is hard to swallow."

"Only one wolf chased him," I said. "I think he killed him."

"The wolf killed Lance, or Lance killed the wolf?"

"The wolf killed Lance. I heard him screaming."

Sam's eyes clouded as he ran a hand over his stubble chin. "We'd best go and get your truck. While I'm down there I can take a look," he added, pulling a rifle off a shelf.

The drive back to get my truck was mostly made in silence. I could tell Sam was distressed, his eyes darting from one side of the road to the other. "Lance's wife is a saint," he muttered at one point. "That man is always screwing around."

"This was rape," I said in a near whisper, a shudder moving through me.

Sam glanced at me before turning back to the road. "Did he hurt you?"

"Didn't get that far," I mumbled.

He let out a sigh. "Glad to hear that."

I was positive the wolf had saved me. There'd been a thread of communication between us, as though he knew I needed his help. I knew better than to tell this version to Sam. He'd just think I was crazy.

My father's assaults reared up in my mind, my hand going to my mouth to keep from screaming. He'd raped me repeatedly. The helplessness came over me, a sick feeling in my stomach as I realized how close I'd come to being violated. "Can you pull over?" I asked Sam, rolling down my window.

He took one look at me and did as I asked, waiting while I retched into the weeds at the side of the road.

When we reached the spot where Lance had pulled off, I told Sam to stop. "It was right here where he parked. I ran up that trail," I said, pointing.

He gave me a glance as he got out of the car. "Wait here."

"Don't worry, I will."

It was about a half hour later that he returned, his face blanched of color.

"He's up there all right," he said, climbing into the driver's seat. "I'll call the cops once we get your truck to the garage."

"You didn't want to carry him out?"

His eyes darkened. "What's left of him, you mean? No."

I gagged and tried not to see what came into my mind. The wolf must have torn him to shreds.

Once we got the truck to his shop it didn't take long to install a new battery. While he was working on it I cleaned up in the bathroom and rinsed out my mouth with a Pepsi I bought from his shop. I hoped it would settle my stomach.

When I drove off to pick up my trailer the sun was still high in the sky, a map of several campsites Sam had given me on the seat beside me. He'd also called the cops, who were now investigating, their cars parked where Lance had pulled off.

"You know anything about this?" one of them asked me when I slowed down and stopped.

I nodded and looked away, not sure I wanted to tell him the story.

"Sam told us the gist of it, but he didn't explain how a wolf came to be there. The man is not even recognizable. I've never seen or heard of a wolf acting this way. We'll have to track him and kill him."

"Please don't. I know this may seem weird, but that wolf saved me from being raped."

"He went after a human and killed him," the cop said, his gaze hardening.

"I can't say that Lance deserved it, but..."

The cop smirked. "But he did?"

I took in a breath. "If it hadn't been for that wolf I might still be lying up there."

He stared at me, his expression impassive. "A rape is just a rape, ma'am."

"Just a rape? Have you ever been raped?"

He shook his head and wandered away to talk into his phone. I heard him say the word 'track' and the word 'rabies'.

I knew they'd never find that particular wolf. How could they possibly know which one he was? I drove past, heading to my trailer. Once I reached it I hooked the trailer back up and pulled onto the highway again, glancing at the cops as I drove by going the other way. I saw two of them coming down the hill carrying a body bag. It was a disturbing sight, but for some reason it didn't bother me that Lance was dead. A short time later I passed by Sam's garage. I didn't stop.

When I glanced at the map Sam had given me, trying to figure out where to camp, I had a feeling the ones he'd listed were miles away from where I was. The day had been long and terrible and I was ready to call it quits. When I came to a dirt road heading to the right, I turned off and followed it downward. From what I'd read in the guidebook about Alaska, it was pretty much okay to park anywhere overnight.

The logging road meandered into a narrow pine forest and ended at a clearing on the other side. When I got out of the truck the silence was immense, the sun hidden behind a mackerel sky. I locked the truck before taking a path that led into the woods, needing the call of birds, the aroma of earth and pine needles, and the feel of a breeze on my cheek to clear my head.

I'd been walking for about fifteen minutes when I heard a snuffling sound. I stopped and hid behind a tree, fear snaking up my spine. It could be anything, I thought, regretting my decision to take a walk. What was I thinking? A moment later a skunk shuffled by. I almost laughed, but held it in until he'd gotten some distance away. And then I hurried back to the rig, my gaze going into the distance where thick clouds were forming, thunderheads rising.

Dinner was a boiled egg and an apple. I had to find a grocery store, especially since I was about to run out of coffee.

May had finally found her niche. There was only one catch. Her parents had arrived from Illinois and were threatening to drag her home—'where she belonged,' they said.

"But I'm famous now!" she pleaded, showing them the write-up in the paper. **May Flowers is on her way to being a star,** *the article said.*

"Famous for being a dancer like that isn't famous, May. You should be ashamed of yourself."

"Why? I wear regular clothes and…"

"You call those outfits regular clothes? They show too much skin, young lady," her father said sternly.

May thought about the full skirts and tight tops. When she twirled the skirts twirled with her, adding to the festive quality of her special choreography. Her tops stayed in place no matter how she twisted or bent. "I don't see how you can say that, Papa."

"Haven't I taught you anything, girl? Dancing is the devil's work."

May thought about her religious upbringing and how hard it had been to move on from the rules. No dancing, no singing, no alcohol. Arms and chest and legs covered at all times. No parties, no dating. Her life had changed so much these past months. She had a boyfriend who often took her out to dinner, and once in a while she would even have a glass of wine. She was happy for the first time in her life.

I read over what I'd written. May was full of joy, just as I'd been before Dean ruined it all again. My thoughts traveled back to the night before my mother died. The chemo was working and she felt better—she was eating again, and her cheeks were pink. We went out to dinner for the first time in months. Dad wasn't around, his absence allowing me to breathe. But when Mom died the next day my world crashed down, the conclusion that happiness was followed by disaster tangling inside my brain.

My past flashed in front of my eyes, the truth of this settling into me. As I'd read in my self-help book, the mind was a tricky place. Half the time people acted on impulse with no real understanding of why. My father's nearly nightly assaults had hurt me badly, on a physical level as well as a psychic level, at a time when I was too young to understand. I had no memory of my childhood before then. And when he finally stopped and spent his nights elsewhere, I felt such relief that I opened my heart, letting the joy of my mother's recovery come in. Three months later my mother was dead.

Dean was another example that filled the bill. I trusted him, loved him. But as the years went by he turned against me, making me feel like I deserved his scorn and abuse. And now I'd let down my guard and allowed Tim into my heart. He'd referred to me as his woman—why hadn't he come after me? Tears welled as I pictured his face, the smile that curled up the corners of his mouth and softened his eyes. I felt bereft and hollow with wanting him. I should never have let myself fall for him. And yet how could I not? He'd given me the time I needed, not ever making any demands—he'd shown me what real intimacy was.

I wiped my eyes and saved my document, glancing at the clock on the computer. It was nearly two in the morning and it was still light outside. I shut the computer down and decided to try and get some sleep.

11

I was actually glad when my cell phone rang in the morning. For one thing it meant I had signal, and for another I was lonely. Rain pattered lightly on the roof of the trailer, the sound of dirt and pebbles pelting the trailer as the wind picked up. It was Mary.

"I'm sorry," she said as soon as I answered. "I don't know what got into me. You're my best friend."

"I thought so, but when you took Dean's side, I..."

"I know. I feel terrible. I want to blame it on Bill, but it isn't his fault."

"What happened since the last time we talked?"

"I remembered what a bastard Dean is. He's been yelling about you for three days now, telling us all about this creep you hooked up with and how the guy shot him. Just so you know, he's gone to the police here about it. Not that they can do anything. He reported you missing at the same time."

"I'm in Alaska and Tim isn't with me. It may be over between us."

"Sorry about that, but you did say he was too young."

"I did say that, but I still miss him."

"So what's happening in Alaska?"

"The sun doesn't go down, so sleeping is difficult. But it's raining today. I'm heading up to Fairbanks for the thingy."

"Burning Night," Mary supplied.

"And I almost got raped."

"What?"

"My truck wouldn't start and this guy stopped and said he'd give me a lift to a gas station up the road. We'd only gone a couple of miles when he suddenly pulled off and grabbed me. I managed to get out of the car, but when I ran for the woods he came after me. He almost raped me, Mary. I was shaking like a leaf. A wolf killed him."

There was a long silence before Mary asked, "What were you wearing?"

"Oh my god! You think it's my fault? I had on sweats and a stretched out T-shirt."

"Sorry, just checking. Seems like you've become quite the sexpot since you left."

"Why would you say that?"

"Dancing in a bar, having some torrid affair with a much younger man— Dean said that seeing you dance is like watching porn."

My face was suddenly hot. I felt deep shame and anger at the same time. "I knew I shouldn't have answered the phone. Please tell me that Dean didn't put you up to this."

"He didn't. I've washed my hands of him. Now what were you saying about a wolf killing the guy?"

"The pack came by when he was attacking me," I said coldly. "He freaked out and one of the wolves went after him. Cops found him torn to shreds."

"Jesus, Mary and Joseph. I knew wolves were dangerous, but I didn't know they killed humans. Maybe you should head home before something really bad happens."

"They don't kill humans. That wolf knew Lance was hurting me."

"The wolf knew? Sounds like you're still caught up in your mystical stuff. Are you on drugs?"

I let a moment pass as I counted to ten. "I don't expect you to believe me, but what Mom said is true. There's more to life than what our senses tell us. I've been reading and learning a lot about myself lately, and I doubt I'll be heading home anytime soon. Maybe never."

"Glad to hear it. I miss you, Collie. Please be careful and don't get into cars with strangers."

I hit the red button, threw the phone down and burst into tears. Tim was gone, Mary wasn't my friend, and Nadine didn't much care what I did. I had no one now.

When I opened the trailer door a while later a wolf was standing there, his tawny eyes glowing in the gray dawn light. "Are you *my* wolf?" I whispered, watching him. He was huge and shaggy, with thick gray brown fur. He stared for a full ten seconds before he turned and trotted off. I watched him disappear into the shadows under the trees. The wolf was still with me, a reminder that I wasn't alone.

A strange thought entered my mind about a spirit animal keeping watch over me, but I quickly dismissed it as ridiculous. But I had to admit that strange things had been happening ever since my night at the medicine wheel. And I'd said as much to Mary. Now I had to trust that there was a reason for it all.

What had Tim told me? *You don't have to figure it out, just live day by day.* But I had to come to terms with my life, had to decide at some point where I was going and what I wanted to do. I thought of the nights he'd held me, his own needs put on hold. His patience had gone a long way to helping me heal. Unfortunately I had the sense that there was a lot more healing to do before I came out the other side.

I opened *Outgrowing the Pain* to a random page and looked

down. *"There is a way past the pain,* I read. *It just takes time and the ability to face the past.* Hadn't I already faced the past? It was the present that was haunting me now—my new life that Tim had been a part of. It had to be love—I'd never experienced anything close to how I felt about him. I was out here to discover my future, I reminded myself sternly, not get embroiled in a love affair with a man ten years younger. But the warning that came from the logical side of my brain fell on deaf ears. I longed for his arms, for his mouth, for his calm support. My body literally ached every time I thought about him. *He's gone,* I told myself. *Get on with your life.*

I inched up the muddy track, hoping I wouldn't get stuck. The rain had stopped now, but the clay-filled earth that made up the logging road, was slick, my tires sliding as I crept upward. I let out a heavy sigh of relief when I reached the top and pulled onto the main road.

Driving was slow, what with animals abruptly appearing, eagles flying by on their way to nest in the trees, and the general feeling of being in another world. There were forested hills on either side of the gravel road, animals darting out and running before I could even figure out what they were. I stopped often to take pictures. In a meadow beyond the wooded area I saw a lynx chasing a horseshoe hare, its body a blur of tufted ears and long legs as it leapt gracefully.

When I reached Tok, Alaska, and found a real campground, I pulled in. A shower sounded wonderful, and it had a café, which was good since eggs and nuts for dinner did not sound appetizing.

The café was full when I went in, the din of conversation loud in the small space. I found one free table and sat down. Around me the RV crowd traded stories that had to do with being in the wilderness. One caught my attention:

"I heard a wolf tore some guy limb from limb," an overweight, red-faced man in his forties told the guy sitting at the table behind him.

"I heard about that. Sounded real scary. If I see a wolf I plan to shoot on sight."

"Is that allowed?" a woman asked.

"I don't care if it's *allowed*," the guy answered. "Wolves should be wiped off the earth."

"No, they shouldn't," I said loudly.

The guy frowned and turned. "What do you know about it?"

"I was there."

"There? You saw it?"

The waiter came over and put a glass of water down. "The guy tried to rape me," I mumbled. "The wolf protected me."

"Those animals don't protect," the red-faced man said. "They're predators and now they've killed a man. Hunters should go out there and exterminate every last one of them."

I shook my head, trying to find a sympathetic face in the crowd. There were none. "They're endangered from over hunting, and I'm telling you the truth. If it hadn't been for that wolf I could have been killed."

"What makes you think he wouldn't have turned on you next?" another man asked.

"Our eyes met."

There was a collective scoff as the men took this in. I had suddenly lost my appetite and wished I'd never spoken up. A second later I pushed my chair back and left the café.

As I drove the rig out of the camp I wondered whether I was wrong to tell them about my involvement in Lance's death. Alaska seemed like a gossipy place, as though everyone knew everyone else's business. What if this rumor made it to Burning Night? The idea was horrifying. I wanted to put the experience behind me, but I could not let them blame it all on the wolf. The wolf had made contact with me. Twice. And I had the feeling that not only was the wolf my protector, I was its protector too.

About fifty miles up I found a turn-off and drove down a rough dirt lane to park. Lack of sleep and worry were catching up with me. Fairbanks was only two hundred miles away, but then I had to get to Eagle Summit, another hundred miles further on. Barring any more strange incidents, and allotting time for shopping, it would take me at least two more long days.

Was my wolf still with me or had his appearance at the forest been a coincidence? For all I knew it was two different wolves. But something inside me wanted to believe that this wolf had followed me and might still be around. I sighed and went to eat my last egg, swallowing it down with one of two bottles of water I had left. I *had* to find a grocery store.

I opened the door and watched the sun for a while, wishing it would disappear, but when it didn't I opened my computer and set to work.

May was dragged away by her parents, tears mottling her pancake makeup, black mascara running down her face to form jagged dark streaks. "Why are you doing this?"

Her father narrowed his eyes, a frown appearing on his face. "Did you think we'd let you parade your body for all to see? The sin of pride, May, the sin of pride."

"What pride? I only wanted to participate in the play!"

"Plays are not part of our religion, nor is dancing of any kind. You know that as well as I do."

"I don't want to be part of your silly old religion," May cried out, sobbing like a child.

Her father smiled. "You belong to us, May. You will come

home and take care of the house as you've always done. And when we grow old, you'll take care of us as well."

"Unless you lock me in I won't stay!" May shouted.

Her parents exchanged a glance. "If that's what it takes," her father said.

I stopped typing, surprised by the nasty turn of events. I'd expected my main character to dance and feel liberated by her freedom, but instead she was allowing her parents to ruin her life again. What was keeping her from saying no? I'd heard of characters taking over the plot, but this was ridiculous.

What was going on with the book had to be connected with my own confusion and feeling shut out by the people I'd counted on. My head was swimming with the past and I didn't trust myself. I saved the document and shut down the computer.

Once I reached the mountain I wouldn't have time to work on the book, especially now that my main character had taken the plot in a different direction. And I had no idea what she was planning next. But then again, the blogs I'd read on writing said that there had to be tension in order to keep a reader interested. What was too much and what wasn't enough? I had no idea.

Not only was my entire life up in the air, now my book was out of control as well? I let out a slightly insane sounding laugh. If I talked to Mary now she would surely send the men in white coats after me.

Morning came too soon. I'd gone to bed late and hadn't slept well, excited about Burning Night, wondering about the slight chance that Tim would be there, and concerned about how my book had got so far from where I'd planned it to go. *May needed*

to get a backbone. Was that my problem too? Maybe if I'd told Dean off years ago he wouldn't be hounding me now. And he *was* hounding me, thoughts of him interrupting my sleep. It was entirely his fault that Tim had taken off.

I made coffee and dressed, stowing things as I wandered around the tiny space. The trailer was feeling more cramped than it had at the beginning—funny how when Tim was with me the space seemed larger. I was looking forward to sleeping outside under the stars. But today I had to find a grocery store and stock up on food. No point in rushing things—I had several days to get there.

When I was walking from the trailer to the truck I was sure I saw a streak of brown-gray fur disappearing under the trees. Tim's face loomed up as I climbed behind the wheel. He knew where I was going, and he hadn't missed a Burning Night in five years. Just the thought that he might be there cheered me up.

12

It was three in the afternoon when I reached Anchorage and checked into a motel. I counted out my cash, more than happy to shell out the money for the large bed, TV, and a real bathroom with a tub and shower.

After heading to a corner market for emergency supplies I took a long hot bath and binge watching TV. My eyes were drooping when I settled into the comfy bed and turned off the light. Unfortunately the loud argument I could hear through the thin wall kept me awake. When the yelling stopped the rhythmic squeak of the bedsprings began, accompanied by moaning. They must have sorted out their problems. Once they were finished with make-up sex I heard the shower turn on and a man's voice singing in a falsetto. I lay awake for hours after that, thinking about Tim and imagining him next to me.

At some point sleep finally claimed me, my dreams taking me places I didn't want to go. Despite being a grown woman in the dream my father molested me, my mother laughing as she watched. I woke drenched in sweat, my heart pounding. When I turned to see the clock it read 7:00 a.m. I rose and took a shower, trying to let go of the helpless feeling the dream had instilled. Tears spilled and tracked down my cheeks, mixing with the water from the shower. I opened my mouth and let the sobs come. I cried nearly every day now.

Once I dressed I opened *Outgrowing the Pain* to another random page. *...memories will surface, ones you don't want to look at, but facing them and knowing what happened was not your fault, goes a long way toward healing.*

I let out a sigh. All well and good, but a dream like the one I just had indicated that the abused little girl still lived inside me. I knew it wasn't my fault, and yet deep down I felt powerless. I thought of Tim and how he'd listened when I explained what I wanted from him. He'd waited, always there if I needed to talk, holding me when I cried. Tim's support and compassion had allowed me to open to him. And when the day finally came, he was careful, asking if this or that was all right, and making sure I got what I needed. No one in my life had ever treated me like that.

I dressed and headed out to find some breakfast, carrying my computer along—I had an idea for my book and wanted to get it down before I forgot it. A block from my room I came upon a café with Wi-Fi and a lively crowd occupying the tables and chairs lining the street. Judging by their hippy attire I figured they were Burning Night goers. Every nationality, color, and age seemed to be represented, ranging from teenagers to over seventy.

Inside I found an empty table next to a wall and ordered. While I was waiting I plugged my computer into the wall socket and brought up Word. The din of the place receded into the background as I reconnected with my main character. *What have you been up to, May?* I whispered as I reread my last paragraph. My fingers flew across the keys as though she'd been poised in time, waiting for me to move her along.

May cried herself to sleep that night, her ability to do something about her situation disappearing with the sound of the lock clicking. Her parents had actually locked her in her room. Memories surfaced from her childhood. This had happened often enough when she disobeyed some rule. She couldn't remember what she'd done wrong, only that they gave her the cold shoulder and delivered her food on trays. Just like this. But now she was of age. They couldn't do this to her. It had to be against the law. But she had no phone and no way to reach out to a friend to ask for help.

It was day three of this when she decided it had gone on too long. Any career she'd hoped for as a result of her debut dance part was washed up. But this was her life, and she deserved to make her own decisions, despite her parents' antiquated rules. When her mother appeared with the tray, May shoved her backward, the tray and soup spilling down her mother's apron and crashing to the floor. Before her mother could get her balance, May was out the door and bounding down the stairs. She flew out the front door and kept going like the hounds of hell were after her.

When the waitress arrived with my food I stopped typing and saved my document. At least May was pushing forward. I stared down at my plate of eggs, toast, and bacon. Would the festival bring answers? What were my questions? Did I still want to dance or did I want something else for my life? I hoped for an experience like the one I had at the medicine wheel but I knew that Burning Night would be very different. I picked up my fork.

Once I finished eating I checked my email, surprised to see a return message from a publisher I'd contacted.

Dear Ms. Morgan,
I have spoken to my colleague about your story proposal and we are both interested. Can you send us either the first few

chapters or an outline that details the storyline with all the plot points?

Thank you for consulting Putney Publishing.
Sincerely,
Louise Putney

I gazed at the email for a long while. Since sending the query letter the plot had shifted and changed. Would she like it now? Instead of attempting to write an outline, a thought that filled me with dread, I would send her chapters one and two. And I would mention the fact that it hadn't yet been edited. Maybe they had editors on staff. And then I remembered how much editors cost. I clicked on the Word document, but my mind was still back on the email when I felt a presence next to me.

"Are you a writer?" the woman asked, glancing at my screen.

"I guess I am."

"I'm sorry to be so nosey, but I read a paragraph or two before you realized I was standing here. It's intriguing."

I took in her narrow face, the wispy brown hair that framed it. Her eyes were a clear gray. "You really think so?"

"I do. I have several friends who are writers. I edit for them. And I have connections with several publishers—I'm also an agent," she said, smiling. "I'm Karen Holt." She held out her hand.

"Columbine Morgan." I shook her hand and gestured for her to sit. "I just got an email from a publisher I contacted when I'd barely started this. I sent her a synopsis of what I intended to write, but now the story's going in a different direction."

Karen laughed. "Every author I talk to says the same thing. Characters cannot be controlled." She dug in her bag and handed me a business card. "Are you travelling through or staying a while?"

"I'm leaving for Fairbanks this morning."

"The festival."

I nodded.

"Well, I hope you have a mystical time," she said, rising. "If you want an editor I'm pretty cheap. And we can do business over the web. I'd love to see the finished product. Good to meet you, Columbine."

"Thanks," I said. "You too."

"The pleasure is all mine. I hope to hear from you." She smiled and headed toward the door.

I was stunned. Now I had two possibilities? Would I have to pay for this bit of good luck with another disaster? I mentally chastised myself for the thought, vowing to stay positive.

I left Anchorage around ten, heading toward Fairbanks and Eagle Summit. The drive was scenic, with lots of places I could have stopped, but I knew it would be a long drive and I was anxious to get there. I thought of my wolf, wondering if he was still with me. Maybe he'd given up when I stopped in Anchorage.

I was on a steep stretch of road when the truck engine began to falter and hiccup, finally stopping altogether. Luckily at the first sign of engine failure I'd pulled to the side of the road, limping along until I couldn't go any further. This was what I got for thinking things were looking up.

I was sitting there trying to decide what to do when a car pulled up behind me. A young couple got out and headed to the driver's side window.

"Are you okay?" the young blonde woman asked.

"I'm fine, but my truck isn't. It just stopped working and I know nothing about engines."

"Pop the hood and let me take a look," the sandy-haired man with her said, stepping toward the front of the truck. I did as he asked, watching him through the gap as he fiddled with this and that.

"Brandon knows a lot about engines," the young woman assured me, watching him check my oil and battery.

He wiped his hands on his already grimy jeans and joined her at my window. "Slide over and I'll give her a try."

I did as he asked. When he turned the key the engine gave a cough but nothing happened.

He glanced at me. "This truck ain't goin' nowhere without a mechanic."

"What's wrong with it?"

He shrugged. "Damned if I know. Oils good, battery seems ok, although it's hard to tell."

I felt a panic attack coming on. "I just bought this battery. What should I do?"

"You'll need to have her towed. We can give you a ride to Randy's—he's got a garage up in Fairbanks."

I let out a sigh. "I'd appreciate that, but it's getting late. He's probably closed."

Brandon looked at his watch. "Susie, do you know what time Randy closes up shop?"

Susie's blonde curls bobbed as she shook her head.

Brandon stared out the windshield, seemingly thinking. "I suggest you get in with us. If nothin' else we can take you to a motel close to Randy's and you can have the rig towed in the morning."

"But I was on my way to Eagle Summit. I'll never get there at this rate."

"That's where we're going," Susie said.

"I'd bum a ride, but I can't leave the rig here that long."

"Climb in with us. Maybe you'll get lucky and Randy'll still be open."

I grabbed my purse, locked the truck and climbed into their

vintage pinto, sharing the back seat with a friendly pit bull. They chatted non-stop about the festival and how excited they were to be going. "Several rock bands will be there. Do you know the Grateful Dead?"

"The Grateful Dead will be there?"

"Well, not the original, but a cover band that's pretty good, from what we hear."

"It's a drug-users paradise," Brandon added. "Psychedelics, weed, you name it."

They prattled on about former years with crazy stories of police busts and famous bands.

"Do the police come every year?"

"Nah—that year was a fluke. They were after some dude who'd robbed a liquor store and followed him up."

⚬⚭⚬⚭⚬

It was nearing six o'clock by the time we reached Randy's garage.

"He's still open," Brandon said brightly, pulling up in front.

I gave the dog one last pat and hopped out of the back seat. "Thanks so much. I'll see you up there?"

"We'll be long gone by the time you get there," Brandon said, one side of his mouth curling up.

"What? You're not staying…?"

"Brandon's talkin' about our heads. There's a lot of good dope," Susie explained, giggling. "Hey, what's your name, anyway?"

"I'm Columbine."

"Columbine. That's different. See you later, Columbine."

I waved and headed inside.

"What can I do you for?" the heavy-set man wearing baggy overalls asked.

"My truck and trailer broke down about twenty miles south

of here. I was hoping I could get a tow and have it fixed."

He rubbed a filthy hand across his face. "Was planning to close up early tonight, what with the festival and all, but seein' as how a pretty girl needs my help…" he chuckled. "Headin' to the festival, are ya?"

"I was. But without a working truck I may be stuck here in Fairbanks."

"Let's get your rig and see how bad things are. Worse comes to

worse you can leave her here for a few days and catch a ride up with someone."

Randy got the truck working just long enough to drive the rig to his shop. I drove his truck, following closely to make sure he didn't get stuck on the side of the road. Once he checked it over he gave me a grim look. "Needs a new carburetor. These Chevy trucks aren't made any more, which means I'll have to locate a used one. I hate to tell you this, but we're talkin' at least a thousand bucks."

I gasped, mentally going through how much money I had left. "I may have to get a part time job," I muttered.

"What kind of work you do?"

"I'm a dancer."

He frowned. "A dancer, you mean like an exotic dancer? I know several clubs in town that would be happy to hire you," he said, looking me up and down.

"I've got enough to pay for the repairs. How much does the festival cost?"

He chuckled. "Festival's free, and there's a lot of people up there who'd give you the shirt off their backs. You'll get by just fine. And if you find you need to work for a week or two, I'll fix ya up with a buddy of mine who owns a decent place."

"But how do I get to Eagle Summit?"

Randy let out a guffaw. "You walk out that door and stick your thumb out, that's how." He smiled at my skeptical look. "Don't worry—she'll be all ready to go once you get back." He nodded at the trailer. "Better take what you need. I'll lock her up at night to keep your things safe." He pointed behind a chain link fence where several cars were parked.

I pulled the money out of my purse and paid him in cash before I grabbed my sleeping bag, my computer, my water and the snacks I'd purchased from the Quick Mart. "Thanks so much, Randy. You're a godsend." I waved and walked purposely toward the street.

It took all of five minutes before a car stopped, two men and a woman leaning out with smiles on their faces. The odor of marijuana wafted out the windows, smoke drifting toward me.

"Need a ride to the festival?"

"I do. My truck broke down and it's spending a couple of days with Randy," I said, gesturing to the shop behind me.

The driver laughed. "Randy gets all the good ones. Why are all my customers overweight and taciturn?"

"Jerry's a mechanic," the woman explained. "He and Randy are competitors."

"Climb in," Jerry said.

I threw my sleeping bag down on the floor and placed my backpack with my computer, all my cash and a few changes of underwear on the seat, and climbed in behind it. The passenger in the back smiled, rearranging his things to give me room. He was hitchhiking from Chicken, a little town toward the southeast.

"You know how it got its name?" he asked once we were on our way, taking a deep drag on the joint he held.

I shrugged.

He let out his held breath, smoke coming with it. "They

wanted to name it ptarmigan after the grouse that lives around here, but they didn't know how to spell it."

I laughed. "Where are you from?" I asked, noticing his accent.

"Australia. I travel in the summer and pick up odd jobs, like baling hay or working in the fields."

"Sounds like a long way to come."

"It is, but I like the change of pace." His hazel eyes met mine. "How about you?"

"I...I ran away from home a while ago. I've been traveling from Virginia. I heard about this Burning Night thing and I wanted to check it out."

"It's pretty cool." He held out the joint. "Want a toke?"

"No thanks. I'm already high from the smoke in here." All three burst out laughing, the giggles going on for quite a while as they fought for breath.

I dozed for a while, waking as we began the long climb up to Eagle

Summit. The sun was a ball of fire hanging low in the sky. Mountains loomed darkly, their shapes reminding me of childhood stories I'd read having to do with trolls and giants. The Burning Night festival was held on a closer range of low rolling hills that were free of ice and snow this time of year.

We joined a line of slow moving cars, inching our way forward with the rest. People were yelling and waving to their friends, the sound of honking, rock music and the odor of marijuana drifting in the still air. I saw a half dozen VW busses painted in bright rainbow colors, as well as several small RV's that had been retrofitted with wooden shakes. Silver Airstreams glinted as they glided by. And interspersed were trucks and trailers similar to mine, almost all of them vintage. The newer and larger RV's stuck out like sore thumbs.

"Not exactly Mt. Everest," Jerry said. "But the view from up there is

spectacular."

"Does it stay warm at night? I have a sweater and a sleeping bag, but not much else."

"You'll do fine—most of the people up here have less than that."

"What's it like—Burning Night, I mean."

My backseat companion grinned. "You'll have to see for yourself."

"But what if it rains?"

"It never rains during Burning Night."

I had no idea what time it was when we rolled into a parking space between two rusted out trucks. A dog ran by as we got out of the car, his hackles rising as he barked and disappeared behind an RV. I squinted into the distance where the sun hung above the horizon, just as it had been for the past couple of hours. People were everywhere, the miasma of marijuana and incense assaulting my senses. I heard rock music, laughter and singing. I turned to ask my companions where to go, but they'd already taken off. I started walking in the direction of the noise.

I wandered around the outskirts of the all night party, trying to find some out-of-the-way spot where I could put my sleeping bag. The ground was hard, and what grass there was had already been taken; there were tents and sleeping bags everywhere. The top of the mountain was very bare—desolate almost. But what it lacked in vegetation it made up in view— three hundred and sixty degrees of it. People ran by me every so often, calling out to long lost friends or just jogging for exercise. A band had set up in the center of a large field and began to play old rock tunes. People were barbecuing. I hadn't eaten since breakfast and my stomach registered the delicious smells; my peanuts, pork rinds, and corn chips didn't sound that good right now.

As I wandered I kept a lookout for Tim, hoping he'd decided to come. I didn't see him. "You want a dog?" someone asked, stopping next to me.

I turned to the dark-haired skinny young man. "A dog? No, I don't think

so."

"A hotdog, not a real dog," he explained, laughing. "We made too many."

I followed him over to a propane barbecue, accepting the hotdog he handed me. "Thanks. I just got here and I don't have any real food. Are there vendors here?"

"Will be tomorrow when it officially opens. Glad I found you. No one should go hungry."

I smiled and took a bite of the mustardy hotdog slathered in pickle relish and onion and encased in the soft white bun. Delicious.

The party atmosphere continued, although by this time many had gone off to their tents to get a few winks of sleep before the real festivities began. I found a spot to set up my sleeping bag that was far enough away for privacy, but not so far that I felt isolated. I climbed in, pulling my pack in with me. I fell asleep almost immediately.

Tim was in my sleeping bag with me, his body warming mine. I put my arms around his neck. "I missed you," I mumbled. "Glad you made it."

I woke to rain, my sleeping bag nearly soaked through. Hadn't Jerry said it never rained?

I climbed out of my bag and looked around. No one was even awake yet. I shivered and wrapped my arms around my chest. No dry clothes and no dry sleeping bag didn't add up to a good day. I headed toward the only patch of trees, trying to get out of the steady drizzle. That's when I saw the wolf. He was standing just where the hill sloped down—a hundred yards away. As soon as I spotted him he turned and loped off, disappearing over the rise. I hurried after him.

He vanished into woods at the bottom of the hill, his bushy tail a flag for me to follow. It was warmer under the trees, and I slipped off my soggy sweater and tied it around my waist. A feeling of the mystical sent a tingling sensation up both of my arms. I couldn't see the wolf now, the dark conifers sending light skittering as shadows melted into shadows. A narrow animal trail led off and I followed it, peering ahead to catch a glimpse of the wolf. There was no sign of him now. Gray mists replaced the shadows, ghostly faces appearing within them, dark eyes watching me. I was suddenly afraid. But when I turned to go back the trail had disappeared. I hurried ahead, trying to ignore my rising panic.

I must have walked for nearly an hour before I spotted a small tent set up under low hanging pine branches. I stopped and held my breath. I was miles away from the festival and had no idea who I might encounter. I was just about to take off in another direction when I heard a rustle. "Columbine?"

The tent flap opened, revealing a familiar face. "Tim? What are you doing here?"

"I came for the festival."

I looked around. "But…you're camped so far away."

He grinned. "Don't like crowds much. How'd you find me?"

I glanced at the trees, the path that wasn't there now. "You won't believe me if I tell you."

His brown eyes met mine. "Try me."

"I followed a wolf." I began to tell him the story, my arms going round my shivering body.

"Come inside the tent," he offered, moving back.

I crawled inside, glad for the warmth and his proximity as I kept talking. His eye color seemed to shift and change, one minute brown and in the next a tawny yellow.

"What ended up happening with Dean?" he asked when I came to a stopping place.

I shrugged. "I left him at the hospital. The last time I spoke with Mary she said he was back home."

Tim pressed his lips together and stared into space. "I thought for sure you'd go with him."

"Why would you think that?"

"You had the strangest expression on your face that night— and then you climbed into the ambulance without even looking at me."

"He was hurt and I felt responsible. He told the cops it was you who shot him."

Tim scoffed. "I know. It's why I took off." He glanced at me. "Now tell me more about this wolf."

I smiled. "He…he led me here. He's been following me since the attempted rape."

Tim let out a huff of concern. "When did that happen?"

"A couple of days ago, but nothing happened. The wolf killed him."

"What?" Tim raised his eyebrows in alarm. "The wolf killed the guy?"

"Ripped him to shreds, according to the cops. They said they'd have to track him. But how can they? They'll never find him."

Tim stared into space, a faraway look in his eyes. "Every wolf here is tagged. If they want to find him, they'll find him." He went silent after that, a frown of worry appearing. When he finally turned back to me his eyes were no longer the brown I knew, the tawny irises scaring me. He had an untamed look.

"What are you thinking about?" I asked, trying not to be frightened.

"Wolves are my spirit animals."

"I thought so. I wondered if the wolf was you." After my comment Tim stared at me for so long I began to fidget. "Is it?" I finally asked.

He let out a low rumbling chuckle that sounded vaguely animal-like. "A man who can shape shift? Really?"

I laughed nervously. "I guess not."

He let out a sigh. "You have no idea what I've been going through. I thought I'd never see you again…and then…" He stopped in mid sentence, a frown appearing on his face.

"And then…what?"

"I don't remember how I got here." When he looked up his eyes were full of a strange light.

This definitely had to be a dream, but I didn't want it to be. "So what's the deal? Didn't you drive here in your truck?"

"Nope. No truck."

"Did you hitch-hike?"

He shook his head and stared at me. "That's what I'm saying. I'm here now, but I was at home not that long ago."

His eyes were pale again and a slightly different shape. I pushed backward away from him. This entire experience was beginning to feel dangerous. "So you just found yourself here? How is that possible?"

His hair had bits of leaf and twigs in it, some of it drifting to the ground as he ran his fingers through it. "What I want to do right now is kiss you and forget all this other stuff..." his words trailed off.

"I...I've been thinking about you every day since the night I shot Dean. I figured you'd decided I was too old for you." I waited for some normal response, like the smile I remembered, or for the color of his eyes to return to brown, but instead he moved his head from side to side as though he was sniffing, a gesture that didn't seem human. My pulse quickened as I inched backward toward the tent flap. This was not the Tim I knew.

"Age is nothing but numbers," he muttered.

A moment later the distance between us seemed to shrink. His arms came around me, pulling me against him, and when I struggled, he held me so tightly I couldn't move. "Tim, you're hurting me."

He didn't answer as his head bent to mine, his lips brushing against my lips. Desire rose up, my resolve slipping as the smell and feel of him worked its usual magic. And when his tongue ran along my lower lip I opened my mouth, tasting him. He moaned, his fingers moving through my hair. I felt his heart beating. The next thing I knew we were stretched out together.

And sometime in between kissing and lying down, our clothes had magically disappeared.

I was in a forest following the wolf, but when I caught up with him he'd turned into Tim, his gold/green eyes glowing as they stared into mine. We melted into one being, our bodies twisting and curving into one another as we connected. I was lost to this world, my mouth open under his, my body meeting his as wave upon wave of sensation rolled over me.

I woke alone in my sleeping bag. There was no tent and no Tim. I stood and looked around, surprised to see the sun shining. I had no idea what time it was. Did I dream the entire thing? It couldn't be. My body was in a state of high arousal; my pulse raced from what we'd been doing together—and yet there was no one here.

⬥

"What kind of drugs are you on?" Jerry asked me later, smirking.

I'd searched for him and his girlfriend, Helga, needing to tell someone about my odd experience. "I'm not on any drugs. That's the thing. I was following the wolf…"

"Wolf? What wolf?"

"There was a wolf standing just down there," I pointed at the crest of the hill. "I followed him."

"You followed a wolf, an animal that never shows itself, and then you were with your boyfriend, except now he's gone? Sounds like hallucination to me. Did you eat anything last night?"

"Just a hotdog somebody gave me."

"Must have been laced with LSD. It's the only explanation." He glanced at Helga. "I say forget about it and enjoy yourself. There's a band about to start."

I focused on the people wandering here and there wearing

112

bathing suit tops and cut-offs. The sun was high and warmed my back. "It's like it never rained."

"Rain? It never rains for Burning Night."

"It rained last night. It's why I was up so early. My sleeping bag was soaked through."

Helga laughed. "Wow. You were on some trip."

When they wandered off I followed them, afraid to be by myself. Had I been drugged the night before? Everything seemed so real, from my conversation with Tim to…and that's when I remembered the oddness of the sex, the sense of being animal and human at the same time.

I put the night behind me and tried to get into the festival atmosphere. When Helga offered me dope I took the hand rolled joint and smoked it, holding the smoke in my lungs and hoping it would stop my thoughts from returning to Tim. I refused to let Jerry and Helga out of my sight, afraid if I did, I'd see the wolf again and be off on some other crazy escapade.

I danced to the music, shed my outer garments and joined with the rest of the scantily clad crowd. When a man commented on my dancing prowess I laughed and performed a short sexy number, holding my hair up off my neck as I pranced around him. He pulled me close and kissed me, his tongue going in my mouth. He tasted of smoke and beer.

I drank a drink someone handed me, not caring what it was laced with. I wanted to put Tim behind me, but the harder I tried, the more the scenes from the night before plagued me. I couldn't get him out of my mind.

At some point late in the evening I saw the wolf again, a hazy gray shape moving in the distance. I grabbed Helga's arm. "See him? He's over there."

She frowned, squinting toward where I pointed. "I don't see anything." A moment later Jerry grabbed her arm and twirled her around as the Grateful Dead cover band played 'Hell in a Bucket.'

My muscles loosened as I danced alongside them, my head falling back as I twirled, stumbling to keep my balance as the world rocked around me. Fairy lights came on around the makeshift stage as men grabbed my hands, tugging me along with them. People were naked, their bodies slick with sweat as they danced. I undid my bathing suit top and shed my shorts—I was a dancer, a wild woman, a gypsy, as free as a bird. When another man grabbed me and kissed me I kissed him back, my arms tight around his neck. A moment later I was spinning away again, my eyes shut as I swayed. When the music suddenly stopped, I opened my eyes, surprised to see the band trooping off the stage.

"What we all came here for is about to begin!" I heard a male voice yell. He stood on the stage naked, his arms lifted to the sky. His leathery skin was sunburned and peeling, his cheeks and nose bright red. Matted dreadlocks fell to his shoulders.

Behind him fireworks rose into the sky, crackling and popping, rainbow colors shifting and changing. I was floating, my arms held up as his were as I screamed with the others, our voices echoing.

"This is Burning Night and now we **BURN!**" the man on stage screamed. A shout went up as a group of men and women dragged over logs and pieces of wood, stacking them against one another until they formed a tall pyramid.

"Who will light our fire?"

I watched from my place thirty feet away as a man came forward, his dark hair a curtain against the copper skin of his cheek. He was bare-chested, wearing jeans, a band of leather tied around his head. His skin glistened in the lowering sun, his profile as familiar as my own. He struck a match and leaned forward. A moment later the dry wood caught, flames licking upward. I stared, my heart suddenly pounding, but before I could hurry toward him he'd faded into the shadows on the other side of the bonfire.

"Where did he go?" I shouted at a man standing close to the blaze.

"Where did who go?"

"The guy who lit the fire."

He pointed into the distance, but all I could see was a crowd of people staring in rapt wonder at the blaze. A moment later the crowd began to move, gathering hands and swaying to and fro. When someone grabbed my hand I was pulled into the movements, my head twisting as I tried to locate Tim. I didn't see him anywhere.

We snaked around the fire, people singing, others shouting. Fireworks placed strategically among the logs exploded as the flames ignited them. They burst into the sky, blue, white, red, the colors mixing as they shot upward. I heard screaming, crying, people laughing, animals whining and barking. I was caught up in it and couldn't get out, even if I'd wanted to.

At one point I was sure I spied Tim on the other side of the circle, but when I looked again he was gone. I realized I had tears streaming down my face. I was overcome with wanting Tim so badly I thought I might die of it. Instead of feeling liberated, I now felt like a balloon with all the air let out. All my hopes for this night had been lost in a dream fantasy that had disappeared with the dark smoke lifting into the air. My sobs were drowned out in the cacophony, the world spinning away from me. Faces appeared in the flames, their mouths open in a perpetual scream. I heard what sounded like gunshots.

I wrenched away to be sick, my belly wracked with spasms as I threw up. I lay like a spent fish on the ground, unsure where I was. It was twilight now, as dark as it would get. The night's activities whirled by me, making me dizzy. I vomited again, my head throbbing, my throat raw. I heard the music start up again, people laughing. Tears had dried on my cheeks—the salt burned my skin. I fell into an uneasy slumber.

The next time I woke I was in my sleeping bag and the sun was a ball of fire in the east. I turned away and shaded my eyes. My head was splitting. I groaned and rolled over. In the distance a pile of ash still smoldered, the stench of scorched wood, alcohol and vomit wafting around me. I gagged and reached for my water bottle, taking a swig while my gaze traveled across the deserted camp. Everyone was still asleep, the silence like a heavy weight pressing down on me. I thought of the alcohol I'd consumed, along with whatever drugs I'd been plied with. I moaned and sat up, holding my head in both hands. Tim had been here—I'd seen him light the bonfire. And yet he hadn't bothered to seek me out. My fantasy of him telling me that age was only numbers was only a story I made up.

I felt drained and sick with disgust about how I'd behaved the night before. I'd kissed two strange men and taken off all my clothes; I remembered hearing the hoots and wolf whistles. I was only glad there wasn't a strange man lying next to me.

And that's when I saw him. A dark-haired man was in a sleeping bag two feet away from mine. My head swam, and for a moment I thought I might be sick again. I did have a vague recollection of rolling around on the ground, the feel of hands on my body, a tongue in my mouth, the feel of…oh god…no. When I rose to my knees I realized I was completely naked. I searched the vicinity for my clothes but couldn't find them. What had I done?

I had the sleeping bag around my shoulders, trying to decide what to do, when I heard a man's voice.

"Collie?"

When I turned toward the familiar voice Tim was on his elbows staring at me. "Are you all right?"

"Not really. What…what happened?"

Tim smiled. "You were a wild woman last night."

I frowned. "I don't remember much. Where are my clothes?"

"You stripped naked and threw them in the fire."

"Good god!"

"Don't worry—lots of other people were doing the same. I'm glad I found you before you were spirited away by some other guy."

"I thought…when I saw you there…"

"That I was a stranger? You don't remember last night?"

I shook my head. "I kind of remember rolling around, but…"

He pushed himself up, a wicked smile on his face. He waggled his eyebrows. "We'll have another chance, don't worry."

"But not now," I said, feeling the sickness come over me again.

"You need food and coffee. I'll find you some."

When he got out of his sleeping bag and searched for his jeans I couldn't stop staring. His copper skin glistened in the dawn light. He was gorgeous and unearthly. "I had this dream about a wolf, and…" I began.

"Yeah, you told me all about it last night. Pretty crazy, Collie." He pulled on his jeans. "I'll be back in a minute. Don't go anywhere."

I grimaced. "Believe me, I won't." I thought about my experience with him in the forest, our conversation—a rational conversation about the things that really happened back in

Lovell. How could it all be a dream? But he was really here this time. I lay back and closed my eyes.

I was dozing when I heard him come back, but when I opened my eyes it was Jerry standing next to me holding out a plate of food. "I brought you breakfast. Figured it was the least I could do after last night."

I pushed myself up to sitting. "Where's Tim?"

"Who's Tim?"

I glanced toward his sleeping bag, but it wasn't there. "He...he went to get me food. He was with me last night."

Jerry shook his head. "Helga and I put you to bed last night. You were a sick mess and I felt responsible for plying you with drugs and alcohol. Sorry, Collie."

He held out a cup of coffee, which I took into my shaking hands. "I think I might be losing my mind."

He scoffed. "Everyone says that after their first burning night. At least you didn't throw your clothes in the fire like some people."

I glanced down, noticing I was still dressed in my cut-offs and bathing suit top. "I remember taking off my top, and..."

Jerry laughed. "Yeah, you did. But you put it back on."

"I didn't take everything off and burn them?"

"Nope. I would have remembered that."

"And I was sick to my stomach."

He nodded. "Helga and I took care of you. We should never have given you that shit. You're a major lightweight."

I had no memory of any of it except the sick part. Apparently I'd completely blacked out. I sipped my coffee, my mind on Tim. This was twice now I'd been with him and had it turn out to be a dream. I glanced at the haggard-looking people with tangled hair stumbling around camp in a daze. "Can drugs make you have lucid dreams?"

Jerry did a one-shoulder shrug. "I never have, but maybe." He glanced over his shoulder. "Got to get back to Helga—she's a bit worse for wear this morning."

"Is this it? Is today the day everyone leaves?"

He grinned. "Hell, no! This is just the beginning."

I watched him walk away before taking a bite of the bread and cheese he left. The first time with Tim was after I'd eaten a hotdog, apparently laced with LSD. And this morning was the result of a drug-induced haze from the night before? I put the bread down. I couldn't take any more of this. I had to get out of here before I truly lost it.

I was staring into space when I saw the wolf again. Our eyes met for an instant before he turned and disappeared over the other side of the hill. I didn't follow him.

⁂

The day wore on, people getting drunk and stoned as the hours passed. I smoked a joint because Helga told me it would settle my stomach. It did, but it also made me woozy. But my idea of leaving was put on hold a few hours later when another band started playing my favorite Jerry Rafferty music. And they were good.

The music lured me on, my inhibitions disappearing as I worked into one of my sets. A crowd formed around me as I danced and swayed, doing impossible moves. When I used the pull of music to do a striptease, I knew I'd gone over the edge. I was now a woman who felt her own power and knew exactly how to use it.

When an exotic-looking black man entered the circle I let him twirl me, his hand on the small of my back. He copied my moves and shadowed me, his body cupped behind mine as he anticipated every move I made. When the music ended he smiled and disappeared into the crowd.

I pulled on my shorts and bathing suit top and left the circle to wander into the crowd. And that's when I saw Tim smiling down at some girl, his arm around her waist. I ran toward them, yelling. But it wasn't Tim—it was another Native man who stared at me as though I'd lost my mind. I was pretty sure he was right.

I had no idea what time it was when I climbed into my sleeping bag and fell asleep.

14

In the morning I was sick again, my stomach clenching as I ran from camp to retch in private. I was emptied out, panicked with the thought of another day of this. It wasn't fun to look back on yesterday and see myself stripping and dancing with some man I didn't even know. I'd embarrassed myself for a second night in a row. It was time to get the hell out of here.

"Come on, Collie, stay," Jerry coaxed. "You were the life of the party last night."

"Do you know that guy who danced with me?"

"You mean Martin? He's a male stripper—he works in Fairbanks. You two looked great together."

I shook my head. "I feel like I've abandoned who I am, or lost myself. I'm seriously freaked out."

"You didn't seem crazy last night. You put on a show, is all."

"But I didn't mean to—I didn't come here to put on a show," I muttered, turning away.

"Why *did* you come?"

"I thought I'd meet up with Tim…and…I thought I'd have a mystical experience and learn the meaning of life or something." I let out a shaky laugh.

He gazed at me. "Maybe you did. You just don't know it yet."

"I was drunk and stoned, and god knows what else. You can't have a mystical experience when you're so high you can't feel your feet!"

He reared back on his heels. "Is that right? I suggest you ask some of these stoners how they feel about that. You might be surprised."

"I have to go, Jerry. I'm afraid of what I might do tonight."

Jerry laughed. "I'd love to see what you do tonight, Collie. You're one interesting lady."

"Where's Helga? I want to say goodbye."

Jerry pointed to where Helga was folding up their sleeping bag. I left him and walked toward her.

"If you came here to have a spiritual awakening you should stay!" Helga told me.

"I can't. My dreams are too weird—these drugs are making me crazy. I've already been with Tim twice, even though he's not here, seen a non-existent wolf wandering the edge of the hillside, and danced naked in front of strangers."

She laughed. "And you think no one else has done that? Did you happen to look around last night? There was way worse stuff going on than you dancing naked." She made a face. "Think orgies. As far as Tim, maybe he was here, just in a different dimension."

"What?"

"I'm serious. Quantum physicists believe that ours is just one of many realities. I saw Jesus last night."

I chuckled. "But did you have a lengthy conversation with him?"

She glanced at Jerry in the distance. "Jesus told me to pursue my dreams. My dreams don't include Jerry. I'd have to move to New York."

"To do what?"

"I want to make hats. I know that sounds crazy, but I've been designing them for years. I have a friend in New York who wants me to go into business with him."

"You have to go. If you don't do it because of Jerry, you'll resent him."

Her pale gaze met mine. "I've had the same thought. This is what happens at Burning Night—anything buried rises to the surface and burns its way into your psyche. You danced naked because you needed to bare your soul. Didn't you say you felt your power?"

I gazed at her. "I did feel powerful, but I don't want that kind of power. I think I did it to convince myself to quit."

"Dancing?"

"Exotic dancing. I want to be a real dancer."

"Any kind of dancing is real for someone like me, who has two left feet. Maybe we should go to New York together."

I frowned, trying to wrap my mind around the possibility. "But first I have to find Tim and decide if there's a future for us."

"Maybe you already have one in another reality." Helga dug in her backpack. "Take my number."

I looked at the card she handed me, noting her email address and a phone number.

Helga Hartman

Hats Unlimited

"Cute card."

"Thanks. I hope you keep in touch. After talking to you I'm leaning toward taking Brent up on his offer."

"I bet Jerry would understand. If you two are serious maybe he'll decide to tag along."

She glanced at Jerry who was talking to another couple. "Not sure that would work out. Jerry's got a business here."

"Oh yeah, I forgot about that. Are you and Brent just friends, or…"

She chuckled. "That's the other thing—Brent and I were lovers before I met Jer."

"And now?"

She shrugged. "Haven't seen him in five years—we Face Time once in a while."

I smiled. "I think you're still in love with him."

"Why would you say that?"

"The look on your face when you talk about him. And he represents a big part of your dream."

She twisted a lock of hair around her finger, gazing into the distance. "You may be right," she said a moment later. Her eyes widened as they met mine. "That's what I'm telling you— Burning Night isn't just a festival, it's a major shake-up!"

I hugged her and went to get my things. But before I reached my sleeping bag Martin grabbed me and tugged me to where another band had begun to play old Fats Domino songs. He was dressed in loose-fitting pants, his upper body bare except for the bright orange scarf around his neck. His skin was very black, the scarf vivid in contrast. He looked flamboyant and striking.

"I like your style," he whispered, looking me in the eye. He took hold of my hand and began to jitterbug.

Before I could say no I'd fallen into the rhythm of the music, letting go of anything but how it felt to move my body. He lifted me into the air and spun me, swinging me between his legs as the music grew faster. We whirled together and apart, mimicking each other's moves. When the song ended there was a round of applause. "You two should enter a contest!" someone yelled. "Dancing with the stars!" another yelled.

Martin winked and gave me a peck on the cheek, "Good dancin', lady—see ya around."

I watched him head off through the crowd, the scarf blowing wildly in the breeze.

"See? I told you not to leave," Jerry said walking up to me. "That was fun, right? You two should seriously work together."

"But this is daytime—something comes over me at night."

Jerry laughed. "You mean like sex, drugs and rock and roll?"

"Two of those things are on my no list," I quipped. "I have to go, but thanks for wanting me to stay."

I hitched a ride to Fairbanks with a couple leaving early to get back to their three-year-old. I sat in the back seat of their SUV and didn't say a word as we sped down the hill and away from what I'd hoped would be the turning point of my life. Instead I was overcome with fear about my hallucinations, disgusted with my behavior, and terrified of the future. I should never have come.

⟡

"You didn't stay for the bitter end?" Randy asked me later with a laugh. "Lucky for you I've completed the repairs. You still want that job I mentioned?"

I dug my coin purse out of my backpack and counted out what money I had left. "Maybe I should, but will the owner care if it's only for a few days?"

"Doug runs a clean place and he'll be happy to get someone like you in, even if it's short-lived." He frowned, looking me over carefully. "What happened up there in the hinterlands?"

I glanced into the distance, wondering how much I should tell him. "To tell you the truth I'm kind of shaken."

Randy frowned. "Let me guess—drugs?"

"Maybe—I don't really know. I had a couple of strange

experiences that I can't explain. It all started when I was at the Bighorn Medicine Wheel in Wyoming. But up at Burning Night..." I shook my head, my gaze going to my feet.

"Don't discount what you can't explain. There's more to this world than we will ever know or understand."

Sounded just like what my mother had told me. When our eyes met I had the feeling there was a lot more to *him* than I realized. "Do you believe in parallel realities?"

He frowned and rubbed a hand across his face. "Haven't really thought about it. But I've read some interesting books on the subject."

"What should I do about what happened up there?"

"Was it scary or dangerous?"

I thought about that. "Maybe a little scary. And I'm ashamed of my behavior. But I don't think it's dangerous, unless I'm losing my mind."

He chuckled. "I'd say go with the flow. But I'd stay away from drugs if I were you. Shall I call Doug?"

I nodded.

❦

Doug was heavy-set and jovial with kind eyes. I liked him immediately. His club had seen better days, but it was clean inside with a decent stage. And it didn't reek of beer.

"Can you do a set tonight? I have a crowd coming in for the game at four, but when it's over the men will vacate unless I have something on offer." He grinned. "You'll help alcohol sales."

"Don't you worry about people driving drunk?"

He scoffed. "These guys mostly live close. I take their keys away if it gets too bad. You need a pole or are you okay with dancing on a stage?"

"Stage is fine. What should I wear?"

He looked me over. "I have some costumes in back—nothing risqué, mind you. Cowgirl outfit and a belly-dancing number."

The belly-dancing outfit was the one I picked, liking how the sequined maroon material sparkled. The skirt was designed to fit low and tight, leaving the belly exposed. The stretchy material hugged my hips before flaring out and hanging nearly to my ankles, and the bra-like top didn't show much cleavage at all. It was the least risqué outfit I'd ever worn on stage. "Music?"

"Whatcha like?"

"Van Morrison or even some East Indian?"

He smiled. "Gotcha covered in that department. The costume looks great on you—ya done much belly dancing?"

"No. But I can improvise."

"I like your attitude. Come back around eight."

That night was the most fun I'd had in years. The crowd was a mix of young and old, men and women. They clapped when I did the splits and when I twirled, as though those things weren't easy to do. The East Indian music was dreamy and put me into a trance as I tried to imitate the belly dancers I'd seen. I incorporated the moves into my normal set and let the spirit take me. At the end of it I realized just how much I loved to dance. It had become as important to me as the writing. At the end of my second set the crowd cheered and clapped. I bowed gracefully, my arms out like bird wings, before I left the stage.

Doug paid me a hundred bucks and I made nearly three hundred in tips.

"Normally I ask for a fee, but after what Randy told me about you I decided to forego it. Will you come back tomorrow?"

"I'd love to. But just to warn you, if I make this much tomorrow night I'll have enough to get me back to Wyoming—unless something else happens to my truck."

"I wish you lived in the area. I could use someone like you on a regular basis." He winked.

I smiled. "I kinda wish I did too. This was fun." My sets tonight had taken me into an ethereal place where the movements came over me—it wasn't about being sexy, it was about expression. And I got the feeling that the crowd saw me as a performer rather than an exotic dancer. My dark mood lifted.

The crowd was even bigger the second night. I wore the belly-dancing outfit again and worked more belly dancing into my two sets. By the end of the night I was covered in sweat and exhausted. The crowd went crazy at the end, and wanted an encore, but I simply couldn't do it.

"You done any performing—I mean at a real theater?" Doug asked me later.

I shook my head. "I've only done clubs and bars."

He cocked his head. "You could, you know."

"I don't have any connections to theater, and I'm too old."

He raised his eyebrows. "How old are you?"

I laughed. "Not willing to say."

"Whatever your age I'd look into it. You're too good for places like this."

I left the club and drove the truck back to the campground, my purse bulging with cash. Maybe my stars were aligned or something—I couldn't believe how well things were going. *You're going to pay for it*, a voice said. I hugged my arms around my suddenly cold body.

Just before I went to sleep that night Helga's words ran through my mind—*not just a festival—a major shake-up.*

Something new was working in the back of my mind, something that hadn't been there before. And it wasn't all about Tim.

I was in a campground close to Anchorage when my cell rang. It was Nadine.

"Collie? Just thought I'd let you know I saw Tim. He said he's been laying low. When I told him you'd been asking for him he got a really strange expression on his face."

"Did he go to Burning Night?"

"He was in the bar last night so don't see how that's possible, unless he can be in two places at once."

I pondered that for a moment. "What did he say about me?"

"He didn't say much of anything."

"And you told him about Dean and why I went to the hospital?"

"He already knew all that. Are you all right?"

"Not really. I may be losing my mind."

She laughed. "Come on back here and I'll put you to work—that'll straighten you out."

"I'm serious, Nadine. Something's going on. I need to see Tim."

"What did I just say? Haven't found anyone to replace you—business is way down since you left."

"If you see him again can you tell him I'm on the way back?

I'd hate for him to disappear before I get there."

"And will you work for me again?"

"Let me think on it." I disconnected, my mind going in several directions at once. How could Tim know about Dean and the ambulance unless I'd really had a conversation with him? A sudden headache pounded inside my temples. I was no longer sure what was reality and what wasn't.

I ran into Karen Holt at the Safeway in Anchorage.

"You're back!" she said, surprised. "I was hoping to run into you again. That story of yours kind of caught my imagination." She frowned. "But isn't the festival still going? I thought it lasted five days."

I placed a loaf of bread in my cart. "I left early—too many disturbing things happening."

"Yeah, the drug scene can be a bit much. Want to get a bite to eat? I'd like

to talk to you about your book."

I hesitated, mentally tallying up my cash. I had plenty, but I also had a long drive ahead of me with possibilities of flat tires and other unforeseen demands for money.

She smiled. "Meal's on me—I can deduct it from my expenses."

"Okay. Where should I meet you?"

She glanced at my cart filled with coffee, bread, fruit, lettuce and cheese—the healthiest food I'd seen in weeks.

"Why don't you ride with me? That way you don't have to find a parking place in town."

After paying for my groceries and stowing them in the ice chest, I locked up my truck and trailer.

We were seated in a café with glasses of wine in front of us before she brought up her idea. "I want to show your manuscript to one of the publishers I work with, but I'll need a copy. Do you need it edited?"

I took a sip of wine trying to decide if I trusted this woman. She had a nice smile, and she seemed genuine, but after what had happened recently I was wary. "I don't have money for that right now. Maybe after I get another job. Right now I'm living off what I made back in Fairbanks."

"If my boss likes it I can get you an advance. The way things are in the publishing world now, it won't be much, but at least it'll pay for editing."

I gazed at her over my wine glass. "I don't understand why you like it so much."

"Maybe because it has the ring of truth to it. I sense that you're writing a memoir of sorts."

I looked down at the table. "It's similar, I guess, but I didn't have a religious upbringing."

"And you're a dancer?"

"Yes, I have been."

"Will you be staying here for a while?"

I shook my head, looking up as the waitress brought our food. "I'm planning to go back to Wyoming for a while," I said when she left. "I may have to resume my work there to pay my bills—my truck needed repairs, and…"

"Finish the book and send it to me over the net. I'll take a look before I show it to the publisher. If it's too rough for his eyes, I'll edit gratis, but from what I read over your shoulder, I don't think that will be necessary."

As we ate our food we chatted about her life in Alaska and how much she loved it, and also about the festival. I didn't share what had happened to me there, sure that it would be put her off me for good. And I didn't want to miss this opportunity.

After dinner she drove back to my rig and dropped me off. "I look forward to working with you, Columbine," she said, handing me another business card. "And I hope you finish that book sooner rather than later." She gave me a winning smile and drove off.

I stood in the middle of the Safeway parking lot until someone honked, bringing me back to my senses. I unlocked the truck and drove the rig to my camping spot, my thoughts going round in circles. Could I, a complete unknown, really get my first ever book published? I could hardly believe my luck. I ignored the warning that came up in my mind, cautioning me to curb my enthusiasm.

Later that night I looked up Karen Holt, happy to see that she was a reputable agent and editor with lots of accolades from satisfied customers on her website. It seemed she worked with several well-respected publishers. And then I remembered the email I'd gotten from Louise Putney. I answered it and sent off the first two chapters. It wouldn't hurt to have a back-up plan. But with the new themes and changes to the plot I figured she wouldn't like it anyway. Once that was done I pulled out my computer and set to work.

May was on stage with several other people. She wore a black leotard with a flowing skirt covered in sequins that glittered when she twirled. The crowd was a blur as she danced, her focus entirely on the intricate choreography. It wasn't until she was finished and bowing with the others that she noticed her father's angry face in the first row.

Backstage her friend Emma told her to hold firm. "Don't let him shake your confidence! Gary needs you, May. You're on your way to becoming a real star!"

May doubted that, but she did know her part in the troupe was important. Gary had told her that a million times. How her father had tracked her down was still an unknown, but he was here and she would have to decide how to handle it.

The next morning I was on my way back to Lovell, my pulse racing in anticipation. Tim had invaded my dreams, his face going from wolf to man and back again. But when he kissed me he was no wolf. I pressed down hard on the gas pedal, barreling down the rutted uneven pavement. When the trailer swerved around a corner, I hit the brakes hard. I didn't want to end up dead in a ditch just as my life was beginning to make sense.

But why was it making sense to me now when it hadn't two days ago? Was it Karen Holt? That was certainly part of it—a woman interested in publishing my work! Mostly it was the idea of seeing Tim again; I hoped he felt the same way about me. I was suddenly elated, my mind rushing ahead to our reunion. And that was the moment the deer chose to run in front of my truck.

16

I slammed on the brakes and swerved to miss her, and ran straight into the guardrail, my nerves completely shattered. Several cars stopped to see if I was all right. I waved them on. My racing heart finally slowed enough for me to get out and assess the damage. There was a dent in the hood and a broken headlight, but the engine worked just fine. My newly filled tires looked good all around. I climbed into the driver's seat, contemplating the situation—again with the happiness and then disaster. The universe must be trying to tell me not to get caught up with Tim—what else could it mean? He was too young for me and I had to come up with a real plan for my life. I was acting like a lovesick teenager. But when I tried to imagine a future without him in it, I felt a distinct drop in energy, a cold knot forming in the region of my heart.

I turned the key and listened as the engine roared to life. The new/used carburetor was working just fine. I glanced in all directions, making sure there were no more animals poised to race in front of me, before I put it in gear and eased onto the road.

May had taken her friend's advice, managing to slip away from her father the night he was in the audience. She couldn't let them stop her again. She was on her way now, her life unfolding like a…of course, her life was unfolding like a flower—a May Flower. She chuckled to herself.

Weeks had gone by since that night and now her name was truly in the lights. She had just gotten her first gig in a Broadway musical. She had a singing part. But her heart was heavy as she walked onto the practice stage. Her former boyfriend from back home had called her and told her all about how desolate her father was, and how his health was deteriorating because of May. "He's sick, May. You need to come home and see him before he dies."

When May called home her mother told her that her father had been taken to the hospital. "You broke his heart. If he dies it's on you."

My fingers stopped typing, my gaze going out the open door on the back of my trailer. A wolf stood there. But as soon as I rose from the bed he loped away. I'd taken another turn-off down a narrow road to find a camping spot. There was not another soul here, but the woods were thick and dense, the perfect place for him to hunt. *Was the wolf Tim?* Watching out for me seemed like something he would do. I was seriously beginning to wonder.

I gave up on May for the night, unable to keep my mind from Tim and my unexplainable experiences at Burning Night.

I was in another campground close to the Trans-Canada highway that ran from Alberta down to Montana before I saw the wolf again. I figured it was sometime between nine and midnight, the light the same as it always was, when he appeared. But when I got up and checked outside, there was no more sign of him. And when I gazed around at all the other campers, I figured I must have imagined him.

I jumped when my cell phone rang, an unfamiliar number

on the screen. For some reason I answered. "You the woman who dances?" a male voice asked.

"Who is this?"

"My name's Pete Carson. Nadine told me about you—said you'd be back here soon. I'd like to see what you got."

"Why?"

"Didn't she tell you about me? I'm a talent scout."

I paused before I spoke again, afraid of what I might say. "I haven't decided if I'm going back to work at the bar...she..."

"No worries. We can have a private session. Just get in touch with Nadine when you hit town."

A private session? I was about to say something snide when I realized he'd hung up. I called Nadine.

"Yup, I gave him your number, and nope, I don't really know him. He seemed a decent sort. I thought he might help you with your career."

"My career? I don't have a career. A private session sounds kind of dicey, don't you think?"

"Could be, or not, depending. People who are looking for dancers have to see them dance."

My mind spun around all the attention I was getting. I'd never been this popular. Right now the only person I wanted to be popular with was Tim.

But then again, Tim was a grown man with a life of his own. He didn't need me complicating things for him. And I had to earn some money, which meant looking for a normal job, not dancing in some sleazy bar. I had to get a grip and think about what made the most sense.

"How far away are you? Tim has some plan to leave for a few days."

My stomach instantly turned into knots. "Please tell him to wait for me. I have to talk to him."

"I'll do what I can."

Tim would most likely be gone when I got there—it seemed par for the course. Maybe this Pete guy could help me get into a dance troupe. *Like May, my character.* Karen Holt was right—our lives were merging into one.

My head pounded, my thoughts twisting down one track and up another. Burning Night Tim seemed better than the real one. At least he cared. Had real life Tim told me his spirit animal was a wolf? Was I really asking myself this question? Oh my god, I was seriously going nuts.

The closer I got to Lovell the more confused I became. Did I want to work for Nadine again? Dancing at Doug's place had been different, more respectable. I felt like an artist there. But at Nadine's bar I was just another aging stripper who had to show skin to get tips. My mind cast back to Burning Night. Despite all my confusion and the drugs, I'd come to the conclusion that I wanted to be a performance artist. Maybe this Pete guy could help me with that. But my first order of business was Tim. I had to know if there was a future for us. *There's no future for you*, my inner voice reminded me. *He's a decade younger than you are.*

"Leave me alone!" I shouted, picking up my self-help book and flinging it at the wall—as if I could stop the logical part of me that was attempting to steer me in the right direction. "I don't want to be reasonable or rational," I whispered, crying. "I love him…I love him…"

When I woke in the morning rain was sluicing off my skylight, jagged streaks of lightning accompanying the booms of thunder rumbling in the distance. My mood matched the weather perfectly. I was seething with indecision, my mind twisting from one thing to the next. I was desperate to see Tim, but afraid at the same time. What if he didn't want me? And then I was off again, trying to be sensible. Was my future to be wrapped around a relationship? I had to get clear about my own life before I attached myself to a man, no matter how hunky he was, or how I felt about him.

Instead of taking off early I decided to work on my book and wait until the weather improved. I had hook-ups, which meant I could plug in my computer. There was a shower at the campground too, and I badly needed one.

May was heartbroken. Her new boyfriend had decided to break up with her just when she was hoping for something more serious. Her mother was calling hourly to guilt trip her about her father's health, and her troupe was about to move on. Gary had given her exactly two hours to make up her mind.

"If you decide not to join us there are a lot of other girls to take your place," he'd told her coldly when she tried to explain her predicament.

"But..."

"We're leaving at noon, with or without you."

Her friend was no help either, telling her that her father's bad health had nothing to do with her, and if she wanted a life she'd better make up her mind right now. May knew she was right, but if her father died...

I stared into space wondering how I could extricate May this time. I'd spent my entire life feeling guilty—I knew this emotion very well. I'd blamed myself for my father's attacks and now my character was blaming herself for her father's illness. There were differences, but the storyline was too close to my own.

But then I thought about the book I'd been reading about abuse. So many women had gone through it, their lives parallel to mine. *Write what you know* was the advice I'd read somewhere. And I certainly knew how May felt. And she was just as confused as I was.

I opened the back door and watched raindrops pinging into the large puddles that had formed, arcing silver as they bounced away, and leaving ever widening circles. The oil from the road had formed rainbow slicks on the surface, the colors shifting and changing as the rain came down harder.

When I heard a rustle I pulled my gaze away, surprised to see a bushy tail disappearing into some brush on the other side of the row where I was parked. For one second I had the strangest sensation that Tim was standing right next to me. But of course there was no one there.

My phone rang, bringing me out of my reverie. "Your house is being foreclosed," Mary said as soon as I answered.

"Hello to you too. How'd you find that out?"

"Dean called Bill. He wants to bunk with us until he can find a place to move."

"And what did you say?"

There was a long pause. "It isn't really up to me, Collie. We have the extra room and Bill…well…you know Bill."

"Not really. He never wanted much to do with me. Are they repossessing the house?"

"Sounds like it. Everything inside is due to be auctioned off by the bank. Dean barely got away with his clothing."

"Poor Dean."

"He is kind of pathetic right now. He looks terrible."

"I don't care what he looks like or what's going on with him. Why do you call me about this stuff?"

"Because he's your husband? And also I thought you might like to keep some of the furniture that belonged to your parents. Are you ever planning to settle down, or will you be a gypsy who lives in a trailer forever?"

"It hasn't even been a year yet, Mary, and if they're repossessing I doubt they'd allow me to take anything, even if I wanted to. The bank will use the sale of the contents to offset their costs."

There was long silence before Mary said, "Just thought you'd like to know that the man you were with for twenty years is homeless."

I let out a huff. "Homeless? Why doesn't he move in with his recent girlfriend?"

"Turns out she's married."

"What a surprise. He's the one that let the house go into foreclosure. He could have done something years ago."

"How is it all his fault?"

I counted to ten. "Are you asking a serious question?"

There was a pause before she asked, "Where are you?"

"I'm on my way back to Lovell."

"Is that guy with you?"

"No, Mary, he's not."

"And how was Burning Night?" she asked in a chirpy voice.

"I have to go." I hit end and placed the phone carefully in my bag. How had I misjudged my best friend for so many years? I'd always blamed Bill. Now I knew who she really was.

A rap on the side of the trailer startled me as I was stowing my things and getting ready to move on. When I opened the door a bedraggled woman was standing there with a duffel bag over her shoulder.

"Can I hitch a ride with you?"

I took a closer look, noting the exhaustion that had drawn lines along the sides of her face. There was a desperate look in her eyes. "Where are you headed?"

She darted a glance over her shoulder. "Anywhere but here."

"I'm just packing up." That's when I noticed the purple bruise on her upper cheek. "Did someone hurt you?"

She shook her head. "No, no. I just need…"

"Is it your husband?" I asked, noticing the ring on her left hand.

She fiddled with the gold band, twisting it around and around, her eyes downcast. "He…he doesn't want me."

In the distance I saw an overweight man with a beer in his hand come out of an RV and scan the area. "Come inside out of the rain."

She slipped past me and I closed and locked the trailer door. "Is your husband in that blue and white RV two rows over?"

She nodded. "Did he see me?"

"I don't think so. Tell me what's going on."

She burst into tears, blubbering on about how he expected her to keep herself young, and how she didn't have the money for plastic surgery. "He wants a younger woman."

"From the look of him he isn't exactly a prize."

She smiled wanly. "I'm Sandra."

"I'm Columbine. I'm running away from a bad marriage too."

Her eyes widened and she dabbed at them with her sleeve. "You are? But you're so pretty, so…"

I shook my head. "I'm not young, if that's what you were about to say. I expect we're around the same age."

"Forty-three?"

"I'm forty."

"I never would have guessed it."

"You've been overworked, and it looks like you aren't getting enough sleep. Am I right?"

"Daryl forced me on this trip, said it would be good for us to get away. But all I do is fix meals and clean up the RV while he drinks beer and hangs out with anyone he can get to drink with him. He got drunk and beat me up last night because I complained. At least I have friends at home, a father and mother who care." Her eyes filled again. "I sound like a child, I know. He's turned me into a whining baby. I'm just glad we never had kids."

I looked her over, noting her trim body, the taut muscles in her arms. She obviously worked out. "Have you ever danced?"

"Danced? I used to love to dance when I was younger…do you mean professionally?"

"Would you like to?"

She frowned, her gaze going to my short shorts and the tube top I was wearing. "Are you a stripper?"

I smiled. "Not anymore, but I was. If you're interested I can teach you how to dance—not as a stripper but as an exotic dancer. I might be able to find you a job too."

Sandra ran agitated fingers through her graying hair. "I'm not pretty like you."

I gazed at her fine-pored skin, her cobalt eyes. Her hair had been blonde once and lay tangled around her shoulders. Yes, she looked tired, but that was only because she was stressed-out. "Yes, you are—you just don't know it."

We talked for a while and then I turned on my phone and set it to Pandora and linked it to my wireless speaker. I tuned in to the Van Morrison station and showed her a few simple moves. She watched me with her mouth open.

I took hold of her hand, dragging her to her feet. "Let the music take you, Sandra. Just let go."

"This is fun," she said a few minutes later, waving her arms. "And you *are* a good dancer."

She shook her head. "I'm not good at much of anything."

"Maybe that's what Daryl told you, but I beg to differ."

She laughed.

We left an hour later.

By the time we rolled into Lovell we were fast friends, with more in common than I would have thought possible. We'd both stayed in bad marriages because of self-esteem issues—neither one of us had children. She'd lost her mother when she was sixteen, and her father had never been around. Her parents were both alcoholics.

I encouraged her, building up her confidence as the hours went by. "If you need money it's the fastest way to make a bundle," I said. "My friend Nadine is expecting me." I glanced at her. "Dancing boosted my self-image. It gives you a sense of control."

"I can't imagine dancing in front of anyone."

"I can dance with you until you get over your stage fright."

She looked skeptical. "All I've ever done is work in an office and play wife to Daryl. Yeah, I sometimes dance to music when I'm home alone, but this is…"

"Just keep an open mind. If it doesn't work for you, no harm done." I couldn't wait to introduce her to Nadine. It was the perfect solution for both of us.

17

"You two gals make the perfect team," Nadine said after I introduced her to Sandra. "The men will love havin' two pretty gals moving across that stage."

Sandra beamed at the compliment.

I gazed at the dark walls with their chipped paint, the scratched up bar that had seen better days, my thoughts going to Doug's place and how I'd felt dancing there. This place wasn't anything like his, and the skimpy outfits didn't appeal anymore. But I had to do it for Sandra's sake. "I'll dance for a day or two, but I'm not staying," I told Nadine.

"You can't leave me here!" Sandra said, her smile disappearing. "I have no idea what I'm doing!"

"I won't leave until you feel confident—I promise." I turned to Nadine. "Did you talk to Tim?"

Nadine took me by the arm and led me toward the bar. "He's not around."

"He's gone?"

She nodded. "He came by yesterday, said he was leaving today."

"And you told him I was on the way?"

"It had something to do with his dad, Collie. He had to go."

I stared into space, any hope I'd been harboring disappearing like a puff of smoke. "What *about* his dad?"

"He didn't say. Oh, I nearly forgot. He asked me to give you this." She moved behind the bar and came back with an envelope in her hand. I took it, looking down at the slanted irregular printing that spelled out my name. I tore it open and unfolded the lined piece of paper he'd ripped out of a notebook.

I'm sorry I'm not there. I wanted to be. My dad is sick and I have to go to the White Mountains for a couple of days. Will you wait for me? I hope so.

Love, Tim

I folded it up and put it in my pocket.

"Well? What did he say?" Nadine asked impatiently.

"He asked me to wait for him."

"Who asked you to wait for him—that hunky guy you told me about?" Sandra asked, walking over.

I nodded.

She grinned. "And while you wait you can teach me how to dance."

Sandra rented a room in the local motel, leaving me on my own in the trailer. I read and reread the note so many times that it began to disintegrate. My tears didn't help. He did care after all. I couldn't wait to see him.

When Sandra met me at Nadine's the next afternoon she'd had her hair colored and cut. I couldn't believe the transformation. "You look ten years younger," I told her admiringly.

"I feel like it too. But…" she glanced at Nadine behind the bar. "I can't wear one of those outfits, Collie. I just can't," she whispered.

"Have you tried one on?"

"No!"

I grabbed her arm, dragging her into the back. "I know one that'll work for you. We can wear them while we practice."

I talked her into the cowgirl outfit, but when I told her about the pull away snap she shook her head. "I can't be seen in my underwear!"

I laughed, relaying some of the more sleazy things I'd done on stage. She stared at me, wide-eyed, when I mentioned pasties and thongs. When it was time to practice I donned a bustier and a pair of satin short shorts, hoping to desensitize her.

Once we were dressed I turned on the music and told her to follow my lead. I began to dance, watching her out of the corner of my eye. When she slipped up I stopped and went through it again. By the end of two hours she had the set pretty well down.

"If you keep an eye on me you'll do fine," I assured her.

"We aren't dancing tonight, are we?"

"I hope to hell you are," Nadine called from the bar. "I've already put out the word. Hate to think what the guys would do if you two didn't show up."

Sandra stared at me, looking like a deer in the headlights. I smiled. "You'll do fine. And we'll have fun."

I thought about how confident I'd become. I was a teacher now.

There were a few slip-ups that night, but mostly Sandra and I worked well together. I got more tips than she did, but I figured it was because the crowd knew me.

As we changed into our street clothes Sandra gazed at me. "I have to say I enjoyed tonight. Being in control was so intoxicating! Maybe I like this more than I thought I would."

I pulled on my jeans and folded the bustier and shorts, placing them in a bag to take to the Laundromat. "I had a feeling about you."

"Yeah? Like what?" She pulled off the skirt and stuffed it into my bag.

"All you need is a moment to shine, Sandra. That husband of yours made you feel like a piece of crap, just as mine did. I know it seems strange that dancing in front of a roomful of men could help, but for some reason it does. It's not about how you look; it's about the confidence you exude. I figure if you can stand up on a stage and do this, you can do just about anything."

Sandra laughed. "You may be right about that."

"Once you have the moves down you have the choice to walk away or keep going. Were you nervous?"

She shook her head. "Not with you there. But I'm not ready to solo quite yet."

As we walked to my truck I told her about Doug's place and how different it was. "When I danced there I felt like a performance artist."

"That sounds even better, but I'm sure it wouldn't work for me."

"Why?"

"Because I don't have your talent."

Our eyes met. "You could if…"

She waved her hand. "Don't try to play it down, Collie. You're really good."

I stared into the darkness, wondering what, if anything, I was going to do about that. It was very hard to admit to myself that I had talent. How could I break into a career I knew nothing about—and who would hire me? And then I remembered the man who called—the talent scout. I hadn't called him back. Perhaps I should.

I was driving back to my trailer after dropping Sandra off at her motel when my phone rang. It was Nadine.

"Pete Carson watched you dance tonight. He came looking for you, but you'd already left."

"Is he for real?"

Nadine scoffed. "As in a true talent scout? I can't really say. He seems on the up and up to me. You'll just have to meet him and see what he has to say. He plans to be here tomorrow night, said he'd come early to talk with you."

"What about Sandra?"

"What about her? She's okay, but she isn't you. Are you still denying what you have?"

"No, I…"

"Just get here early and speak to the man. Okay?"

May took a taxi to the hospital, tears streaming down her cheeks. The troupe was gone, leaving her behind to live her horrid life. Her mother greeted her in the waiting room. "I'm so glad you decided what was important, May. Your father may not have much longer to live."

When May followed her mother into the room to see her father, he was sitting up in bed, his cheeks flushed. When he saw her he frowned. "So you decided to let go of your selfishness for once?" he asked, glaring at her. "I hope you can see fit to take care of me when I come home. Your mother has better things to do than wait on me."

May had a sinking sensation in her stomach. She was trapped and she knew it. She'd been blackmailed with guilt.

"Come give your old Dad a kiss," he demanded.

She moved close and gave him a quick peck on the cheek.

"There now, that wasn't so bad, was it? You'll get used to your life, May. I'm going home today. The doctor needs some assurances that I'll have help."

"What was wrong with you?"

"What kind of a question is that? I had heart palpitations because of you. I was sure I was having a heart attack. Luckily it was only stress."

May glanced around wildly, feeling like a trapped animal. Her life closed in around her, the view of the future as bleak as the dark sky she could see through the window. "But what about my life?" she whispered.

No one answered her, and when the doctor came in and told her how much her father needed her, she fought hard not to cry.

May was in trouble again. Why did these things keep happening to her? I thought of my life and how one minute everything was headed straight toward something wonderful, and in the next I'd fallen down some rabbit hole into hell. Every day was a challenge of uncertainty. But when I thought back on my life with Dean, the uncertainty I had now was a cakewalk. With Dean I knew exactly what each day would bring, and it wasn't good.

Pete was younger than I expected, his body cut and trim. He was wearing a jacket over a black T-shirt and tight jeans. A scruffy beard, that he'd obviously cultivated, made him seem exotic, and his eyes were a piercing blue. His slight southern drawl did not go with his appearance. Funny that I'd pictured him heavy-set with glasses. He stood next to the bar, a beer in front of him.

"Glad you could make it," he said, looking me over.

"I'll leave you to it," Nadine said, disappearing into the back.

I cringed under his scrutiny, my wrinkled skirt and loose-fitting top feeling dowdy. I hadn't bothered with my make-up yet, figuring I could do it when I dressed for the gig. "Good to meet you, Peter," I managed, holding out my hand.

"Please call me Pete," he said, smiling. When he took my hand he didn't release it, staring at me as I fought the urge to rip my hand away. Luckily Sandra arrived, breaking the spell.

She gazed at the two of us, a blush creeping her cheeks. "Oh, sorry. I thought…"

I pulled my hand out of his and wiped it on my skirt. "It's okay. This is Pete Carson."

Pete turned to her. "You're the gal she's helping along?"

Sandra nodded. "Have to go get ready," she mumbled, stumbling away.

"So, Columbine—nice name, by the way. Is it a stage name?"

"No."

"Well, it's a good one. Let's talk business, shall we? How long until your set begins?"

I glanced at the clock behind the bar. "I have a half hour before I need to get ready. I haven't done my make-up, or…"

"I watched you last night and I have a proposal for you. Come with me to L.A. and I'll set you up in one of the hottest new dance clubs."

I kept my voice even. "I've decided to be a performance artist, Pete. Dancing in clubs doesn't appeal to me anymore."

He watched me as he reached for his beer. "I was led to believe you were an exotic dancer. You certainly looked like one last night."

"I was led to believe that you were a talent scout who wanted to help me go legit."

He let out a bark of laughter. "Fair enough. I deal with many types of artists. If you let me, I can help you. But I'm on a tight schedule. You need to make up your mind tonight. I have other places I need to be. I have a friend, Ward Banks—he runs a place you might be interested in. He hires all sorts of talent."

"How did you hear about me?"

"A man I know told me about you—said you were really talented."

"A man? What man?"

"His name's Martin. Said he connected with you in Fairbanks?"

"Martin—oh, the black stripper. He's good."

"He's pretty well known in dance circles. He brings me leads from time to time."

I glanced at the clock. "Can we talk again after my set?"

He nodded. "Join me here for a drink afterwards. I think you'll like the options I have to offer."

I slid off the barstool. "See you later."

He smiled and gave a perfunctory nod before picking up his glass and taking a swig.

My mind swung from one thing to another as Sandra and I moved past each other, doing identical moves. I could see the concern on her face whenever I veered off of our prescribed routine, but I was having a hard time concentrating. After the third time of this I noticed Sandra doing her own thing, a look of annoyance on her face as she moved away. After that we were completely independent of each other, doing our own moves to the music as it flowed over us. I closed my eyes and let myself go.

The applause at the end was loud in my ears, money thrown at us as we finished up. I watched Sandra bend to pick it up, her back arched. The pull away skirt lay bunched up on the stage. She'd done it. A few minutes later we were in the back.

"Did you do that on purpose to test me?" she asked, frowning.

"I couldn't keep my mind on our routine—I was thinking about Pete."

"He was out there, and I didn't like how he was looking at you."

"What do you mean?"

"He had this expression on his face—like he wanted to get in your pants."

I laughed. "Isn't that what we're trying to evoke?"

Sandra stared at me. "He's supposed to be a talent scout, isn't he? A professional? I'd be careful if I were you." She turned away to finish dressing.

"You let the skirt go tonight."

She turned. "I had to do something—our routine was a mess."

I smiled. "Good for you for improvising."

As I dressed I thought about what she said about Pete. What we did on stage was meant to arouse. It was why I didn't want to do it anymore. Pete was a man, just like the rest of them, but he was also a talent scout, and despite how he'd looked at me, I had to find out if he could help me find a real dancing job.

Pete and I were in the bar having a beer when Sandra came by. "Should I find another ride to the motel?"

"Oh shoot." I glanced at Pete. "Can you give me a ride back to my trailer?"

He shrugged. "Sure."

I handed Sandra my keys. "Come get me in the morning, okay?"

"Thanks. See you bright and early." She gave me a warning glance before she walked away.

"Have you come to a decision?" Pete asked.

"No. You haven't given me enough information. Do you expect me to just follow you to L.A.?"

"I told you about Ward. I can give you his phone number. I've found other dancers for him. And if you don't like what he has to offer there are other places; L.A.'s a big town."

I couldn't leave Lovell before I spoke with Tim. The note

he'd left indicated he still had feelings for me. But I had the sense that Pete wouldn't wait around forever. "Can you at least give me until tomorrow? I have to sleep on it."

He nodded and upended his beer, finishing it. When he paid and slid off his stool I followed him. His black Range Rover was parked right outside, and when he unlocked it I climbed into the passenger seat.

Once we reached my trailer he cut the engine and followed me to my door. "You want some company tonight?"

He was more than a little drunk. "No, Pete, I don't."

His eyes narrowed and grew hard just before he grabbed my arm. "You're a tease and I don't like to be teased."

When I tried to wrench away he pressed me against the side of the trailer, one hand going to his zipper.

"If you don't stop I'm going to scream," I hissed.

He glanced around the empty trailer park. "Good luck with that."

He was strong and didn't react at all when I bit his shoulder. "You deserve this, you slut," he said, slapping me hard. "You've been asking for it all night."

He flung me to the ground, and a second later he was on top of me. I let out a shriek, my hands pressing against his chest as hard as I could. I couldn't budge him. My skirt was now bunched up around my waist, one of his hands tugging my underwear down before he pressed my legs apart with his knee. All my fighting and screaming was doing no good at all. Tears streamed down my face. He was going to rape me.

I shrieked as loud as I could, hoping someone, anyone, would hear me. I wriggled beneath him as he grunted, arranging himself. He was nearly there and there was nothing I could do about it. I braced for the pain, knowing it would happen in the next few seconds.

When I heard a warrior's yell I thought I must have been

dreaming. A second later Pete was dragged off me, his arms flailing as Tim pulled him backward through the dirt. I saw the glint of a knife, watched Tim move it up next to Pete's throat. "Don't kill him!" I screamed.

Tim hesitated, and in that moment Pete managed to jerk away from him. He pushed to standing and sprinted for his car, Tim in pursuit. I couldn't see them in the dark, but I heard the grunts as they fought. I yelled then, sure that Tim would kill him. When Tim turned toward me Pete jumped into his car and slammed and locked the door. The engine roared to life and the Range Rover spit gravel as it sped away.

Tim was by my side a second later. "Jesus, Collie! Are you all right?"

"Barely."

He put his hands on either side of my face. "What in hell were you doing with that guy?"

"Pete gave me a ride home. He's a talent scout. I had no idea..." I felt shaky and weak, tears welling as the shock took hold. "I should have known. Sandra warned me..."

Tim held me against his chest, one hand stroking my hair. "You're okay now. But I'm glad as hell I got here when I did."

"I'm just glad you didn't kill him," I mumbled.

He scoffed. "I wasn't going to kill him. I just wanted to scare the bastard."

Tim stayed with me that night, holding me against him while I cried. When I woke in the morning he was resting on one elbow, watching me with a worried expression.

I smiled, reaching for him. "I'm okay, Tim. It was just a fluke."

He frowned. "I can't deal with it anymore. I can't be worrying about you like this."

"What do you mean?"

"You need to stop dancing."

I sat up. "You can't tell me what to do."

He shook his head and glanced into the distance. "If we're together I should have some say."

"We're not together."

He frowned. "What the hell is this, then?"

"It's you arriving in the nick of time."

"And you don't think that means something?"

"I'd say it was pretty lucky for me. What else?"

Tim stood and pulled on his jeans, his jaw clenched. "It's more than that. We're connected. I've had a couple of dreams…"

I gazed at him. "I have too. We were together at the festival—you lit the bonfire, and…"

"I was camped down by the forest."

We stared at each other. "Right. And we talked about the night I went with…"

"Dean to the hospital, and…"

"Oh my god! What's going on?"

"I told you. We're connected."

"What does it mean?"

"It means we share something beyond this reality."

"And the wolf? Is it your spirit animal?"

Tim sat down on the bed. "Yeah, it is. Did I tell you that?"

"A wolf followed me. He killed a guy who was trying to rape me."

"And this time it was me who saved you."

When his gaze hardened I put my hand on his arm. "Despite what I said a minute ago, I don't want to dance like this anymore—last night made me see that. I don't know what's wrong with me. I missed you so much, and then Burning Night and all those weird dreams—I didn't know where you were, or even if you still cared about me."

"Didn't you get my note?"

I gazed into the distance, all my confusion and feelings for him rising up. "I did get it, but…I feel like I need to sort out my life."

"You need to trust, Collie. And believe me when I tell you how I feel. Why would you even consider taking off with this Pete guy?"

I stared at him bleakly. "Because I don't want to dance in bars anymore, and he offered a way out."

"And you were planning to go?"

"I… was still thinking about it, even though Sandra warned me not to trust him. What's wrong with my intuition these days?"

He frowned and looked down. "You overrode it."

"I guess I did." When I examined his face I noticed the dark circles under his eyes. "You look tired. What happened with your dad?"

"He's got cancer. He's been smoking his whole life."

"I'm so sorry."

Tim shook his head, his clear eyes meeting mine. "I know what you've been through, and why you can't trust, but I thought we had something."

"We *do* have something."

Tim glanced away. "I told my dad about you. He approved."

"He doesn't think the age difference is a problem?"

"He said age has nothing to do with anything. We need to be together. If you don't know that by now, you're…"

I grinned. "Either stupid or not paying attention."

He scoffed. "Something like that."

A moment later we closed the gap between us. I clung to him as he kissed me, my body melting into his. He smelled like pine needles and fresh air.

He pressed me back on the bed. "Is this okay?" he asked worriedly.

"Why wouldn't it be?"

"Because you almost got raped last night."

"Not by you."

He made love to me like I was made of glass, each touch as soft as a feather along my skin. His hands slid along my arms, my belly, awakening a hunger I hadn't known was there. He whispered words I didn't understand—Apache words, his voice taking on a different timbre. It felt like a dream as we moved together and apart, my heart beating in rhythm with his.

When I woke later there was no sign of Tim. If I hadn't felt the ache of what we'd done together I would have figured I was dreaming again. I rose and dressed and checked for him outside. His truck was gone.

When Sandra drove up in my truck a few minutes later I rushed outside. Her eyes went wide when she saw me. "What's wrong? What happened?"

When I told her about Pete she looked horrified. "I knew it. I could tell he wasn't what he said he was. Did he hurt you?"

I shook my head. "Tim got here just in time."

"Oh my gosh." She glanced around the empty park "Where's Tim now?"

"I fell asleep and when I woke up he was gone."

"Maybe he went to get you some coffee."

"I hope he didn't go after Pete. He was pretty angry last night. I thought he might to kill him."

"My goodness," Sandra whispered. "You do lead an exciting life." She glanced at my trailer. "Do you have coffee or should we go get some?"

"We better go and get some—I don't have the energy to make it." She slid over and I climbed into the driver's side. "This is the second time I've almost been raped," I whispered. "Am I doing something that makes men act like this?"

Sandra scoffed. "You mean besides dancing half naked?"

"If that was the reason it would happen every night."

Sandra sighed. "Pete's just one of those guys, Collie—his brain's in his pecker."

I laughed and headed to the closest coffee shop, a small busy place a block off the main street.

"Tim wants me to stop dancing," I told her while we were sitting together in the café. "And I want to stop too."

"You can't stop until I feel confident."

I smiled. "I told Tim I want to go legit, but I'm not sure he understands what that means. I also promised that after the thing with Pete I was done with this type of dancing. But I can't just quit. I need the money."

"Too bad Pete wasn't on the up and up."

"I think he was who he said he was—he mentioned this guy I met up at Burning Night—a male stripper. It was Martin who told Pete about me."

"Then why did he try and rape you?"

"He said I was a tease and I'd been asking for it."

Sandra pursed her lips. "An entire roomful of men watched us last night and only one went after you. I was kidding before—don't feel like you did something wrong."

"But what if Tim took off again because of the dancing? He was pretty upset last night."

She shrugged. "You have to do your thing, Collie. If you let him dictate your life he'll be just like the bastards we married."

It was the first time I'd heard her swear. "If I quit would you keep dancing at Nadine's bar?"

She gazed into the distance. "Maybe. Lovell seems like a decent place to settle. I've checked into rentals and the rents are pretty low. My husband hasn't even called. I guess he's happy I skedaddled." She turned, grinning. "It feels good here."

I thought of Tim again, realizing I'd never seen where he lived. I had no way to get in touch with him. There was restlessness in me, a need for something I couldn't identify. I felt itchy and unsettled. "You could work for Nadine until you have enough money for rent and than look for another job. There's a bookstore in town. I could see you working there."

Sandra laughed. "I guess I am more of a bookstore girl than an exotic dancer."

"You like the dancing?"

"To tell you the truth, I don't know. It's nice to get the attention. But if I want a relationship I can't see taking up with one of the men who tucks a twenty into my satin boxers."

I laughed. "You never know, Sandra. The men who come to the Bighorn are different than the ones who frequent a strip club in the city."

"I hope you don't quit on me, Collie. I'm not ready for that."

I glanced at her as I swallowed down the last dregs of my latte. "The problem is I don't know how I'd live if I didn't dance. Making minimum wage doesn't cut it any more."

Sandra chuckled. "It does spoil you. Three or four hundred a night goes a long way to making up for the sleaziness."

18

When Sandra and I left the coffee shop we decided to look around town for possible rentals for her. It was around three, and we were on the way home, when we heard the local news on my truck radio.

"A man in his thirties was found dead in his car early this morning," the announcer said. "He was wearing a black T-shirt and jeans and had no identification. The car is a black Range Rover with California plates. If anyone has any information regarding this man, please contact the local authorities."

Sandra let out a gasp. "Isn't that…?"

"It might be," I managed to whisper. I shuddered, remembering.

Sandra turned to gaze at me. "His car was a Range Rover, Collie. And you said that Tim…"

"I know what I said," I snapped.

"You have to go to the police."

"But what if it was Tim?"

"You have to go," she said firmly, placing a hand on my arm. "We don't know what happened. The guy could have been in an accident or had a heart attack…or…"

I pulled over to the curb, trying to take in a deep breath.

"The police station is right down there," Sandra said, pointing.

I eased back into traffic and headed toward the low-slung building in the distance.

⁂

"The man I met had dark hair and blue eyes. He was supposedly a talent scout, but he tried to rape me last night."

"Did you report it?"

"No. He didn't get that far. He was fine when he drove out of the trailer park."

He looked me over. "How did you stop him? You're a small gal. The guy they brought in was in good shape."

"I locked myself inside the trailer."

The officer gave me a skeptical look and wrote something down. "And what was this man's name?"

"Pete Carson. He lives in L.A."

"Lived," the officer corrected. "And where did you first come into contact with him?"

"I...I was at the Bighorn Bar."

"He picked you up?"

"No. I had an appointment with him. I told you, he was a talent scout."

"And what kind of talent are we talking about?"

"I'm a dancer."

He glanced up at me again, his dark eyes shrewd. "So you're saying you were dancing at this bar and had an appointment with this Pete Carson afterward?"

"Yes. I know it sounds dicey, but he told me he could get me a gig in L.A."

"A gig—like a stripper gig?"

"No. I'm not a stripper."

"You could have fooled me," he muttered, writing something else down.

"How did he die?"

The man glanced up from his notes. "He was stabbed."

My hand went to my mouth. "Oh my god."

The officer's eyes narrowed. "What do you know?"

"Nothing—nothing. I didn't know he was murdered."

"Do you own a knife, Miss...?"

"Morgan. Columbine Morgan. And no, I don't own a knife."

Sandra appeared looking worried. "You parked in a no parking zone," she hissed.

I handed her the keys. "Can you move it?"

She nodded, glancing at the officer before she walked away.

"I think that's all we need for now," the officer said a moment later. "What's your phone number?"

I gave it to him.

"If we need anything else I'll contact you. Thanks for coming in."

When I walked away I had the distinct impression he was watching me. I was pretty sure I was a suspect.

I hurried to where Sandra waved from the driver's side of my truck and I relayed the conversation as best I could.

"Knifed? Tim must have done it!" she said, sliding over so I could get in.

"The police know Tim. He's friends with half the force. They all hang out at the bar. But the guy who questioned me isn't one of them." I gazed at her. "I can't believe he'd really kill the guy. Last night he told me he only wanted to scare him."

"Maybe he tried to scare him again and things got out of hand." She let out a sigh and turned away. "I'm not sure I'm up to dancing tonight."

"We need to act like everything's fine. For all I know the police will be staking out the place. I'm sure I'm a suspect."

"You? Why?"

"Because the guy tried to rape me?"

Sandra glanced at me. "This is getting a bit too exciting for my taste."

"Go back to your husband then. I'm sure he misses you."

Her head whipped around, her eyes dark with anger. "That's uncalled for. I'm just not used to being involved in murder."

"You aren't involved in murder, and neither am I. Sometimes things happen that are out of our control."

"If Tim killed him you have to tell the police. You can't let him get away with it."

"I have to think he didn't do it. And besides that, I have no idea where he is."

When we reached the bar and told Nadine about it, she took the news in stride. "The guy had it coming."

"Because he tried to rape me, you mean?"

"Because I'm sure he's pulled this countless times and probably got away with it. As far as Tim goes, it's hard to believe he'd kill a man."

"But you said he could be violent."

"Violent like beating someone up, not killing them."

"Has he been in today?"

Nadine shook her head. "Are you gals dancing tonight?"

I glanced at Sandra and nodded.

We were on stage when I saw Tim come in. He found a table in the back and ordered a beer, his unsmiling gaze on me. When I had the chance to glance at him again his eyes were as dark as thunderclouds, an expression on his face I'd never seen before. He looked positively dangerous. What did I really know about him? Fear made me stumble, my steps unbalanced as I tried to remember what I was doing. From then on I was lost, my body stiff with nerves. Sandra glanced at me as we passed, her eyes questioning. I gave her a tiny shrug and tried to focus. As soon as our set was over I rushed into the back, my hands trembling.

"What happened to you?" Sandra asked, pulling off her outfit.

"Tim happened. He was out there." I pulled on my bra and hooked it, reaching for my T-shirt. "He…"

"He what?"

I turned to Sandra, trying to seem normal, but I was shaking all over. "He seemed scary. I hardly recognized him."

Sandra didn't say anything for a moment. Finally her eyes met mine, her voice pitched low. "You have to go to the police. He could hurt you."

"He wouldn't—he couldn't…we're connected, and…"

"You hardly know him. Good sex can blind a person."

I tried to smile. "Amazing, unbelievable sex."

Sandra scoffed. "Yeah, that too. What are you going to do?"

I pulled on my jeans. "I'm going to see if he's still out there and then I'm going to talk to him."

"Please be careful, Collie."

I found Tim sitting at the bar talking with Nadine, a pint of beer in front of him. He turned when he saw me, a wary look coming on his face. I slipped onto the stool next to him. "Nadine, can I have a Dos Equis, please?"

"Sure, honey," she said, winking.

Once she placed the beer down she headed away to help another customer.

"Where did you go this morning?" I asked Tim.

"Had to see a man about a horse."

"What?"

"Yeah. I bought a horse this morning."

"You…you ride?"

"Yup. All Indians ride, just like cowboys."

I gazed at him as he picked up his beer. The wary look was still there. "Did you hear about the murder?"

"Yeah. Nadine just told me. Unfortunate."

"Unfortunate? Tim, did you do it?"

He frowned and slammed his beer down, some of the liquid sloshing out of the glass. "You think I killed him?"

I glanced at the faces that had turned toward us. "Who else had a reason to kill him?" I whispered. "And he was knifed."

His mouth turned into a thin line. "So, just because I own a knife I killed the guy? You don't trust me at all, do you?"

"You were angry, Tim. And tonight when you came in, you…"

"I was pissed at how the crowd was ogling you, Collie. I told you how I feel about it. That guy tried to rape you because of your dancing."

"No one else has tried to rape me because of it. Is that why you disappeared this morning?"

"I told you—I had to buy a horse. But I also had to figure some shit out. If you're planning to dance after you told me you were quitting, I have some serious thinking to do."

"I am quitting. I'm only staying for Sandra."

"Sandra looked better than you did tonight. She's got the moves down."

"It's your fault I looked bad. You rattled me."

He chuckled. "Me in the audience rattled you after what we've done together?"

"Tim, you had this terrible expression on your face… it…scared me."

"I explained all that. Think how you'd feel if I was up on stage dancing half naked in front of a roomful of sex-crazed women."

I giggled, visualizing it. "Women who wanted to jump your bones?"

He scoffed. "Of course they'd want me."

I laughed. "You have a good opinion of yourself, don't you?"

"What did you call me—some Greek god? It's your fault."

I gazed at him. "If you didn't kill Pete, who did?"

"How the hell should I know? Did he know anyone here?"

"Nadine!" I called out.

She turned and walked toward us. "Need another beer?"

"Did Pete have friends here?"

"I don't know. This was the first time I met him."

"Were there police in the audience tonight?"

She leaned forward. "I noticed a few regulars, but there were also a few who didn't seem to belong. They were standing along the back wall."

When Nadine went to help another customer Tim stood and grabbed his hat. "I've got to deal with the horse. Will you be around tomorrow?"

"You're not coming by tonight?"

He frowned. "I have some thinking to do."

"Don't think too hard," I said, trying to lighten the sudden dark mood.

Frustration sharpened the angles of his face as he pushed his hat on his head and walked toward the door.

"Is he mad at you?" Nadine asked.

"He doesn't like me dancing."

Nadine nodded. "He's possessive."

"Did you talk to him about the murder?"

"A little. He seemed genuinely surprised."

"Can you give me a ride to the motel?" Sandra asked, arriving from the other end of the bar,

"Thought that guy down there might take you home," Nadine said, winking.

Sandra glanced at the brown-haired man who was staring

into his glass. "He wanted to, but I told him I'm married."

I laughed. "I guess you weren't attracted to him."

"I am, but I'm afraid what might happen."

Nadine chuckled. "He'll be back tomorrow night. Mark my words."

19

When I opened my computer later I noticed an email from Putney Publishing.

We were happy to receive your chapters. From early discussions we are in agreement about publishing your work. I'll be in touch as soon as we've made our final decision. In the meantime please know that we have editors in house. There are always changes to be made in any work we take on.

Thank you,

Louise Putney

When I opened the Word doc and stared at the last page I'd written the words blurred—too much going on to concentrate on May. Would I let Tim decide my future? Did I trust him? I closed my computer and shut out the light.

A knock on the door woke me. When I looked at my phone it read 1:00 a.m. "Who's there?"

"It's Tim."

I turned on my battery lantern and opened the door. "Thought you weren't coming by tonight."

"When did I say that?"

"Last night at the bar?"

Tim frowned. "I wasn't at the bar last night. Can I come in?"

I stepped aside to let him in and then closed and locked the door. "What do you mean you weren't at the bar? We had a beer together. You told me you had to deal with your horse."

"My horse? Which horse?"

I stared at him, exasperated. "The one you just bought?"

"I have three horses, Collie, and I didn't buy any of them recently."

"Pinch me."

"What? Why?"

"Because I'm pretty sure this is a dream."

"How about I kiss you instead," he said, moving close. He pulled me into his arms, his lips finding mine.

Next thing I knew we were stretched out naked on my bed, our bodies finding their own language. My mind went blank as we connected fully, my gasping breath the only thing I could hear.

It was light when I woke up, soft rays of sunlight sifting down through my skylight. When I rolled over Tim wasn't there, nor was there any sign he had been. I was still wearing the pajamas I'd put on the night before. Was Tim with me last night or not? The only way to find out was to ask him. He said he'd see me today—would he come by?

I made coffee, pondering this newest dream. It was so real. I thought about Burning Night and the conversations Tim and I shared during our time…where? Alternate reality? We hadn't had time to discuss it, what with murders, and…oh my god—Pete's murder. I'd been so caught up with the sex I hadn't even asked last night's Tim about it. *Last night's Tim—do you hear yourself?*

My computer taunted me—I had to finish my book. I was supposed to be sending it to Karen Holt, but how could I concentrate with all this craziness going on?

I had opened the back of the trailer and was sitting there drinking my third cup of coffee when I saw Tim's truck drive in. He waved and got out, strolling toward me.

"How's the horse?" I asked, expecting him to look puzzled. Instead he smiled.

"Doing well. He's getting over the long haul from New Mexico."

"Do you remember us having sex last night?"

Tim frowned and shook his head. "I would have enjoyed that, but I had to deal with Firebird."

"Nice name. I had another of those lucid dreams—you were here and you told me you had three horses, and hadn't bought any of them recently."

"I do have three horses…this last one makes three." He cocked his head to one side, looking puzzled. "What else did I say?"

"Not much. We were too involved in having sex."

Tim grinned and raised his eyebrows. "That sounds about right. Maybe you missed me so much you made it up."

"I thought this might be like the other shared dreams—but if you don't remember…"

"Sorry. I'd *like* to remember."

I stared into space for a moment trying to collect my wayward thoughts. "Tim, please tell me the truth. Did you kill Pete or do you have an idea who did?"

He frowned and rose from where he sat next to me. "I told you last night, Collie. Why would I lie to you?"

"But if it wasn't you, who did it? He didn't know anyone here."

Tim's eyes narrowed. "The police already questioned me. The man was robbed. He had no wallet or identification. The guy who stole his money had a knife, that's all."

"When did they question you?"

"Early this morning—banged on my door and woke me up."

"What do you do, exactly? And where do you live?"

"I raise sheep. I have a small ranch outside of town."

"And you make a living from this ranch?" I asked in a tone I regretted.

His mouth turned thin. "Who are you to judge?"

"I'm not judging, I'm asking. I haven't even been to your house."

"How could you? You've barely been here."

"We hardly know each other."

He gazed at me for a long moment before he said, "I thought we connected on a different level. Guess I was wrong." He turned on his heel and walked back to his truck. A second later it roared to life and he drove away.

I felt sick for a second, wondering if I'd just pushed him out of my life for good. I'd never felt like this about anyone.

I called Sandra's cell phone.

"You didn't know he raised sheep or had a ranch? That seems odd."

"I thought so. He was pissed at me when I asked if he made a living from it."

"Maybe he's doing something illegal. Do you believe him about Pete?"

"I think I do. The police questioned him this morning. There are lots of people who carry knives."

"True."

"I had another dream about him last night."

"Let me guess—incredible sex?"

"Well, yes, but also in the dream he didn't know anything about the horse he said he was buying."

"It was a dream, Collie."

"I'm not so sure anymore."

There was a long pause before Sandra asked, "What else could it be?"

"Another reality? I don't know. I'm heading to the bookstore. Want to come along? Maybe you can ask the owner if she has any work for you."

"Sure. Come by and pick me up, okay?"

I picked up a book called *The Hidden Reality* by Brian Greene and thumbed through it. *Theoretical physics, quantum physics, cosmological physics have all led scientists toward the idea of parallel universes. But there is so much that isn't known and can't be proven.* I shoved the book back into its slot, realizing that nothing I read would help me. Whatever was going on was beyond any one simple explanation. What I really wanted to know was why Tim remembered the dreams of us together at Burning Night, but not the one I had last night. What was different about them? The only thing I could come up with was my drug use. Would Tim be willing to go to the medicine wheel with me? I was determined to find out what was going on.

When I turned toward the door Sandra was talking with the owner, an earnest expression on her face. I walked toward them, waiting while they finished their conversation.

When we left the store a few minutes later, Sandra was elated. "Liz said I could work part time for a couple of months. She's having a financial crisis right now that should be cleared up by early next year."

"Does she know about the dancing?"

"I told her all about it. She didn't seem to care, said that we all have our unique ways to get through this life."

I laughed. "Very true."

"So what did you find? Anything explain it?"

I shook my head. "Physicists have been talking about parallel universes for a long time, but of course no one can prove anything. I think I'm on my own."

"What will you do? If it were me, I'd be scared."

"I am scared, Sandra, and I feel like I'm losing my mind. It all started when I was at the medicine wheel. I hope Tim will go up there with me."

"What about the bar?"

"You can dance on your own for one night, can't you? You'll have to do it sooner or later." I let out a sigh. "It all depends on Tim now. The way he left this morning I'm not sure he's speaking to me."

"See if he comes to the bar tonight and talk to him after."

Tim was there all right, his glare making me so nervous I tripped several times and ended up falling flat on my face. The crowd laughed and clapped, like it was part of my act. Sandra stared at me wide-eyed as she glided past. After our two sets I hurried into the back to dress, afraid I'd miss him, but when I came out he was sitting at the bar, a girl on the stool next to him.

"This is Maggie," he told me. "My girlfriend."

My mouth dropped open. "Your...I thought you broke up."

He grinned. "We did, but Maggie came around last night." He turned to gaze at her. "She wants me back." Maggie smiled and kissed him on the mouth before giving me a sideways glance.

I couldn't move for a second, my mind going completely

blank. By now their heads were bent together and Maggie was whispering something in his ear. His eyes met mine for an instant before he smiled, turning back to her. A second later I collected Sandra and hurried to my truck.

Tears were streaming down my face by the time I had the key in the ignition.

"Do you want me to drive?"

"No," I muttered, wiping my eyes. "Why is he doing this, Sandra? Why?"

"I don't know, but they looked pretty cozy to me."

I let out a howl and banged my fist on the steeling wheel.

20

My heart felt squeezed as I worked my way through our sets. Tim hadn't been in the audience for over two weeks. I imagined Maggie in his arms, visualizing him removing her clothes and taking her to bed. She was very pretty and way younger than I was, and she suited him with her dark hair and eyes. I felt sick all the time, barely able to eat.

After dancing I tried to work on my book, but every time I began to write, Tim's face would appear in my mind and I'd burst into tears. Sandra worried for me, trying to cheer me up by telling me things I already knew. Tim was too young, he had no visible means of supporting himself, and he was more than likely a drug dealer, and maybe a murderer as well.

Nadine didn't say a word as I stumbled across the stage every night, my mind scattered. But after a week of it she finally took me aside.

"You're chasing the customers away," she hissed after one particularly bad night. "If you can't keep it together, I'll have to let you go. Sandra will fill the gap. She's getting much better."

On the way to Sandra's motel that night I thought about my options. I either had to forget about Tim, or find him and let him have it.

"And how will you do that?" Sandra asked. "You don't know where he lives and he doesn't have a phone."

"Nadine will help me," I muttered, staring into the darkness.

But Nadine was no help.

"He's a private person, Columbine. He doesn't confide in me. And now he's taken up with Maggie again it's anyone's guess where they might be."

"But why? Why did he do it?"

Nadine's lips pressed together. She shook her head. "I really don't know. I thought he was finished with her."

"Did they find Pete's killer yet? Do you think Tim did it?"

"They haven't found the killer, but I doubt Tim had anything to do with it. He wasn't serious enough about you to kill someone over it."

"Thanks a lot!"

"Just telling it like it is. If you want to continue working here you have to get a grip. Tonight is your last chance."

That night I danced like I'd never danced before, putting all my anger and upset into my intricate moves. I left Sandra in the dust as she struggled to keep up. When it was over I was exhausted and drained, feeling like a limp rag. I pulled the wad of bills out of my bustier, counting it out—nearly five hundred dollars.

"I'll keep you on," Nadine told me, "but if you screw up again you're finished."

I gazed at her, hoping to find the approving expression of my friend, but instead her eyes were narrowed. I had the sense she didn't like me and was only putting up with me because of the crowd I brought in. I'd talked Sandra into this, and now I'd created a total mess.

There was no way I could think about going legit when I felt like this. I couldn't write, I couldn't think, I couldn't plan. I deserved to dance in skimpy see-through outfits in front of a roomful of leering men. I was stuck here until I could work my way out.

"What's with you?" Sandra asked on the way to her motel. "You shut me out tonight. I almost left the stage."

I turned to her. "I'm sorry. I guess I had to work out my frustrations on stage. I'm so unhappy right now."

"I can tell. If you want to quit, please go. I'm ready to be on my own. And frankly, dancing with you isn't doing me any good."

I stared. "You want me to quit?"

"You told me you were quitting as soon as I was up to speed—now you're saying you want to keep doing this?"

Tears welled and I wiped them away. "I don't know what I want anymore. I can't concentrate on anything. I haven't worked on my book in weeks. Tim's gone, and..."

"Yes, Tim's gone. You have to face it, Collie. You left your husband and now you're mooning over a man who doesn't want you. You're stronger than that."

I heard her words, taking them in. I let out a long sigh. "I'm so unhappy."

"You said that already, but I know who you are, and I know you can be that person again."

Later that night I looked up dance schools on the Internet. I found a few in Caspar, Wyoming, and several in Billings, Montana. When I looked up agents for dancers I could only find ones for strippers and exotic dancers. I was sure if I contacted them I could make a bundle of money, but that wasn't what I wanted. To go legit I had to move to a big city. And I had to find a real agent. Without Tim there was nothing to keep me here, especially with Nadine's attitude. I stared at the screen for so long my eyes began to cross. I finally closed the computer and decided to sleep on it.

"Why don't you trust me?" Tim stared at me, his liquid brown eyes confused.

"But you..."

"You know how I feel—we're connected."

"So you said, but you and Maggie are..."

"You think I love her?"

I woke suddenly, my face wet with tears. The dream was only a dream. Tim was with Maggie and I had to accept it. I was crying again, my sobs muffled as I pressed my face into the pillow.

⧼⧽

The next night Tim was in the audience, his gaze riveted on me as I crashed into Sandra and tripped. I couldn't stop myself from meeting his angry gaze, my movements clumsy and ill timed.

Once we were backstage Nadine grabbed my arm. "You are out!!" she hissed.

Sandra frowned at me. "You ruined tonight. Thanks a lot."

"Tim was out there."

Sandra shook her head. "So what? He's with that gal, Maggie. Didn't you see her sitting next to him?"

"No."

Sandra turned away and pulled on her skirt.

A half hour later I walked by Tim in the bar, trying not to see how Maggie was draped all over him, her coquettish gaze on his face as he sucked down a beer.

He glanced up and grabbed my arm as I went by. "I need to talk to you for a second."

When I jerked away and kept going he jumped up and

followed me outside. "Sorry about this, I was…"

"I don't want to talk to you. Please leave me alone." I was walking away when he grabbed me again.

"Just listen," he hissed. "Maggie has a brother who may have killed Pete. The guy is a serious loser and hooked on drugs. I wouldn't put it past him."

"Why tell me? Just go to the police."

He bent close. "I'm only with Maggie to get information."

I frowned. "Why should I believe you? It's been weeks since I've seen you."

He stared into the distance. "Tell me about it. I'm doing what the cops asked me to do."

"So you're sleeping with her to extract information? Seems easier for the police to question her."

"She'll lie for him, Collie. The guy is as slippery as an eel. They want to know where he is."

"Your pillow talk isn't working?"

"I haven't slept with her. I only do one woman at a time."

"Only do…? Whatever."

He chuckled. "I'm a one woman man—does that sound better? I'm with you."

I glared at him. "With me? You could have told me about this weeks ago. You could have come by."

"She watches me like a hawk. She's suspicious as hell."

"And how is she taking you turning her down for sex?"

"I told her I have a venereal disease," he mumbled, staring down at his feet.

A sudden realization popped into my mind. "That you got from me?"

He glanced up, embarrassed. "You're an exotic dancer."

"So basically she thinks I'm a prostitute."

He shrugged. "It was the easiest explanation."

I narrowed my eyes. "You are a real jerk, you know that?"

He grinned, and was about to reach for me when the door opened, revealing Maggie. "What's going on out here?" she asked, annoyed.

I faced her. "I just told your boyfriend that he didn't get his crabs from me." I gave Tim one last scathing look and stalked toward my truck.

I was about to put the key in the ignition when Sandra appeared, running toward me. "Were you planning to leave without me?"

"Sorry. I was in a fog. I would have remembered before I drove off."

"You and your fogs—was this one about Tim again? That girl can't keep her hands off him."

I made a face. "According to him he's with her to extract information."

Sandra climbed into the passenger side and slammed the door. "What kind of information?"

"Tim thinks Maggie's brother killed Pete—he's a drug addict."

Sandra looked skeptical. "And this isn't for the police to figure out?"

"Tim says Maggie will lie for her brother."

Sandra stared at me. "Now you're going to tell me he isn't sleeping with her, right?"

"He isn't sleeping with her."

"Oh brother. Just take me back to the motel. For a woman who seemed like she had her shit together, you've certainly gone off the rails."

Had my shit together? What a laugh that was.

21

I was preparing for my trip to the medicine wheel when Tim drove up in his truck.

He jumped out and hurried over. "Where are you going?"

"Medicine Wheel. I got fired. I need answers."

Tim frowned. "What kind of answers?"

"Answers to my life questions—what do you think?"

He looked me over. "Jesus, I've missed you."

"Could have fooled me."

"You remember that night when you basically accused me of murder? I took that kinda hard."

"Is this your excuse for being with Maggie?"

"I told you why I was with Maggie. But I'm not now. The police got her brother last night. He confessed."

"I'm glad to hear it. How did she take it when you broke up with her?"

"She destroyed my truck," he said, pointing to several dents, a missing bumper, and a broken side window.

I laughed. "Her temper's as bad as mine."

"You are nothing alike." He grabbed me and pulled me close, and when I tried to wriggle free he wouldn't let me go. "Can I go with you?" he whispered, his breath warm on my ear.

I pulled away. "Do you have any peyote?"

He chuckled. "You think all Natives have peyote?"

I shrugged. "Not necessarily—but when I was there the last time…"

"The Native dude from the past gave you some."

"It helped, I think."

"You mean it helped you hallucinate. When are we going?"

"Now?"

"I have to take care of some things first. Can we go later this afternoon? I'll meet you here around 2:00."

I gazed at him, trying to decide if I was still angry or not. I wanted to be mad at him, but I could feel myself softening. "If you aren't here by 2:00 I'm leaving without you. Bring a sleeping bag."

"I know what to bring." He walked toward his truck.

"You told me you hadn't been up there!" I yelled.

But he didn't hear me as he started his truck. He waved and took off.

A few minutes later my cell phone rang. "I'm dancing tonight. Are you planning to give me a lift?"

I hesitated, realizing I'd entirely forgotten about Sandra. "I'm about to leave for the medicine wheel."

"Let me guess—Tim's going with you?"

"You don't approve?"

She sighed. "You have to do what you have to do, Collie, but it seems like you're willing to believe whatever the guy says."

I remembered what he'd told me about breaking up with Maggie and how he'd lied to save her feelings. I was suddenly ashamed of myself for doubting him. "I do believe him. He's the most honest person I've ever met."

There was a long pause before she said, "Maybe you're right.

Nadine seems to think highly of him. She told me the police love him. I guess I'm just jealous."

"I don't think it's jealousy—more like you're looking out for me. And I appreciate that. Can you take a taxi tonight?"

"It's only a couple of miles. I can walk."

⚜

Tim arrived back at exactly 2:00. When he knocked I was in the middle of writing a passage about May. I'd finally moved her on, but she was still trapped, taking care of her sick father. I closed the file down and stuck my computer under the bed.

"Where's your gear?" I asked when I opened the door.

"Didn't know if you wanted to go in my truck or yours. You want to drag this trailer up the mountain?"

"I did it last time."

He gazed at me, his eyes soft. "Do we have to leave right this minute?"

"Oh no—I recognize that look." I backed away but it was too late. He'd already moved inside the trailer and his fingers were reaching for my buttons. When his lips went to my neck I tried hard to resist, but I was already melting, the familiar ache of wanting him back with a vengeance. "I don't want to do this now," I murmured. "I'm still mad at you."

He didn't reply as he unhooked my bra, his heavy-lidded gaze on my breasts. He looked up at me. "You've lost weight."

I nodded. "Upset about you and Maggie."

He moved his hands from my breasts to my ribs, a worried look on his face. "Shit, Collie. I'm really sorry. I should have told you what I was doing." His gaze met mine. "You're too thin."

I tried to smile. "No one's too thin."

"And it's my fault," he continued.

"Are you still attracted to me?"

He scoffed. "Hell yes, I'm attracted. I can barely contain

184

myself. But you need to start eating more." When his lips moved to where his hands had been, my resistance vanished, overtaken by the feel of what he was doing. What he'd said, the worry on his face—I was completely undone.

His fingers traced across my skin, each caress a letter that led on to the next letter. I struggled to understand what they were spelling out. At some point I lost concentration, our bodies moving together as though we were two halves of the same whole. We moved and crested and moved again until we both arrived on the other side, our arms tight around each other. He stroked my hair and murmured words I couldn't understand until I fell into a post-coital sleep.

When I woke later he was still there, his beautiful naked body sprawled across my bed like the Adonis he was. I heard the patter of rain on the metal roof, glancing up to see dark clouds moving across my little skylight. I hadn't heard the wind, the rain, or anything else.

When I kissed his shoulder his eyes opened, his sleepy gaze on mine. He pulled me close.

"No more of that," I said firmly. "We need to talk."

He pushed himself up to sitting. "I apologized about Maggie. I used her, and I don't feel good about it. I'm sorry, Collie. I know I hurt you. Are you still mad at me?"

"I'm not mad, Tim. I just think it's strange that I've never seen where you live. I don't know anything about you."

"I told you all about my childhood, my father, my brothers, my mother…"

"But what about where you live, what you do all day?"

He rose from the rumpled bed to pull on his jeans. "How about I take you out to my ranch tonight and we can go to the Medicine Wheel tomorrow?" His dark eyes held my gaze, his eyebrows lifting.

I glanced at the skylight, noticing that the light was fading fast. By the time we reached the Medicine Wheel it would be too dark to do much other than eat and sleep. And I did want to see where he lived. I nodded and grabbed my pack.

By the time we drove out of the RV Park the rain had stopped. There was a clear look to the air as we drove north and west out of town. I sat close to him on the bench seat, my mind going back to dates in high school. I felt just like that breathless girl. He kept one arm around me as he drove, steering with his left hand, his elbow propped in the open window. The radio was blaring a country western tune, the cool breeze blowing my hair all around my face.

"I'm surprised you like this kind of music," I said.

"I like all kinds of music. What's your favorite?"

"I like all the classic rock, Van Morrison and Dylan and Fleetwood Mac, Eagles. I also like rhythm and blues and new age and east Indian chants—sitar music."

"Most of that's good dance music."

"Yeah—I love to dance."

He turned, surprised. "I didn't know that. I thought you did it for the money." When the truck lurched to the right he pulled his focus back to the road, straightening the wheels.

"I told you about Doug's place in Fairbanks, right?" I continued. "I felt like an artist there—not a stripper or an exotic dancer or a pole dancer. It was really different."

He glanced at me. "It's the idea of all those dudes hard for you that gets my blood boiling."

I laughed. "Good thing I got fired." But it wasn't good. My money would run out and I had no way to make more unless I found some low paying job somewhere.

We drove by farms and fields and through a couple of tiny towns. I watched the light change, shadows filling in the spaces under the trees as the sun dipped toward the horizon.

I had no idea how much time had gone by when he pulled off the road and stopped in front of nondescript green metal gate. All I saw beyond it was a meandering dirt road and undulating waves of grass. He got out and opened it, hopping in to drive through. "I keep it closed because of the sheep," he explained before exiting the truck again.

Once it was closed we drove slowly down the rutted road. "How many acres do you have?"

"Maybe a thousand? Not sure, exactly."

He owned a thousand acres of land? Didn't he tell me he had a small ranch? I watched the terrain shift as we rounded a bend and began a descent into a wooded area. In the far distance I spotted mountains with snow on their peaks. "What's that range?"

"Part of the Rockies."

"It's beautiful out here."

A few minutes later we approached a log cabin nestled in the trees, several outbuildings behind it. Wooden fences surrounded pastures on either side, horses grazing in one of them, sheep in the other. I heard the skree of a raptor, looking up to see a Red Tail hawk flying in lazy circles. Everything glistened from the recent rain.

He pulled up in front of the cabin and cut the engine. A wide porch ran the length of the building with several Adirondack chairs facing out. A Mexican style runner in blues and grays and reds lay in front of them, a table for drinks in the middle of the seating arrangement. I felt like I'd come across an ad for Architectural Digest, a vision of sitting in one of them with a mint julep on the table arriving in my mind.

He jumped out of the truck and came around to open my door. "Welcome to my home."

"Did you…did you build the cabin?"

He smiled. "I did. It's been a few years now."

"How old are you, Tim?"

He frowned. "I'll be thirty in August. I thought we went over the age thing."

"I'm just trying to wrap my head around this house, this land, your horses, the sheep."

"You're wondering how an upstart redskin has the money for all this?"

"It isn't that. You're so young."

"Yeah, well, I had some luck in my short life."

"What kind of luck?"

"This place belonged to my grandfather. I inherited it."

"What about your brothers?"

"My grandfather on my mother's side. He was white. He offered it to Jake too, but he wasn't interested."

"What about Mohin?"

"Mohin isn't related to my Mom. He's full Apache."

I gazed at the land stretching into the distance. There was no other house in sight. When I turned back Tim was headed toward the cabin. I hurried after him, climbing the few steps up to the porch and toward the front door. A tree in full leaf had been carved into it, limbs branching from the wide trunk at the bottom and spreading gracefully outward toward the top. "Did you do this?" I asked, pointing.

He shrugged. "I designed it. A woodworker friend of mine carved it."

A dog appeared from behind the house and ran up to him, wagging its fluffy tail. He reached down to place a hand on his head. "Hello, Scat."

"Who's this?" I asked, bending down to pat him when he came forward.

"He's my sheepdog."

Scat was black and white with long hair and soft brown eyes.

When Tim made a motion with his hand the dog dropped onto his belly. Tim opened the door to the cabin and ushered me inside.

"Scat doesn't come in?" I asked, watching the dog as he closed the door.

"He's a working dog—he lives in the barn."

The walls inside were logs chinked with plaster. Clerestory windows sat high on either side of the stone fireplace and casement windows stood open, a sweet-smelling breeze wafting in. A brown leather couch covered with a Pendleton blanket faced the fireplace, and the rug on the floor in front of it looked Navajo. A basket next to the couch held magazines and books. Several photos on the walls caught my attention—landscapes of wide vistas and rushing rivers done in black and white.

When I turned to Tim he smiled sheepishly. "One of my hobbies."

"They're beautiful."

"Thank you."

"Do you have help here?"

He nodded. "I have two employees who help with the sheep around shearing time, one other who comes when they drop their lambs. With eight hundred head I can't keep up with it all. And they'll start lambing in January."

Eight hundred sheep?

"Want a beer?"

"Sure," I said gratefully, sinking down on the couch. I leaned against the wool pillow covered in a geometric pattern of turquoise and reds, wondering how I could have misread this man so completely. I felt like I was meeting him for the first time. I reached into the basket and pulled out a well-thumbed book on astronomy. It was filled with pictures of the night sky, all the stars that made up the constellations named:

Orion's belt, Cassiopeia, Cygnus the swan, Scorpios, Taurus, Ursa major. I was suddenly nervous—out of my depth. I didn't know this man at all.

I'd replaced the book in the basket when he arrived with two frosty glasses, placing one down on the rough wooden coffee table in front of me. He looked older and competent, and scarily handsome.

"What? Do I have dirt on my cheek?" He wiped absently at his face.

"I'm just in shock. Why didn't you bring me out here when we first met?"

"I didn't want to scare you off."

"I thought you were just some drifter who lived in a doublewide somewhere outside town."

He let out a low laugh. "That's what I am at heart. This place has nothing much to do with who I am inside."

"But it keeps you from starving."

He took a swallow of beer. "You could say that."

I sipped, my gaze going to a craftsman style bookcase filled with books. I'd read about this furniture. "Is that a Stickley?"

He nodded. "Belonged to my grandfather. It fits the house."

"Did your grandfather live on the property?"

"His house is a couple of miles back. It's too big for me. The workers live there during shearing time. I can take you out to see it tomorrow, if you'd like."

"So, when Nadine told me you go hunting...do you really hunt, or is it when you have to work with the sheep? Does she know about this place?"

"Sometimes I hunt on the property. I have to cull the deer from time to time. And other times I head into the backcountry on one of the horses. Nadine knows."

"And she didn't tell me?"

"I told her a long time ago not to share my life. I'm a private person. You're one of only a few people who've seen this place."

"Maggie?"

"Hell, no! She would have moved her stuff in. I rent a couple of rooms in town."

"And entertain your guests there?"

"That's right."

"But not me."

He put his glass down on the table, his dark eyes meeting mine. "For some reason I didn't want to take you there. Maybe I knew I'd eventually bring you out here."

"I still can't believe this," I said, looking around.

"That's why I keep it a secret. It can ruin a good relationship."

When I glanced at him, his gaze was wary. "It's just a surprise, Tim—not a turn-off."

"Want something to eat?" he asked, jumping to his feet.

"Don't tell me you cook too?"

He grinned. "A little."

I followed him into the kitchen, watching him take things out of the refrigerator. "Can I help?"

"Chop this," he said, handing me a broccoli head. "Stir fry size."

He moved around the kitchen with ease, seasoning the vegetables with chopped up garlic and soy sauce as we talked.

"I almost bought a book about parallel universes," I told him later over our dinner of broccoli, carrots, onions and chicken. "I wanted to find an explanation for the dreams."

He shrugged and forked a piece of meat into his mouth, chewing and swallowing before he answered. "I try to make sense of what I experience, not read what others have to say about it."

"Is that how you feel about the dreams?"

He nodded. "I don't know how to explain what happened

between us, Collie. But it did happen and we both remember it. My dad thinks there's a spirit bond between us. He says we travel between worlds."

"So, we traveled to another dimension?"

"Maybe. I wasn't really there and yet we were together."

"You lit the bonfire."

"I don't remember that. I only remember being with you."

"And the wolf?"

"My spirit animal—maybe he stands in for me when I'm not around."

"So you killed that creep up in Alaska who tried to rape me?"

His eyes widened. "I wouldn't go that far."

But I remembered the expression on his face when I said they'd never find that particular wolf. He'd looked worried when he told me all wolves were tagged. I found myself leaning forward to examine his neck for evidence of a chip.

"What's wrong now?" he asked, rubbing a hand over his neck.

"Nothing."

After we cleaned up he showed me his bedroom that looked out on a meadow of grass, dark trees lined up like sentries in the distance. The sun had set by now and the sky was a pale rose color. "If this was my bedroom I'm not sure I'd ever get out of bed," I murmured, gazing out the open casement windows. I breathed deeply, picking up the aroma of roses and meadow grass and a hint of manure.

He laughed. "If you lived here I probably wouldn't."

The four-poster double bed was covered with another Pendleton blanket with a pattern of running horses in turquoise red and black. A black rug lay on the red tile floor next to a Stickley leather chair, a lamp with a gorgeous stained glass shade on the table next to it. "That couldn't be a…?"

"Tiffany? 'fraid so."

I just gazed at him, unable to utter one word. I was suddenly shy, nervousness filling my belly with butterflies. When I glanced at him the angles of his face had changed, his eyes mysterious and darker than I remembered. He moved in an easy relaxed way, like he belonged here.

"If you want to take a bath the bathroom's there," he said, pointing toward a partially opened door. "I don't have a TV, but I have some books if you like to read."

I jumped at the chance to be on my own for a few minutes, the sense of being with a stranger making me more and more anxious. "A bath sounds amazing. I haven't had one in at least a month."

He'd brought our packs in and put them on the bed. I grabbed mine and hurried to the bathroom. Once inside I turned on the lights and locked myself in, breathing a sigh of relief as I looked around. A claw foot tub sat against one wall, a huge window next to it revealing pasture and the shapes of trees. The sun was gone, shadows racing to fill in the darkening landscape.

"Towels are in the cabinet," Tim called out. "And if you want me to wash your back, let me know."

"Thanks," I called out. Right now I needed to process this new version of Tim.

I glanced at the antique wooden cupboard and pulled the heavy doors open to find folded stacks of black towels on one shelf, crisp white sheets on another. Not only was he rich, he was also neat. And he cooked. I plucked out a washcloth and a towel, placing them on a chair.

As I undressed and waited for the tub to fill I stared out the window, watching a thin line of orange lingering at the horizon. When it disappeared the world went mauve and gray. Crickets began to sing. When I turned back to the tub the water was at the right level, the temperature perfect. I climbed in, warm water closing around me, the softness like velvet on my skin. I washed, using the bar of soap lying inside the metal soap basket hanging over the tub's rim.

"What's happening in there?" I heard Tim call.

I opened my eyes, realizing I'd been dozing. "I'm just getting out!"

"Hurry up. I'm lonely."

I pulled the plug, dried off with the fluffy towel, and put on my pajamas. After I brushed my teeth I cleaned the steam off the mirror, confronting my face. My nervousness was back. I felt like I'd never had sex before, and definitely not with the man waiting for me in the next room. My hazel eyes were like stranger's eyes as I undid the clip holding my hair up and let it settle around my shoulders. I felt separate from myself, as though the image reflected there wasn't me at all. "You know this man," I whispered, seeing the tension appear around the wide eyes staring back at me. "He's the same Tim." But the expression in the mirror didn't change. I gathered my clothes and unlocked the door.

When I came out of the bathroom Tim was stretched out on the bed with a pillow behind him and a book in his hands. He was naked and looked completely relaxed, the soft light from the lamp accentuating his copper skin and the angles of his cheekbones. He'd pulled his hair back and secured it with a piece of leather. When he saw me he put the book down on the table and rose to pull the blanket back, inviting me in.

The butterflies were flying so fast I could barely take in breath, and my heart was pounding so hard I thought it might fly out of my chest. I stumbled toward him. "You sleep naked? Night's are chilly now."

"I do when you're here," he grinned. "And I expect the same from you. Don't worry, I have plenty of blankets on the bed."

My hands shook as I fumbled with the buttons of my top, unable to get even one of them open.

"Come here," he finally ordered. When I reached him he pushed away my hands, his fingers brushing against my skin as he undid each button. When they were all open he pulled the material back to expose my breasts, bending to kiss each one in turn.

I felt like jelly, my knees trembling, my pulse racing. Instead of coming back to myself I was spiraling out of control. When I glanced up at him I was glad to see his familiar grin. "I...I feel like I don't know you at all," I stuttered. "I'm really nervous."

He raised his eyebrows, tugging at the string that held up my shorty pajama bottoms. They fell to the floor around my feet. "I can tell you're nervous, but I don't get why," he said.

You...you're different here."

He shook his head. "I'm the same man—it's only your perception of me that's changed. Close your eyes."

When I closed them my body relaxed under his familiar touch.

"Is that better?" he whispered, his fingers tracing along my inner thighs.

"Yes," I murmured, my eyes opening.

He pulled me into bed with him, stretching out alongside me. "Keep your eyes closed," he ordered, resuming his slow exploration. When I felt his lips touch mine I melted into him, lost inside the world he created with his touch. This was definitely the Tim I knew.

22

I woke in the morning with a start, unsure where I was for a moment. And then I heard the steady breathing, turning to see Tim sleeping next to me. The night came back in wonderful detail—my sudden acute need for him fueled by my earlier tension. I remembered him laughing as I took over, the bed banging against the wall as I let myself go.

I sighed and gazed out the window, watching the early dawn creep across the waving grass. I was about to get out of bed when Tim grabbed my arm. "Where are you going?"

"Just to the window. It's so beautiful out there."

"It's beautiful in here too," he said, pulling me toward him.

"I love you," he whispered afterward, his eyes still at half-mast.

"That's just the sex talking."

He pulled back to stare at me. "No, Collie, it's not. I've felt this way for a long time."

"I feel the same."

He watched me, a frown appearing. "Say it. I want to hear you say it."

"I love you, Tim, even though I don't even know your last name."

He laughed. "It's Roman."

"Roman? Is that Indian?"

He shrugged. "Don't know."

"I expected something like Cochise or Geronimo, or…"

"Those are Anglicized names of famous warriors. The Apache version of Geronimo is *Goyathlay*—one who yawns."

I giggled. "How did you get your name?"

"Beats me. You'll have to ask my father. You still want to go to the medicine wheel or would you rather hang out here?"

I snuggled against him, reveling in his warmth and the knowledge that we had the entire day to spend together. "We can always go to the medicine wheel tomorrow."

"You want to go for a ride?"

"Horses or truck?"

"Horses."

"I don't know how."

"I'll ride Firebird and you can ride Duncan. He's gentle."

Duncan plodded along behind Firebird, who was prancing around and snorting, obviously eager to run. I held on to the pommel of the western saddle with both hands, dreading the moment when Firebird took off and Duncan went after him. Tim sat straight, his entire body in synch with the horse's movements. I had a vision of him bareback wearing a loin cloth, his face painted and dark hair flying as he took off across the plains. I was immediately caught up in a reverie of making love with him in long grass somewhere in the backcountry.

Tim turned in the saddle. "You okay back there?"

"So far, but Firebird seems like he's barely containing himself."

Tim grinned. "He's young. It's good for him to deal with walking for a change. Usually I let him gallop, but today I thought I'd take it slow."

"Thank you for that. Gallop is not in my vocabulary."

"Want to stop and take a swim? There's a pond just up there." He pointed toward a copse of trees in the distance.

"What about the horses?"

"They'll graze."

We'd come several miles by now, and the idea of having to walk back was not appealing. "Are you sure?"

"I'm sure. With a buddy they're more likely to stick around."

Firebird pranced a few feet ahead and then broke into a trot. I let out a shriek when Duncan took off after him, my body bouncing with the unfamiliar movement. I was sliding off when he reached Firebird and came to a sudden halt. "Okay, that was a bit too exciting."

Tim jumped down and helped me off before he unsaddled both horses, placing the tack down under a tree. My legs felt like rubber. "How can I be so weak after dancing like I do?"

"Riding uses different muscles, Collie. Keeping balanced is a lot of work if you're not used to it." He pulled his shirt off over his head. "Water's cold but it's a sunny day."

When he threw his shirt down and ran toward the woods I hobbled after him. The pond was surrounded with trees, the water dark and still. I heard a birdcall, looking up to see an enormous jay rising from a tree limb. Tim was already slipping out of his jeans.

He dove in just as I reached him, his body like a seal in the water. When he surfaced his dark hair was slicked back, ripples forming from the sparkling drops landing in the still pond. He treaded water and watched me undress.

I spent time folding my jeans and shirt into a neat pile and went to the edge, but when I stuck my toe in I pulled it back a second later. "Too cold."

"If you aren't in here in two seconds, I'll throw you in," he warned.

I slid off the bank, letting out a screech as the cold water took away my breath. A moment later he was pulling me along with him, his arm around my waist. We swam together for a long time before climbing out to perch on a boulder in the sun. I gazed at him lying on his belly next to me, feeling like I was in a romance novel. If I wasn't careful I could give up any dream I'd ever had just to live here with him. But so far he hadn't asked me to move in.

My mind was racing in circles, trying to figure things out, when his hand came onto my leg. "Relax," he murmured. "There's lots of time to figure out the rest of your life."

I settled on my back next to him, feeling the sun warm all the parts of me that were still cold. "How'd you know?"

"You get a certain energy," he mumbled, turning his head to look at me. "If you're still cold I have a remedy."

I giggled. "Not on this boulder, I hope."

He pointed toward the trees. "Over there."

"Ticks?"

He shrugged, watching me make up my mind, which didn't take long.

It was late afternoon by the time he re-saddled the horses and helped me onto Duncan's back. I was thoroughly sated, in mind as well as body. I'd never felt like this.

My blissed out mood lasted until we got back. But as soon as the horses were fed and watered and we were walking toward the cabin my thoughts began to circle around like vultures. "I have to go back. Sandra probably needs me."

Tim pressed his lips together. "You want to dance?"

"I don't know—maybe."

His eyes turned dark. "Didn't you say you were fired?"

"Yeah, but I don't know if she meant it. It was just a bad night."

He scoffed. "You like the attention. I can see it when you're on stage. You like performing."

"What's wrong with that?"

He opened the cabin door and waited while I walked through. "You did say you want to be an artist, not an exotic dancer. When do you plan to pursue that?"

"If I knew how to do it, I'd be pursuing it now."

He closed the door and headed to the kitchen, pulling two beers out of the refrigerator. He popped the caps and led the way into the living room and slumped onto the couch. I joined him, accepting the cold bottle he handed me.

He took a swig and faced me. "What do you want from life?"

I looked at the bottle in my hands. "That's what I'm trying to figure out. There's something about dancing..." I turned away, not understanding myself what drove me.

"Thought you wanted to go up to the medicine wheel tomorrow. Is that still your plan?"

"Well, I...I guess so. Being here with you, and..."

"You have a restlessness in you, Collie. It's like you're going in circles all the time."

I glanced at him. "That's exactly how I feel. Did I tell you I'm writing a book?"

He stared at me in surprise. "No. What's it about?"

"A woman kind of like me—a dancer. She's trapped with her parents who won't let her dance because of their religion."

"Do you feel trapped?"

I glanced out the window where the light had faded. The day was nearly gone. "Kind of. I don't want to dance like I've been, but I don't know how to stop. I need the money."

"You can stay here with me."

There it was—what I'd thought about and hoped for earlier. Living in this idyllic place with the man I loved. But instead of jumping at the chance, I found myself shaking my head. "No, Tim, I can't. I love it here, but this isn't my life. I have to sort things out." What in hell was I saying?

"Could you be happy writing?"

"You mean just writing, no dancing?"

He nodded and took a swig of his beer.

"I don't know. Dancing makes me feel good—and yes, you're right—I do love the attention."

"How about an audience of one?" he grinned.

"I have to go," I said, standing up. "Can you give me a lift into town?"

We hardly spoke on the trip in. I knew I'd alienated him, but I wasn't sure what to say. And I was too confused to even try. When he dropped me off at the bar he didn't say goodbye, just put the truck in gear and drove away.

"What are you doing here?" Nadine asked when she saw me.

"I...am I really fired?"

"Yes, Columbine. And your friend is doing quite well. You're not needed." The look on her face was less than friendly.

"Is Sandra here?"

"She's in the back," she said coldly, turning away to serve a customer.

Sandra was facing the mirror and putting on her make-up. When she saw my reflection her mouth opened in surprise. "I thought you were going to the medicine wheel."

"I went to Tim's place instead. It's unbelievable, Sandra. He's rich."

"Are you moving in with him?" she asked, tracing kohl along her lash line.

"He asked me to but I said no."

Her eyes met mine in the mirror. "Why ever not? You love him, don't you?"

I nodded. "But I don't know who I am yet. It wouldn't be fair to either one of us."

She scoffed. "Couldn't you figure it out while you're living with a hunky guy?"

"I was tempted to say yes. I think he's angry with me."

She focused on her other eye, beginning to trace kohl along the top. "I'd be angry too. You've been sleeping together, spending time together." Her overly made-up eyes met mine. "And now you don't have a job. What are you planning to do?"

"I have no idea."

23

It was not even dawn when I finally got up and made coffee, the sky outside a pearly gray. I could just see the outlines of the trees, my gaze going under them in hopes of seeing the wolf. But why would he be here? I hadn't seen him since I'd been back in Lovell. I'd spent a sleepless night in my trailer going over the past weeks and wondering what in hell I was doing. So far I'd lost my job, alienated the man I loved, and done nothing about my future. My novel languished as I ran around in metaphoric circles like a crazy person. And if I didn't get another job my money would run out.

I was drinking coffee when my cell phone rang. "Collie? Do you have a moment to talk?"

It was Karen Holt. "If you're calling about the book, it isn't finished," I said defensively.

"I am calling about the book, but I'm not planning to hound you. I just thought you might like to meet this new publisher I just connected with. He's looking for books in your genre."

"My genre? What is my genre?"

"From what I saw it's a coming of age story. They're hot right now."

"You mean drive up there?"

"He's in Billings."

"Would you be there?"

"Of course. I can fly down and meet you. What's your schedule like?"

"I have absolutely nothing going on."

"This is Friday. How about we plan for next Tuesday? Will that work?"

"I don't know how far Billings is, but I'm sure it can't be more than a few hours drive."

"Once you reach Billings punch this address into your phone." She rattled off an address, which I copied down. "And bring something nice to wear. He's an old-fashioned guy. And don't forget your computer."

Something nice to wear? The sparkly six-inch heels I occasionally wore on stage probably wouldn't do. Guess I needed to go shopping.

When I got off the phone I thought about this new development. Maybe I didn't have to sort out my life after all.

I pulled out my computer and opened Word. I'd been working feverishly ever since I talked to Karen, hoping to get the thing finished before my trip to Billings. But it was hard to herd my main character anywhere she'd didn't want to go. So far she'd fought me at every turn, our stubborn natures clashing as I sought to bring the novel to a close.

May ran down the driveway without looking back. She wasn't sure how she'd come to this point, only that she knew if she didn't do something she would surely lose her mind. She shut out her guilt and kept going, her fingers on her pocket where she'd stuffed the money she'd stolen from her mother's stash. Should she give up her life for these people? No. Her life was her own. She'd learned that when she was dancing. Now if she could only get on a bus before her parents came to find her.

I paused for a second, wondering where I was going with the story. Was May like me? Would she find the perfect guy and then give him up because she needed to pursue her own life? A second later I was crying.

It was Sunday now and I'd heard nothing from Tim. Twice I'd debated heading out to his place, but I wasn't sure I could find it again. I'd been too caught up with him to remember the details of the trip. I wiped my eyes and turned back to the manuscript. Going to see this publisher had spurred me on to finish the damn thing, but that was easier said than done. At least May was clear about what she wanted, which was more than I could say for myself. And unlike me, she would find a way to do it. I began to type.

I was dozing later when I heard my door creak. When I opened my eyes Tim was standing there, my turquoise beads around his neck. I sat up. "How'd you get those?"

"You gave them to me. Don't you remember?"

I frowned. "No. Why would I give them to you?"

"Because they represent what we have together. We live on the other side of the veil."

I was dreaming, but when I tried to wake myself up I couldn't manage it. "This is a dream."

"I know it is. But it's the only way I can talk to you. You have a wall around you and I can't climb that high. What do you want from life?"

"You asked me that the other day. I want you and I want to dance and I want to write. What do you want?"

"I want you."

"That's all?"

"I hate to be hokey, but what's more important than love?"

I thought about that for a long moment. "Fulfillment."

"You think dancing or writing will give you that?"

"I do."

"And if we never see each other again?"

"That would make me really sad."

"But you don't mind giving me up."

"I don't want to give you up. I'm in love with you. Can't I do all of it?"

His eyes clouded. "Can we try and figure out how to make that possible?"

"I'm going to Billings in a couple of days. When I get back I'll be clearer about some things."

"About the writing."

"Not sure how you know that, but yes."

"This is a dream, Collie. That's how I know it."

"The Columbine flower represents a portal between two worlds. Is that why we can do this?"

He grinned. A second later I woke up in darkness. When I turned on my lantern and checked for the beads I always wore, they weren't there.

It took me less than two hours to get to Billings. And on the way I thought again about Tim's visitation and my beads. We'd made a plan to meet on Thursday when I got back. I laughed at myself. *It was just a dream, you idiot.* And yet we'd shared dreams before. And what about the missing beads? I must have dropped them somewhere.

Once I reached the outskirts of the city I pulled off the road and punched in the address Karen Holt had given me. We'd talked early this morning and set up a time to meet at the office downtown—the office that belonged to Mountain Publishing. I was wearing a suit, the first one I'd ever owned. It was gray linen with a fitted jacket that nipped in at the waist, and a straight skirt that landed sedately just below the knee. I'd never worn stockings in my life until today. My thick unruly hair was twisted and held off my neck with a black clip. Dark pumps and a black leather shoulder bag containing my computer and a notebook completed my businesswoman look.

I parked the truck as close as I could get to the brick building and walked down the street to where I'd seen the Mountain Publishing sign. Karen was waiting for me out front, dressed in a navy suit with a white blouse underneath. Pearls hung around her thin neck.

"Very nice look," she said, gazing at me. "You clean up well."

I laughed. "I don't feel like myself, but I guess I can stand it for an hour or two."

Daniel McClure smiled warmly when he saw Karen, standing to give her a hug. The way they looked at each other gave me the feeling there was more to their relationship than mere business. When Karen introduced us he shook my hand and then pointed to the two chairs in front of his desk before seating himself.

"Karen has said lots of good things about your writing. I look forward to reading your manuscript. How close to finished are you?"

I glanced at Karen before answering. "Pretty close. I'd say I have maybe one more chapter to go?"

"We need to strike while the iron's hot. The market for this type of book is intense at the moment. If we can do a quick write-up and get your name out there, perhaps we can streamline your book before the feeding frenzy is over."

"I...I could probably finish it in a few days, but I think you should read it first. Maybe it isn't what you want."

"Of course I'll read it, my dear girl. But I trust Karen's judgment. Do you have it with you?"

"It's on my computer," I said, fishing it out of my bag.

"Can you email it to my secretary? She'll print it out for me." He handed me the email address.

I got on his Wi-Fi and sent the doc to the address he'd given me. "It hasn't been edited yet."

"I'm fully aware of that. We have an editing staff to read it over and decide what needs to be done."

I glanced at Karen. "Should I get a room for the night?"

"I've already booked one for you," she said, her gaze going to Daniel.

"Let's meet tomorrow around one," he said, standing.

Karen and I rose to leave, but before we reached the door he was there, his hand on Karen's arm. "Can you spare me a moment?"

He opened the door and when I walked through he closed it quietly behind me. His secretary looked up. "You should consider yourself very lucky. Mr. McClure doesn't usually do this for new clients. You must be very special, or," she continued, glancing at the door, "you have a very good agent." Her savvy gaze met mine.

It was twenty minutes before Karen emerged from the office. She straightened her suit jacket and glanced quickly at the secretary before she herded me out.

"What's going on?" I asked once we were in the elevator.

"We made dinner plans," she murmured.

"He's in love with you."

Karen turned, her cheeks going pink. "We do like each other, but I wouldn't go that far."

"I hope he didn't agree to read my book just because of you."

Karen laughed. "He won't take it on if it isn't good."

Karen told me where to park my truck for the night, and gave me a ride to the hotel where she'd booked me a room.

Before she left I grabbed her arm. "Is it really ready for prime time?"

She chuckled. "Maybe not prime time, Columbine, but certainly it's ready for a knowledgeable publisher." She patted me on the arm. "Don't fret."

The next day Karen picked me up at my hotel at twenty minutes to one. I was wearing the same suit, now wrinkled, with a different blouse. I was sleep deprived from worrying about what Daniel would say about my book, and also about my promise to Tim to be back on Thursday. *You promised dream Tim,* my little voice reminded me. Dream Tim, real Tim—I was beginning to think there wasn't much difference. *Except when one Tim doesn't remember what other Tim has been up to.* I laughed out loud, startling Karen behind the wheel.

"What's so funny?"

"It's too complicated to explain."

"The book is good," Daniel told me right away, pushing his grey hair off his forehead. "It needs a few tweaks here and there, but I think it will make a fine novel. What's the title?"

"I…I haven't chosen a title."

"I'm sure we can come up with one to fit the story." He glanced at Karen. "You came up with something last night— what did you call it? April Showers?"

I laughed. "April showers bring May Flowers. I love it."

Karen smiled shyly. "Didn't mean to step on your toes."

"I'm serious, Karen. It's perfect."

"As soon as the edits are complete I'll contact you with a contract to sign," Daniel said. "In the meantime you must finish it. My editing team is already working on what you gave me. I'll need the last chapters by the end of next week. Can you manage that?"

I counted up the days. "I'll try."

He stood. "Good, then. We'll go from there." He shook my hand again. "It was good to meet you, Columbine. I think my office can handle the rest, but if you have any questions or concerns don't hesitate to contact my secretary."

I rose and left the office, feeling dazed as I walked slowly toward the elevators.

Just before the elevator arrived Karen appeared next to me. "Are you happy?"

"I don't know what I am. It seems too easy."

She gazed at me, her expression serious. "It's a good book, Collie, but there are lots of things wrong with it. You're new to writing and your style is hardly polished."

I suddenly felt deflated. "But Daniel…"

"He likes the story. But your ability to plot properly, the story arc, and your character development leave a lot to be desired. Grammar and sentence structure will also need a good hard look. No publisher worth their salt would publish a book without thorough editing."

"But that's what I told him—I haven't had the chance to edit it myself."

"They'll do the editing for you. All you have to do is rewrite once they send it back." She looked away for a second before her eyes met mine again. "And you must be prepared for substantial changes. If you don't like what they decide, there will be no contract. Do you understand?"

"But Daniel said that…"

She scoffed. "I've had experience with these things. Many authors refuse to give up their vision and lose the chance to be published."

Once we reached the lobby she shook my hand. "Get those

last chapters done as quickly as you can. As Daniel said, the market is hot right now and we don't want to miss this opportunity. And don't feel bad. You're a new author." She smiled. "Wait until you've written book number fifteen."

Book fifteen? A fluttery sensation moved through my belly. I attempted a smile before I walked outside, but once I reached the sycamores that lined the street I stopped for a moment to collect myself. I wondered what the editors would want me to change. What if it really didn't jive with my vision—would I give up the chance to have it published? The story was being written through me, or so it seemed. I was merely the conduit for May to write her story. And yet it was also a way for me to revisit my early life and come to grips with it—and to reconcile now with then.

I heard the call of a mocking bird, looking around for the first time. The leaves were turning color. When had that happened? When I glanced back at the office Karen was in the glass-fronted lobby talking to Daniel, their heads close together. I was suddenly nervous, feeling like I just left my baby at daycare for the first time.

24

I t began to rain on my way home, the steady drizzle on the windshield making it difficult to see as my frayed wipers slid across without doing much. I reached the trailer around seven that night, exhausted and not a little freaked out. On the way home I'd fretted about the story, wondering what changes they might want to make. Part of me felt like I was betraying May by giving the book over to these people. Karen had basically told me the book was garbage. And yet they wanted it? And Karen was the one who'd come up with the title, *April Showers*. She'd obviously been thinking about it for a while. I tried to let go of my rising anxiety, telling myself I knew nothing about this process. As the secretary had said, I was lucky.

I worked on the remaining chapters that night, trying hard to convince May to go where she was supposed to go—a way to end the story. But every time I sent her one way, she went in another. She wasn't ready to make up her mind about anything. Instead of shoving it to a conclusion I went back to the beginning, editing out passages that didn't belong and adding things to round out scenes. It was two in the morning before I closed my computer and climbed into bed.

Someone banged on my door early the next morning—or at least I thought it was early until I looked at my phone. I'd slept until 9:30? When I pulled on a robe and answered the door Tim was standing there, a worried expression on his face.

"I thought something happened to you. I've been knocking for fifteen minutes."

I moved back to let him in. "I must have been dead asleep. I was up late trying to finish the book."

He let out a sigh and lowered to my bed, his head in his hands. "I'm sorry for rushing off like I did. I've had a few days to think about things." He glanced up at me. "How did the trip go?"

I sat next to him and reached over to touch my beads hanging around his neck. "You remember the dream."

He nodded. "You went to meet a publisher in Billings."

"And you asked if we could try and work out a solution when I got back."

He frowned worriedly. "Can we?"

I didn't say anything for a minute, trying to collect my thoughts. "I don't want to lose you, Tim, but…"

"But you don't know what you want. You already told me that. I'm asking if together we can figure out a way around this. I have an idea about how to go about it."

"Are we just accepting this dream stuff now like it's perfectly normal?"

He chuckled and rubbed a hand over his face. "It's easier to talk to you in a dream than it is right now."

I let out a sigh and stared at him. He looked deeply exhausted. "You aren't sleeping."

"No, I'm not. There are several things causing it—one, my father needs me, two, the woman I love can't make up her mind whether she loves me enough to commit, and three, someone poisoned a bunch of my sheep."

"Your father...is it bad?"

He nodded. "He may be dying."

I moved closer and put my arm around him. "I'm so sorry. Will you go there?"

He gazed at me, his eyes dark with pain. "Will you go with me?"

I thought of my book, the deadline. "Now? I have to finish the book and send it back in a week."

"Bring it along. You can work while I drive. And despite how primitive you imagine it to be, there is Wi-Fi on the rez."

"I never really thought about it. Yes, I'll come along. But what about the sheep?"

"I've hired an extra hand to watch over them. And he's a good shot."

"Who would do such a thing?"

He shrugged. "Someone who doesn't like me much."

The first person I thought of was Dean. But that was impossible. Last time I spoke with Mary he was about to move in with them.

"I thought of Dean too."

"You can read my thoughts now?"

"No, but whenever you think or talk about him your face takes on an expression like you just ate a lemon."

I laughed. "I'll call Mary and see what she knows. The man is relentless when it comes to things he thinks he owns."

"How soon can you be ready?" Tim asked.

"An hour or so? But don't you have to go and pack?"

"It's all in my truck. I brought camping gear for the trip out and back. It'll take us a couple of days each way."

"We could go in my rig, if you'd rather."

"I wouldn't."

He made coffee while I collected what I needed for the trip. We were on the road an hour later.

I typed as he drove, both of us quiet. When I came to a stopping place I saved the doc and shut the computer down. It was getting low on battery anyway. When he drove off the highway to get gas I headed into the ladies room, not surprised to see dark circles under my bloodshot eyes. I looked like hell.

I was in the truck again when he came out loaded with elk jerky and several bags of chips. "This is a good place for jerky," he told me, sliding into the driver's seat. He handed me a stick. "Not like Dad's, but good enough."

"Your dad makes jerky?"

"He used to before he got sick. He used to hunt too." His eyes took on a remote look as he drove onto the highway.

I didn't say anything as I chewed on the jerky, wondering what we'd do for dinner.

⁘

We were somewhere in Colorado when Tim turned off the main highway and drove down a rutted road leading into the National forest. We'd been travelling for at least eight hours and it was nearly dark. "Looks like you've been here before," I said when he chose a narrow track on the left that led deeper into the forest.

He nodded, turning the headlights on. "About half way and a good camping spot." He stopped the truck next to a narrow rushing stream and pulled the camping gear out of the back.

"Need help?"

"Nope. I'm used to doing this by myself. Grab the cooler though, would you?"

I picked it out of the back of his truck and carried it close to where he was setting up the tent. It was seriously heavy.

When I opened it I found two six-packs of beer, several small bags of dehydrated food and a bag of coffee. "Want a beer?"

"Love one," he said without turning from where he was hammering in the stakes.

I opened it for him, memories of my time with Dean coming back in lurid detail. "I never called Mary," I said as I handed it over.

"About Dean?"

"Yeah." I pulled out my cell phone, surprised to find I had signal. "Guess I'll do it now."

I walked twenty feet away and punched in her numbers.

"Didn't expect to hear from you," she said in a chirpy voice. "Is this about your husband?"

"Well, yes. Is he still around?"

"He took off a week ago, said he had some serious business to attend to."

"Did he fly?"

"Yes, I think he did. Why?"

"No reason, really. How have things been going?"

"Besides Dean going on and on about you? Just fine, I guess, although I'm about to divorce Bill."

"Are you serious?"

"I am. He's been hanging around with Dean and drinking every night. They do drugs too, when Dean scores them. It's been a nightmare."

"I'm sorry to hear that. Do you think he flew out to Wyoming?"

"Could be. He's fixated on you and what you had together, Collie. He's a very angry man. I planned to call and warn you, but then Bill and I had another knock-down drag-out and I got distracted."

"What we had? Is he delusional?"

"He does seem like he's gone round the bend a bit. If you're still with that guy I suggest you lay low."

By the time I hung up my stomach was filled with knots. I walked back to the tent where Tim was on his knees rolling out our sleeping bags. "I think Dean poisoned your sheep."

He turned. "Dean's in Wyoming?"

"Mary said he took off a week ago. He's been ranting about me and she said he's in a rage."

Tim stared into the distance. "I wonder how he found my place."

"Maybe he asked at the police station. He can be very persuasive when he wants to."

"Shit. I shouldn't have left Jorge alone."

"Didn't you say he's a good shot? And what about the other workers?"

"I gave them a week off. Jorge may be a good shot but he shouldn't have to take care of my business."

"Does he have a cell phone?"

"I have no idea."

"You have friends on the force, right?"

"Yeah, so?"

"I bet you didn't report the poisoning."

He stared at me, his eyes taking on the shadows from under the trees.

I was already on Siri asking for the Lovell police station. "Who should I ask for?"

Tim didn't relax until he'd organized one of his cop friends to join Jorge on the ranch. "Tell him that Dean is armed and dangerous." I whispered while he was talking.

He added that, his eyes meeting mine for an instant before he turned away again. "She's here with me," I heard him say. "Yup. We'll be back in a week or so. Thanks."

He handed me my phone. "He'll call your cell if there's anything to report."

I let out a sigh of relief and pocketed my phone, watching Tim make a fire. He pulled out his camping pots and made a meal while I listened to the call of birds and the chirp of crickets as night deepened. I shivered in the cold night air.

"Come eat," he called a while later.

He'd made rice and beans, which I gobbled up. "Sorry for not helping."

"Nothing much to do. Thanks for calling the police."

We bedded down not long after that, both of us done in from the stress and the long day of driving. When he turned on his side facing away I placed a hand on his shoulder. "You don't want to…?"

He turned to look at me but I couldn't see his eyes in the darkness. "I'm too tired."

A moment later he was snoring. I lay awake for a long time wondering what it meant. Was he sick of me? Had the age thing become too much for him? I'd noticed in the gas station bathroom how haggard I looked from the weight loss and lack of rest. I finally fell into a restless sleep, chasing May down as she laughed in my face.

When I woke Tim was sitting on his heels by the fire making coffee. I wrapped the sleeping bag around me and joined him.

"What's wrong?" I asked, noticing the brooding look on his face.

"If you don't know, you're less intuitive than I thought," he said, his eyes on his tin cup.

I poured cowboy coffee into my mug and sipped. "I guess I'm not very intuitive because I really don't know. Is it your dad?"

His dark gaze met mine. "That's part of it."

I thought back to our conversation after I got back from

Billings. He'd told me three things that were bothering him. "You're upset with me."

"I'm not sure I'd categorize it that way."

"You're tired of me?"

He frowned. "That's not it either."

"Tim, I want to connect with you. I feel..."

"What? Lost? Hurt?"

"Yes."

"Join the club."

And then it came to me. He was waiting for me to make up my mind. His exact words were: 'the woman I love can't make up her mind whether she loves me enough to commit'. "It isn't about how much I love you, Tim. I just have to get clear on..."

"What you want for your life...yeah. I've heard all that." He rose from where he sat on his heels and began to take the tent down. I went to help him.

We drove in silence for what seemed like hours as I struggled to find the right words. Finally I said, "You said the two of us could figure this out, remember? I can't do it alone. I'm too confused."

"There's nothing to be confused about. You either want to be with me or you don't."

"I do want to be with you. But..."

He shook his head, glancing at me. "That sentence can't be followed with the word, 'but'. When we get back we can go our separate ways. I'm sorry I asked you along on this trip."

I sat back, stunned. He was willing to end it because I couldn't give him a definitive answer? "I love you, Tim. Doesn't that count for anything?"

He didn't answer. By the time we neared the White Mountains I was so depressed I could barely speak. Tim had been silent and cold for the entire trip. I'd dissolved in tears a couple of times and he'd said nothing, letting me sob quietly next to him.

When we reached Fort Apache he turned onto a dirt road, driving for another fifteen minutes or so before pulling up in front of a small cabin next to a dense wood. The air was thin here and very cold. I followed him out of the truck, but before he reached the door a young man appeared, a smile lighting up his face when he saw Tim. They did some sort of handshake and spoke quietly in another tongue before disappearing inside. I went back to the truck, found a heavy sweater in my pack, and climbed into the passenger side.

I had my head back with my eyes closed when I heard the truck door open. "Dad wants to meet you."

When I tried to see his expression he was already striding away. I jumped out and ran after him, the man I'd seen earlier nodding to me as I followed Tim inside the house. He looked a lot like Tim, especially his jawline and the shape of his eyes. And he had the same sweet smile—the smile I hadn't seen for a while.

"You're Collie," he said.

I turned. "And you must be Mohin."

He nodded and disappeared into the kitchen, emerging a minute later with a sage bundle. A chemical odor assaulted my nostrils before I smelled the smoke he waved around, trying to clear and purify the air. Gray tendrils drifted, curling upward.

Tim glanced at me before disappearing into the bedroom, his dark head bending toward the man lying in the bed. I waited, feeling like I didn't belong until I noticed the old man gesturing for me to come in. His high cheekbones stuck out of his ravaged face—a face that had once been handsome. I saw Tim in his eyes and around his mouth. "I'm Kuruk," he said in a low gravelly voice. "You must be Collie."

"I am. I'm very glad to meet you. Tim's told me a lot about you." I glanced at Tim, but his gaze was on his father, a worried frown on his face.

"You are as I imagined," Kuruk continued. "I see the strength of your spirit." He had a coughing fit and reached for the water glass on the table next to the bed. "I am old and ready to follow my ancestors into the next world," he said once the cough was under control. He glanced at Tim. "It is not a time to be sad."

"No one wants to lose the ones they love," I said.

"It is a time for rejoicing," he said, his eyes meeting mine. "Singing and dancing. Will you dance for me?"

"Now?" I asked.

He laughed and broke into another coughing fit. "No, not now. When I die."

"Well, I..." I looked to Tim for help.

"She will if she's here," Tim supplied.

"I want her to dance," Kuruk said in a stronger tone, staring at Tim. "It is for me and for you that she does this. I see the light between you. I see the darkness that has crept in. You must repair what is broken before it is too late." His eyes closed and he let out a raspy breath.

"We should go now," Tim said, nodding to me.

I took another long look at Kuruk before I followed Tim out of the room, my heart going out to both of them. I could see Kuruk's strength, the wisdom behind his eyes, and his connection to something greater—not God, exactly, but spirit. When the door closed behind me I was in tears.

"You want to eat?" Mohin asked, glancing at me.

"Thanks, but I'm not very hungry."

Tim gave me a sharp look but didn't saying anything before he followed his brother into the kitchen.

When Mohin served bowls of beans and rice at the linoleum table in the kitchen I came in to join them. Instead of eating I drank a beer, glad of the bubbles that seemed to settle my roiling stomach.

"He's close to the end," Mohin said, looking down at his bowl.

Tim didn't answer, his gaze on the closed door to the bedroom.

"Was he serious about me dancing?"

Mohin smiled. "Very serious. He's been asking about you for weeks now. He seems to think you're part of the family."

"We aren't together," Tim said.

Mohin blinked and stared at his brother. "If you aren't together, why is she here?"

"It was a mistake."

Mohin glanced at me quickly before he shook his head and looked down at his bowl.

I didn't say a word, but my heart felt very heavy. I finished my beer and left the house to take a walk, all my dreams and hopes for a future with Tim disappearing into the dark clouds massing above the trees in the distance.

When I got back Tim had pitched the tent, but when it came time to bed down he disappeared into the house. I was freezing cold all night without his warmth, unable to sleep. In the morning he arrived with a cup of coffee for me. "Dad's asking for you."

"Why?"

He shrugged. "He's been having visions—says we should be together."

"Did you tell him what's going on?"

"He knows."

"What should I do?"

"Talk to him."

I cleaned up in the little bathroom in the house, not surprised to see the many bottles of pills lined up along a shelf above the sink. When Tim showed me into the bedroom, Kuruk used great effort to push himself up to sitting.

"Dad, don't," Tim said, trying to help him.

Kuruk waved him off. "Leave us alone now."

Once Tim was out of the room the old man gazed at me with bright eyes, despite the disease that had ravaged the rest of him. "You must come to a decision."

I sat in the chair next to his bed. "I'm confused. I love your son, but…"

"But you love other things as well. We all do. It is not something to feel ashamed of—it is the way of the world. Is that what's holding you back?"

"I was in a very bad marriage for nearly twenty years. I'm afraid of making a mistake." As soon as the words were out of my mouth I realized the truth of what I'd said. I was terrified of being hurt or hurting him. I was in love for the first time in my life, and utterly petrified. And somehow Kuruk had brought it to the surface.

He nodded. "This is a difficult problem. It is your soul that has been damaged by this bad marriage, and also what went before. But it is also your soul that will be healed by a good one." He reached for his water glass, his hand shaking.

"I'm so afraid. I've never felt like this about anyone. And there's the age difference, and now he's…"

"Behaving like a hurt little boy?" He chuckled, which turned into a cough. "Tim is young, but he loves with all his heart. I have seen him struggle with others. He does not struggle with you. He is clear about his feelings. What has come between you is not real. When the truth is revealed the shadows between you will be chased away. As far as age, I have told him it means nothing. You must promise me one thing," he said urgently, leaning forward.

When he began to cough I moved closer and handed him his glass of water. "What is it?"

"Tim may push you away, but do not let him turn your heart cold. He needs you and you need him. When you dance at my funeral you will see the truth. Until then you must remain unconcerned about his behavior."

I gazed at his over-bright eyes. I was pretty sure he had a fever. "I'll try."

He shook his head and reached for my hand, holding it between his hot palms. "Trying is not enough. Promise me that you will not give up on him."

"I promise."

"Then I will die a happy man." He let go of my hand and fell back, his gasping breath turning into a spell of coughing that I didn't know what to do about. Less than a minute later Mohin hurried into the room and waved me out. Tim passed by me, his worried gaze on his father. The door closed, leaving me alone in the living room.

The coughing went on and on, but the silence that came after was what scared me the most. When Mohin emerged from the room his eyes were filled with tears. Fifteen minutes later Tim came out, his cheeks wet. I hurried toward him, but he waved me away and left the house. I'd just met Kuruk and now he was gone.

I held myself very still and remembered what Kuruk had asked me to do. I promised to dance for him and I would honor that promise. I hoped he was right about 'seeing the truth', because at this moment I was as desolate as I'd ever been.

I was sitting on the couch, trying to control my tears, when Mohin walked over and sat next to me. He handed me a beer. "He spelled out exactly what he wanted," Mohin said, his sad eyes meeting mine. "Except for the part you will play, the ceremony will follow tradition."

I wiped at my eyes and focused on him. "Will my dance be allowed?"

Mohin looked down at the bottle in his hands. "Kuruk was a visionary, a medicine man. He was sought out because he could see into the future. Whatever he wants for his funeral will be honored." He took a sip of beer, and pushed his long hair back from his angled face. "I worry about Tim. He hasn't been around enough to be prepared for Kuruk's death. He needs you, but he's walled himself off."

"Kuruk said we're supposed to be together, but Tim is so angry with me right now. And Kuruk's death will surely make matters worse."

Mohin nodded. "Tim's hurting badly."

"Will others come to the ceremony?"

"There will be many people there—tribe members and those in the community he's touched."

"How can I dance in front of them? I'm not part of the tribe."

"Because he asked you to. You must honor his wishes."

Sometime later a gray-haired Native man arrived and went into the bedroom. I heard chanting, the sound of a rattle. When he came out he nodded to Mohin. "Kuruk is ready," he said. "I will tell the elders. We will sing tomorrow."

That night I stayed alone in the tent, hoping Tim would show up. When I finally fell asleep I dreamed of moles burrowing deep into the ground where it was moist and cool and silent. I was there with them, wishing I could stay forever in the dark and quiet where pain couldn't reach me. In the morning I woke early, shivering. When would the ceremony happen? I had a book to finish and Dean was skulking around Lovell, doing bad stuff. My trailer was there.

How could I dance in front of a group of Apache? I was a white woman with no right to be here. And from the way Tim was treating me, I knew he felt the same way.

It was late morning before Tim arrived back at the house, his face looking nearly as ravaged as his father's had been. His hair was tangled and matted, his clothing covered in dirt and leaves. Instead of speaking to me he talked to Mohin, making plans for what was to happen later on that afternoon. I stayed out of sight as much as I could, knowing that my presence disturbed him. But I had done as Mohin instructed, preparing myself for what Kuruk had asked of me.

Thin afternoon sunshine was sifting down through the changing cloud cover when Mohin and Tim, and two other tribe members, wrapped Kuruk's body in a brightly colored wool blanket and placed him inside a wooden casket. His arms were folded in front of him, and he was dressed in a white linen shirt, a necklace of heavy turquoise beads with a large piece of silver in the shape of an eagle around his neck. His gray hair had been braided and lay on either side of his peaceful face, a bright band of fabric tied around his head. He seemed merely asleep, as though his eyes might open at any moment. I cried when I saw him, wishing I had known him longer.

A long line of people followed the four men carrying the casket up a steep hill. I kept my distance, feeling unwanted and uncomfortable, not sure I could do what I'd promised. Tim had not even glanced at me since his father's death, an expression of utter desolation on his ravaged features. It was a long trek up the mountain, the air growing chillier the higher we went. I wrapped my arms around my shivering body and hoped I would make it through this day.

We finally reached the top where boulders looked over the deep valley below. The wind whipped across the mountaintop, stirring up dirt and making my eyes water. When the casket had been carefully lowered between two sections of rock, Tim bent to open the lid. It listed to one side until Mohin placed stones underneath to keep it level. Someone began to chant and the rest of the group joined in, raising their arms to the sky and moving together to sing their sadness. Mohin brought a pitcher of water a plate of food, placing them next to the casket. He bowed his head for a moment before rising to allow Tim to add a hunting knife and a beautifully carved bow and arrows to the offerings. Tim's expression was one of deep grief, my heart going out to him.

A few minutes later Mohin came to stand next to me. "Food and water for his journey into the afterlife," he explained, "his hunting knife and bow too. The casket stays open so the owls can carry him into the next world."

Mohin glanced up at the gathering storm as a rumble of thunder rolled across the sky. "When the storm is overhead you will dance."

Nerves filled my stomach. "How do I dance? Where?"

He gestured to the sloping hillside where we stood. "Kuruk assured us of your connection to lightning. Lightning power is only bestowed on those who use it wisely."

I stared up at the gathering clouds, watching jagged strikes in the distance. "I'm not a shaman and I don't have any powers. We're at the top of the mountain, Mohin. If lightning strikes up here it could kill us."

His solemn gaze met mine. "It will strike."

I looked past him to where Tim chanted with the others, his profile turned toward me. Tears came into my eyes and I brushed them away. *When the truth is revealed the shadows between you will be chased away.* I hoped Kuruk was right. "I made up a dance in my head, but…"

"You don't have to make anything up. It will come on its own, just as the storm will."

And come it did, with a vengeance. Rain poured down, wind whistling through the branches of the tall pines. My hair blew into my face, my loose pants whipping about my legs. I shivered with nerves and cold, sure I would be struck by lightning at any moment. Clouds moved and bumped above me, dried pine needles and dirt whirling in little eddies as the wind increased. Leaves and twigs caught in my hair, tangling it further. When I scanned for Tim I couldn't find him.

The chanting grew louder, a drumbeat starting up. When my gaze went to the casket, Kuruk's face was wet from the rain. It looked like tears to me—tears of joy brought by this ceremony and the full life he'd had. My face was wet too. I wanted him to open his eyes and smile at me the way he had in his bedroom. I wanted to know him.

When Mohin gave me a nod I forced myself to move, sluggishly at first and then faster, as the spirit seemed to take me. Lightning struck a tree fifty yards away. It caught fire. I kept going, following what the lightning dictated. I was one with it, all parts of me electric as I twirled and danced, my legs swinging as I moved around the circle I'd created for myself. The tribe members disappeared as I whirled, my focus turning inward as I moved in time to the steady beat.

The chanting continued, the drumbeat growing louder with each rumble of thunder. I came out of my trance long enough to locate Tim, his eyes wide as he watched me. And then the conscious part of me was gone, into the storm, into the lightning—I was a spark that had no substance—charged, explosive, volatile. I heard strange sounds come out of my mouth, words that made no sense to me. As I whirled by I saw Kuruk rise from the casket, his ghost watching me as my movements grew wilder and wilder. My hair and clothes were drenched, my face turned up to the sky that seethed and swam with static electricity.

And then Kuruk was there with me, his ethereal body filled with light, a wide smile on his face as he danced alongside me. I smiled back, so glad to see his eyes opened and the joyous look on his face. The turquoise beads glistened, electricity sparking around the silver eagle that lay against his chest. Tim had stopped chanting to watch us, an expression of astonishment on his face. As we danced the others stopped chanting, standing still to stare at us. Kuruk followed my movements perfectly—or maybe I was following his movements. It was hard to tell.

I don't know how long we danced before I heard the call of owls in the distance. The sound grew louder, blocking out the hiss of raindrops as they pelted the flames, louder than the thunder booming across the sky. My fingers itched with electricity. More strikes, more flames. The forest was burning. And still we danced, our movements perfectly synchronized, as though some god had imparted the choreography.

The storm gathered force, sending many of the group stumbling away. Kuruk's lined face was suffused with happiness, a dark shadow lifting from him to dissipate into the storm. We were still at it when silence came over the mountaintop. The storm was gone. Sunlight streamed though the trees, sparkling across the grass and lighting up all the faces of those who had come to take part in this man's funeral. Flying silently on wide wings the owls had gathered above us to wait. Kuruk faced me and pressed his hand to his heart before he floated upward to be carried away. Tears streamed down my face as I watched him grow smaller and smaller until he disappeared from view.

I was suddenly so weak I couldn't hold myself up. I was back at the medicine wheel, falling through the earth. I was in this world and then I was gone.

25

I opened my eyes to see Tim leaning over me, his brows pulled together. I was lying on a bed in an unfamiliar room, a blanket covering me. When I tried to sit up Tim pushed me gently back.

"Take it easy. You've been unconscious for a while."

"What happened?"

He sat down next to me and picked up my hand, holding it close to his chest. "I've been a fucking idiot. I don't what in hell I was thinking."

I frowned, trying to remember the recent past. I did recall walking up the mountain with the tribe. After that there was a large blank.

Tim stared at me. "Do you remember dancing?"

"Dancing? Why would I dance?"

Tim's expression grew even more worried. "You might have a concussion. I should call a doctor."

"No doctors, Tim. I'm okay. Just tell me what happened. Last I remember you weren't speaking to me. Did I miss the funeral?"

Tim let out a low chuckle. "You *were* the funeral, Collie."

"I...?"

"You danced for Kuruk and with Kuruk—his ghost danced with you. He asked you to dance just before he died. Do you remember that much?"

I nodded, trying to recall my last conversation with Kuruk. "He...said when I danced things would change."

Tim scoffed. "They changed all right. You have lightning power. There was a storm up there."

"Lightning power—what does that mean?"

"It means you're powerful and connected to the tribe. Not sure how that could be, but it was pretty obvious up there."

"Owls. I remember owls."

"The owls took Kuruk away. But before they came you had electricity coming out of your fingertips. What you and my dad did together..." He shook his head, his eyes going wide. "I've never seen you dance like that."

Bits and pieces were coming back to me—flashes. "That wasn't me, Tim. I don't know who it was."

"You were an Apache shaman, Collie. You didn't even look like yourself. Your face was as Apache as Dad's."

I thought about that. "When I was at the medicine wheel there was a lightning storm. I could see electricity coming out of my fingers."

"Jesus." He let out a heavy sigh. "I thought I lost you. Carrying you down that hill...I've never been so freaked."

"I'm sorry."

"For what? I'm the one who's sorry. I've been an ass."

I smiled, gazing up at him. "So now that I'm a shaman you like me again?"

"Don't even joke about it. You could have died up there. And just to be clear, I never stopped loving you. It's your stubbornness that makes me crazy."

"Nothing's changed, even though Kuruk said it would."

Tim stared at me in disbelief. "Nothing's changed? You

danced Kuruk into the afterlife, nearly died in the process, and discovered you had lightning power. You're connected to the tribe—my tribe—which means we're even more connected than I thought."

"Our connection has nothing to do with it. You know how I feel about you. Kuruk told me the truth would come when I danced. But it hasn't. I'm still confused about my life. I can't give up everything I want just because I'm in love with you."

He gazed at me, his eyes welling. "I wasn't ready for Dad to die. I knew he was sick, but…" He shook his head and turned away to hide his tears.

When I placed a hand on his arm he turned back to me, wiping at his eyes. "Just before he died Dad told me you and I were destined to be together. He saw us with a child."

"A baby? I'm forty years old!"

Tim smiled sadly. "I can't help that. I'm only repeating Dad's vision."

"So if our destiny is to be together, why can't you give me the time I need?"

Tim grimaced. "Because I'm afraid you'll follow your dream and move to some remote place and we'll never see each other again."

I pushed myself up. "I need to use the bathroom."

Tim put his arm around me, helping me hobble across the living room. "Do you need me to come in with you?"

I shook my head and closed the door, leaning against it for a few seconds. I saw Kuruk in my mind's eye, his eyes bright as he smiled at me just before he lifted into the air. And that's when I remembered the rest of it.

I stayed in the bathroom so long that Tim finally knocked. "Are you okay in there?"

"Not really," I muttered, taking a look in the mirror. Dark

circles lay beneath my eyes, and my hair was a tangled mess and filled with leaves. There were bruises along my collarbones and my shirt was ripped. I opened the door. "I remembered something."

His eyes narrowed slightly. "About the funeral?"

I nodded. "I think I might need coffee before I tell you about it."

Tim left me on the couch in the living room and went to make coffee. When he returned a short time later with two mugs, he looked worn out, his eyes red-rimmed, his skin gray with fatigue. He sat next to me and handed me one of the mugs.

I sipped and collected the bits and pieces of what I remembered. "I think I may have gone to the afterlife with Kuruk," I began, placing my mug down on the coffee table.

"The afterlife? You were concussed, Collie."

"There were natives there, men and women, and they greeted Kuruk, welcoming him into their midst. He knew them. They welcomed me too, but Kuruk told me I had to go back. He said I had to make up my mind, that time was slipping away for us. I wasn't sure what he meant by that, but I think he was saying there's a moment when things come together, and if you choose to ignore the opportunity it won't come again." I gazed at Tim who was staring at me with a look of concentration.

"You're saying that this moment…is our moment?"

I nodded. "If we don't grab it, it'll be gone."

"That's what I've been trying to tell you."

I glanced at him, trying to smile. "I've been so confused. I still am. The only thing I'm not confused about is how I feel about you."

Tim grinned. "I'd say that's a sign. I think you should move in with me and give yourself time to figure out the rest of it. You don't have a job right now. What harm will it do?"

I gazed at him, love welling up and bringing tears to my eyes. "We're both emotionally overwhelmed right now. Is this a good time to make such an important decision?"

"Nothing is set in stone. If you decide to take off for New York or L.A., I'll have to deal. But between now and when you figure things out you can stay with me and finish your book."

I let out my held breath, something heavy lifting from my chest. I thought of his house, the fields of waving grass, the horses. A respite from the constant worry sounded pretty good.

We were kissing when Mohin walked in from outside. "Glad to see you two made up," he said, heading for the kitchen.

We stayed one more night in order to give me time to recover and allow Mohin and Tim to discuss what came next. Tim plied me with food, insisting that not eating enough had caused my unconsciousness. I dutifully ate the beans and rice, stuffing buttered cornbread into my mouth, but I knew what happened to me had nothing to do with starvation. I needed to hear what Kuruk had to say, and to see where he'd gone in order to say goodbye.

"Kuruk told me to burn the house down. He was set on following the old ways," Mohin said over dinner.

"At least he didn't kill his horse. Where is the old roan, anyway?"

"He died a week ago. He was nearly thirty years old."

"Dad must have figured it was a sign."

Mohin chuckled. "Yup. He said he wanted to follow the old guy into the afterlife. He loved that horse."

"If you burn the house where will you live?" Tim asked.

Mohin smiled. "I have a girlfriend, Tim. We've been together for a while. I only stayed because Dad was sick."

"I didn't know that. What about the furniture, his things?"

"I'll contact the tribal council and give what I can away. Will you stay for the burning?"

Tim shook his head, glancing at me. "Collie needs to get back. And someone poisoned a bunch of my sheep."

Mohin's eyes went wide. "What the hell?"

"I've got help for while we're gone, but I should be the one guarding the place."

⟨ornament⟩

We were in the truck the next morning when I asked about the house burning. "What's that about?"

"The horse is killed so he can carry the warrior into the afterlife, and since he no longer needs them, all his worldly goods are given away. Not sure why the house is burned." He glanced at me. "Maybe so his ghost won't be tempted to come back?"

"From what I saw there would be no reason to come back. It was a beautiful place."

He glanced at me. "Can you deal if we drive straight through? I kind of need to get back."

"How long will it take?"

"Probably sixteen hours or so, depending on how many times we stop. Are you up to it?"

"It's not yet six a.m. I say let's go for it. Driving will give me time to work on the book."

I typed as we drove, ignoring May's insistence on following her separate agenda. I figured out a suitable ending and pointed her that way, hoping the rest would fall into place. Unfortunately she grabbed the reins and took off in an entirely different direction. I closed the computer and laid my head back against the seat. This was at least the third time I'd attempted to end the thing.

"What's wrong?"

I kept my eyes closed, speaking in a monotone. "My character refuses to do what I want her to do."

Tim laughed. "Sounds like your character takes after you."

26

It was past midnight by the time we reached my trailer, both of us bleary with fatigue.

"Get what you need for tonight. Tomorrow we'll haul the rig over."

When I hopped out I noticed the trailer door was open. And when I turned on the flashlight on my phone, I saw that the inside had been ransacked, most of my belongings missing. The foam mattress had been hacked into pieces and my travel toilet had been upended on the floor, a pile of something dark spreading across the rug. I held my nose. I distinctly remembered cleaning it before we left. When I checked outside all my tires had been slashed—including the truck tires.

Tim joined me by the trailer, his gaze on the mess. "Dean did this."

I nodded. "Looks like his work. I'm glad I had my computer with me."

"And your cash."

"Yes, that too." I went to check the truck, not surprised to see the driver side window smashed and my glove box hanging open. The interior smelled bad, but I couldn't identify what it was.

Tim opened the door, his hand going to his nose. "He pissed inside your truck? What kind of pervert does that?"

"The same kind who craps in my trailer. He marked his territory," I muttered.

Tim pressed his lips together. "If I get my hands on that fucker…"

"Don't say it. Let's go home."

Tim gazed at me, his eyebrows rising in surprise. "You just called my ranch home."

I shrugged. "This certainly isn't my home anymore. Dean made sure of that. I'll cost me thousands to fix it up, and frankly this trailer isn't worth it."

"I can help. I'm good with my hands."

I smiled and raised my eyebrows. "Don't I know it."

He chuckled, leading the way to his truck. Once we were on the road he turned to me. "I expected you to be more upset. You're taking this pretty well."

"I have everything I need."

He grinned and pressed down on the gas pedal, speeding down the dark deserted road.

Once we reached the cabin he parked the truck and we grabbed our packs and stumbled inside. I didn't even brush my teeth, just took off my clothes and climbed into bed. Tim was already there, his eyes at half mast. "Tomorrow I'll talk with Jack and Jorge, find out what's happened."

"And tomorrow I'll deal with my truck and trailer and the rest of my life."

Tim let out a snort. "Right. Sleep well, babe."

Babe. I liked that. I closed my eyes and snuggled against him.

Instead of hurrying out to catch up with ranch business, Tim woke with an urgent need to connect. It was not yet dawn when I felt his lips on my bruised collarbone. "Trying to make it all better," he murmured when my eyes opened.

His mouth moved downward, his hands on the parts of me that needed attention. He knew exactly where they were. I kissed his chest, tracing my fingers along the line of soft fuzz that ran downward. When my fingers reached that magical part of him he pulled my body on top of his. From then on I was in another world, all thought drifting away as we re-discovered each other.

Tim took a shower afterward and then hurried out the door. "I'll be back in a while," he yelled as he ran for his truck. Dawn light was sifting across the grass, the call of birds breaking the silence. I heard the truck engine start and the spit of gravel as he took off down the road in back of the house. I rolled over in bed and buried my nose in the sheets, reveling in the smell of him. I dozed then, sated and content.

I was making breakfast when he appeared in the doorway, a grim look on his face. "Two more sheep killed, and slashed tires on the tractor."

"Oh no! Did you talk to Jorge and the cop?"

"Cop's name is Jack. And no, I couldn't find them."

"But weren't they supposed to be...?"

"Yes, they were, but something must have happened. I've got to go into town. Do you want to come along or stay here?"

I turned back to the eggs. "Can we eat first?"

He came inside and pulled the door closed. "Guess I'd better. We didn't have much yesterday."

I thought of our elk jerky and the bag of salty greasy potato chips we'd consumed while we barreled down the road. I forked eggs and toast onto a plate and handed it to him. "You need to eat if you're planning to go on a rampage."

"Rampage. Good word," he mumbled between bites. "What does it mean, exactly?"

"Go berserk, get out of control, go postal."

He stared into the distance. "Perfect."

"Dean should be behind bars," I said as we sped toward Lovell a half hour later.

He slanted me a glance. "If we can prove it's him."

"I know damn well it's him."

"The law doesn't work that way, Collie. Innocent until proven guilty, remember?"

I thought about the disgusting mess in my trailer, my slashed tires. "I might be able to prove it."

Tim frowned. "How?"

"I'm still thinking." I thought of DNA tests on the feces, or something he might have left behind that would implicate him. But even the thought of being inside my trailer after what he'd done made me feel sick to my stomach. I planned to have the thing hauled off to the dump. If someone wanted it, they could have it.

Tim's hand went to the knife on his belt, his fingers closing around the hilt. "Tell me when you've figured it out."

I shivered as an image of him bare chested and covered in war paint went through my mind. "You won't do something stupid, will you?"

He turned. "Not unless I have to."

"Police station first, right?"

He nodded. "Got to find out what's going on and where the bastard's staying."

"Jorge was there yesterday afternoon when I left," Jack told Tim.

"He's not there now. Two more sheep are dead and my tractor tires were slashed. Were you planning to come over today?"

"Jorge told me he'd call. He said he expected you back last night."

"We got in late. Have you heard any news about Dean?"

Jack's eyes narrowed. "He's been hanging out at the Bighorn—took up with that new gal there—Sandra, I think her name is? He may be staying with her."

"Sandra? Didn't Nadine warn her?" I asked, horrified.

Jack's pale eyes turned to me. "Nadine had to go to Colorado to take care of her sick mother."

I grabbed Tim's arm. "I need to talk with Sandra—she could be in serious trouble."

Jack trained his gaze on me, his forehead creasing. "What's this man capable of?"

I swallowed. "I don't know for sure. But he's a charmer and he wants to ruin my life. He ransacked my truck and trailer and slashed my tires—I'm sure he's the one killing the sheep."

Jack turned to Tim. "Never saw a soul the entire time I was out there."

"Dean's not stupid," I piped up. "He must have known you were watching. That's why he waited until you weren't there. I hope Jorge's okay."

Jack frowned and glanced into the distance. "I'll put out an APB. In the meantime you need to get me some real evidence. I can only hold him on suspicion for forty-eight hours."

I gave him Dean's full name and a description. "He's driving a rental."

"Can we go by Sandra's motel?" I asked Tim when we left the station. "It's not far."

Tim nodded and climbed behind the wheel. "After we talk to Sandra I need to get back. I'll drop you off at the trailer park and you can drive your truck out."

"With four slashed tires?"

"Oh crap—I forgot. I'm worried about Jorge."

"You can leave me. I'll call a tow truck and have them replaced. Hope I have enough cash with me."

Tim reached into his back pocket and pulled out his wallet. "This should cover it," he said, handing me four one hundred dollar bills.

"Are you sure?"

He made a face. "Come on, Collie—what do you think?"

"Sorry. It's just a lot of cash."

"It's what you make in one night of dancing."

"I have cash but I left it at the house."

He shook his head dismissively and pressed down on the gas pedal.

When I knocked on Sandra's door there was no answer. And when I checked with the manager he told me she'd checked out. "Guess she was plannin' to move in with that fella she was with."

"Thinning slicked back hair and beady blue eyes?"

He chuckled. "That's the one. He had his arm around her, so I figured they must be a couple."

I didn't say a word as Tim drove toward the RV Park, worry taking away any possibility of rational thought. Tim dropped me off and leaned out as I headed to my truck. "If you're not back in an hour and a half I'm coming to look for you."

"It might take longer than that to replace four tires, Tim."

"Okay—let's say two hours."

"If you find Jorge borrow his phone and call me." I rattled off the numbers, watching him copy them onto a piece of paper.

"Be careful," he yelled before taking off in a cloud of dust.

He was seriously worried. And to be honest, I was too. I pulled out my cell, looked up the closest garage and punched in the numbers.

The tow truck arrived twenty minutes later and loaded up my truck. "You got an enemy, lady?" the skinny man in grease-covered overalls asked, examining the tires, the smashed window and the deep scratches dug into the paint.

More damage I hadn't noticed until that moment. "I might," I muttered.

He chuckled. "Climb in the truck. We'll get her fixed up for ye."

I was in the garage waiting when my cell phone rang, Sandra's name displayed. "Where are you?" I asked her. "I went by the motel and they said you'd checked out."

"I met a man, Collie. He's handsome and smart and I may be falling in love. He took me to the best hotel in town and he's paying."

I took in a deep breath, trying to find the right words. "I hate to tell you this, but I think that man is Dean."

There was a long silence and muffled talking. When she came back her voice sounded different. "His name is Toby. He doesn't know you. Why would you want to hurt me like that?"

"Sandra, I..." The call ended.

"It's ready," the tire man said, wiping his hands on his jeans. "Pay in there." He pointed to a small office.

I perused the bill and handed over all of Tim's cash and a twenty that I'd luckily left in my jean's pocket. "Thanks so much."

The older man looked up. "You should get that window fixed before winter sets in."

"I will. I just don't have the cash today. Can you guys haul away my trailer? If someone wants it, it's free."

"Free? Hell, yeah."

"I have to to warn you, it's been vandalized, and there's literally shit all over the inside."

He shook his head and pressed his lips together. "These young people—I don't know what in hell they're thinking."

"It wasn't young people who did it—it was my ex."

"You must have pissed him off pretty good." He stared at me. "Hey, ain't I seen you at the Bighorn? You're a dancer, right?"

"I used to be. I got fired."

"Fired for what? You was pretty good, as I recall."

"I got distracted—made too many mistakes."

"Sorry about that. Next town up has a decent bar. If yer lookin' for a job you should try there."

Cold wind blew my hair into a tangled mess as I drove out to Tim's. When I reached the gate he had just swung it open, his truck idling on the other side. "Where are you going?" I asked.

He stared at me, his eyes opaque. "I was coming to find you and then head to the police station. Jorge's dead."

I was stunned into silence for a long moment. "You...found him? What happened?"

"Scat found him—led me there. He was shot, Collie. Point blank in the chest."

"Oh my god."

"Pull the truck over and climb in. I'm not leaving you alone out here."

While I parked on the side he drove his truck through the open gate and got out again to close and lock it. I was in the passenger seat when he climbed behind the wheel. His face was dark with rage and pain, his lips pressed tightly together. He put the truck in gear and sped off.

"Do you think it was Dean?"

"Whoever it was needs to pay. Jorge didn't deserve this. I should be the one lying out there."

"I'm glad you're not," I said, putting my hand on his tense thigh. "Where was he?"

"Out behind the horse barn." He wiped his eyes. "Shit." He beat his fist on the steering wheel.

"Sandra did take up with Dean."

Tim turned. "Take up? What does that mean?"

"She's with him now. They're together. He told her his name is Toby."

"Goddamn it. It just keeps getting better."

Jack listened as Tim relayed details, jotting down notes as Tim went on. "It's a crime scene. I hope you didn't move him or disturb anything."

"I didn't touch him other than to make sure he wasn't breathing. He was ice cold."

Jack nodded, turning to speak to an officer behind him.

Tim gazed at me, his hand reaching for mine. "I'm not letting you out of my sight."

Jack was back, his hard gaze on the two of us. "We're heading out there now. Is the gate locked?"

Tim nodded, reaching into his pocket for the key.

"We'll need to see your weapons, Tim."

"So now I'm a suspect? Jorge was like a brother to me."

"It's just procedure. You'd best follow us out."

"But we have a lead on Dean. What's the best hotel in town? He's with my friend Sandra and they're staying there."

Jack turned to me. "Don't...do...anything," he said, each word enunciated. "This is a police matter now."

Like it wasn't before? Why did it always take a death to spur the police into action? When I glanced at Tim his expression had turned hard. His cheekbones jutted, his jaw was set and his eyes narrowed. Despite knowing him, I felt a shiver. He looked capable of just about anything.

It wasn't until we were in the truck again that I realized that today was Friday. My manuscript was officially due. And I still had at least a chapter to go.

27

The day dragged on, police cars arriving, an ambulance behind them. The coroner followed Jack around the barn, Tim with them. I went into the house and made coffee, vowing to finish my book no matter what was going on. An hour later two cops arrived with Tim and came inside to examine his guns. There were several.

"One's missing," Tim said after he'd handed over a hunting rifle, a shotgun and two handguns. He frowned, turning to search again.

"Which one's missing?" one of the cops asked.

"A pistol. A Walther PPK."

One of them wrote something down, turning to his partner. "Better get this info out to Jack," he muttered. They left.

Tim glanced at me and then away, his mouth set in a thin line. I put my hand on his arm. "They'll figure it out."

He shook his head, his eyes dark with worry. "I think Jorge was shot with a Walther."

"We weren't here, Tim."

"We don't know when it happened."

"When could he have stolen the gun? The house was locked, right?"

"The house wasn't locked. I never lock it. And I thought Jorge would stay here."

I was suddenly cold all over.

When Tim left the house I opened my computer and tried to focus. But all I could see was Dean sneering, a look of triumph on his face. And now he had Sandra in his clutches. I knew he was a creep, but was he capable of murdering a man to get back at me? I'd misjudged his actions before, trying to gloss over what he'd done to me over the years. I'd excused him over and over, blaming the abuse on alcohol. He was a selfish and cruel man who would stop at nothing to get back at me for leaving him.

After thinking about it for a while I was sure Dean had killed Jorge and set it up to implicate Tim. The only thing that would save Tim was the coroner's report. Unless they found out he was killed before we arrived home, or found some other evidence to link the murder to Dean, Tim would surely go to jail. My stomach clenched. I had to run to make it to the bathroom in time to throw up.

It was late afternoon before the ambulance drove through the gate with two cop cars following it out. Tim arrived at the house looking drawn and exhausted. "I have to go to the station."

"What did the coroner find?"

"Inconclusive. He wants to examine the body in the morgue."

"Are they arresting you?"

He pulled his fingers through his tangled hair. "Not yet."

"Don't say that. They'll discover the truth. What does Jack say?"

"Not much, except that Jorge was shot with my gun. They found it in one of the stalls."

My hand went to my mouth. I thought I might be sick again but the feeling subsided. "But they haven't matched the bullet yet. Right?"

He scoffed. "Only a matter of time." He glanced at Jack approaching the house. "I don't want you staying out here alone," he whispered.

"Should I follow you in?"

He nodded. "If they keep me you can get a room in town for the night."

"They can't keep you—they don't have enough evidence."

He shrugged and shook his head, turning to talk with Jack. I ran to get my computer and my backpack.

I waited at the station, attempting to work, while they questioned Tim. It was an hour and a half before he appeared again, the normally coppery skin of his face leached of color. He nodded to me and the two of us left the station. Once we were in his truck he put his hands over his face and began to sob. "They think I did it. They actually think I'd kill a man who's worked for me for nearly ten years. Jorge was my friend."

"What possible motivation would you have?"

"I asked them that. They didn't answer. The only reason I'm not in jail right now is because the coroner wants to do a more thorough examination."

"What can we do?"

He looked over at me, his expression bleak. "We go home and hope for a fucking miracle."

"You mean the truth?"

Tim tried to smile. "Why in hell would I kill my own sheep, slash my tractor tires and murder my hired help?"

"If it goes to trial that's what your lawyer will be asking."

He looked wild for a moment, his eyes widening. "Maybe we should get the hell out of here."

"And who will feed the sheep and the horses?"

He let out a heavy sigh and started the truck. "If you weren't here I'm not sure what I might do tonight."

"Drink too much?"

He glanced at me. "No, not drink too much. Find that piece of shit who set me up and…"

"And kill him? Not a good plan, Tim."

"And beat the crap out of him."

"That wouldn't look good either."

"That's what I'm saying." He pulled out of the lot and headed slowly down the road in the direction of the ranch.

It was deep in the night when I woke up and felt for Tim. His side of the bed was empty. I turned on the light and called out. There was no answer. After searching the house I put on my robe and checked outside for his truck. It wasn't there. He'd left me alone? He was so adamant about not doing that. He must have had a really good reason. Oh no. There was only one reason it could be. He was going after Dean. I grabbed my phone and called the police and asked for Jack. Luckily he was still on duty.

"I think Tim's about to do something stupid."

"Which is?"

"He's going after Dean. You have to know that Tim didn't kill Jorge. He…"

"Where is this Dean located?"

"You said you were putting out an APB. My friend mentioned the most expensive hotel in town."

"The Crown, then. And what does Dean look like?"

I described him again, adding a description of Sandra, and trying to keep from breaking down. "You have to hurry. I don't think Tim is capable of murder, but he could hurt Dean pretty badly. He's really pissed off."

"I know that from talking to him this afternoon. He doesn't think we're on his side, but he has a lot of friends on the force. He's always been a straight arrow."

"Dean set him up, but how do we prove it?"

"We examine the evidence with a fine tooth comb and we wait for the coroner's report. But at this moment I think I should take a little drive out to the Crown Hotel."

"Thanks, Jack. Dean is a…"

"I know. I saw what happened the last time he came to town."

The next few hours were hell as I paced up and down, my mind racing in circles as I conjured up horrible scenarios. Dean dead, Tim standing over him with a knife—Tim dead, Dean standing over him with a gun. Sandra dead or severely injured from interfering. I let out a scream of frustration. Seconds later my cell phone rang. "Thought you'd like to know that Dean's in custody," Jack said.

"What happened?"

"I'll let Tim tell you once he gets home."

I rang off and sat down heavily on the bed. The relief had drained me, turning me into mush. When I heard his truck a while later I rushed out in my robe, throwing myself into his arms as soon as he stepped out. He held me close for a long moment, his breath ragged. When he finally released me he looped an arm around my shoulders and walked us slowly back to the house.

It was nearly four a.m. when I made coffee, taking mugs into the living room where Tim lay half slumped on the couch. "So tell me what happened."

When he looked up I noticed some color had returned, and his eyes were tired but bright. "I taped him, Collie. I remembered I had this tiny tape recorder from years ago. I put it in my pocket and turned it on before I went to his room."

"How'd you know which one was his?"

"Asked the night manager."

"He didn't mind telling a crazed man who arrived in the middle of the night?"

He chuckled. "I told him Toby was my long lost dad."

"Your dad?" I realized suddenly that Dean was nearing fifty, old enough to fit the bill. "And then what?"

"I knocked on the door and when he opened it I punched him and barged inside. When he came after me, I sidestepped and he fell. Sandra was there cowering behind a chair. When he stood up she ran over to him, but he shoved her away and pulled a gun out of his robe pocket. He yelled something about me bullying him and taking what what was rightfully his. And then he admitted the entire thing."

Tim looked lost for a second, emotions racing across his features. "He bragged about Jorge, going into detail about how he set it all up, and the stupidity of the police. He laughed about how I didn't lock my doors—how trusting I was. He had the gun cocked and was about to shoot me when Jack and another cop slammed through the door."

"Where's the recording?"

"The police have it." He frowned, gazing at me. "Did you call them?"

I nodded, afraid he'd be angry about it, but instead he pulled me close. "You saved my life."

I was crying now, sobs of relief. "I hope they throw the book at him."

He held me and stroked my hair. "I have to go to the station in the morning and give a statement."

"Would you have killed him?"

"Not unless it was self defense."

28

*M*ay's former boyfriend found her at the bus station. He was winded, his face red from running. "Your parents' sent me," he gasped.

May turned to face him. "I'm not going back."

Jeremy watched her, a smile moving onto his face. "I hoped you'd say that."

She stared at him in surprise. "Since when do you stand up for me?"

"Since I realized what they're about. They want to keep you a child."

"No, Jeremy. They want me to be their slave."

"That too. Where are you headed?"

"I'm going back to New York. I'm auditioning for a dance part in a play."

"And you have enough money?"

May laughed. "Right now I do. I stole all the cash I could find."

"I'm coming along," Jeremy said, pulling out his wallet. "There's nothing for me here."

"This is my gig, Jeremy. We aren't an item anymore."

Jeremy watched her, a frown on his face. "I know that, but

I'd like to be. I should never have let you go the first time."

May shrugged. "Suit yourself, but my feelings for you disappeared a long time ago."

Jeremy grinned. "Feelings don't just disappear, May. You used to love me. Maybe we can resurrect what we had."

May waved her hand. "Go get a ticket," she told him. "But don't expect anything from me."

He smiled and took off for the ticket office.

May let out a long sigh. She did still care about him, but she couldn't see them together that way. She'd moved on in her life. But when he hurried toward her waving a ticket, she had to laugh. "Don't expect anything," she told him sternly. "I'm working, not fooling around with you."

He nodded and gestured toward the bus where people were lining up. She went ahead of him and didn't look back.

When Tim walked into the bedroom I stopped typing and closed the computer. "How'd it go?"

He smiled for the first time in days. "He's being held on murder charges. I'll be a witness when the time comes."

"Hope I can testify too."

"A wife can't testify against her husband."

"I hope to be divorced by then."

"Want to get married?"

I laughed. "No, Tim, I don't."

"What if you get pregnant?"

"Why would that matter? We don't need a piece of paper. And besides, I'm too old." He came close and pulled up my heavy hair, burying his face in my neck. Shivers went down my spine. "Do you want to celebrate?" I murmured.

"I would," he whispered. "But don't you have a book to finish?"

I pulled back to stare at him. I couldn't believe he'd just said that. "But..."

"Don't worry. I'm not going anywhere." He strolled out of the bedroom and I heard him whistling, the sound of drawers opening in the kitchen. I opened my computer and continued where I left off.

It was mid afternoon by the time I sent the manuscript off to Mountain Publishing. Thank goodness for email. Daniel McClure would have it today instead of sometime next week. The ending was a little forced, what with me hurrying to get May where she needed to be for the story to make sense. She'd fought me tooth and nail, the writing going in one direction while my mind pulled it in another. In the end we seemed to compromise. Her journey was only beginning—perhaps a sequel? I couldn't believe that thought had just crossed my mind.

I was staring out the window when Tim came into the bedroom with two flutes filled with bubbly golden liquid. "Champagne? I didn't know you drank champagne."

"I don't. It just seemed appropriate for today. A murder charge dropped, a book finished. The woman I love sleeping next to me at night." He handed me a glass.

"How'd you know I finished?"

"Your energy changed. I could feel it all the way into the kitchen."

"Come on, Tim. You can't feel my energy like that."

He shrugged and raised his eyebrows. "I was right, wasn't I? You sent it off?"

"I did." We clicked glasses and both took a sip.

It was after we'd eaten the meal he prepared that he asked me about the dancing. "Are you missing it? What are you thinking?"

"I miss it, but not in the same way. I have the sense that the dancing I did at Kuruk's funeral changed something; I don't feel the need to perform anymore. Why do you think that would be?"

"Maybe that's what he was trying to tell us. Didn't he say that when you danced at his funeral the truth would arrive?"

"I thought he meant between you and me."

Tim stared at me. Rays from the setting sun hit his glass, his dancing eyes reflecting it back. "This *is* between you and me."

I glanced out the open window to see the orange ball disappearing over a hill in the distance. A chill wind blew my hair back. I pulled it closed. "Can we have a fire tonight?"

"Don't change the subject."

I stared into my glass, hoping to find answers there. Maybe the bubbles would act like tea leaves and tell me my future. When I looked up again Tim was watching me. "Did I tell you why I've been so afraid to commit? Kuruk drew it out of me."

"No. When was that?"

"When you weren't speaking to me—the day he died."

"Go on."

"It was because of Dean. We had a horrible relationship— a horrible marriage. I didn't know it until that day, but I've been terrified it would happen again."

Tim frowned. "But I'm not Dean."

"Nope, you're not. And now that he's behind bars…" I glanced at him. "I feel like a weight has lifted. I can actually breathe now."

"I don't want to push you, Collie. I'm not asking for a lifetime commitment. We can take it day by day. I just want to know you're really with me—that I won't wake up tomorrow and find a note that says you decided to go dance in Timbuktu."

I laughed. "Maybe the need will come back—the need to be seen. Or maybe the writing will fill that place. But at the moment I'm content and everything feels right."

"We have dances out here—barn dances. They happen on the full moon."

I raised my eyebrows. "That sounds fun."

"A lot of good people around these parts—and good bands too."

"Your barn?"

"Mine and others. A bunch of us chip in to pay for the bands."

I nodded slowly, imagining it. "A place for me to release my pent-up urges?"

"As long as you don't take off your clothes."

"Ha ha. Very funny."

"Except when you're with me," he added, taking the glass out of my hand.

29

In mid October I found out about a dance studio in town that was up for sale. When I looked in the window at the pristine wood floor, mirrors with a ballet bar along the length of it, I wondered—could this solve my need to dance?

I met with the owner a few days later, surprised by Sylvia St. Clair's agility and muscle tone for a woman in her late sixties. She described the classes she taught, enumerating the benefits of having a studio like this.

"It gives you the freedom to pass along what you know."

"But I've never had any formal training. I taught myself. I was a stripper and then a pole dancer."

She looked me over. "Good muscle tone—a nice body. I can see it. What kind of dancing would you teach?"

"That's the question."

"So why does this intrigue you?"

I thought about that for several minutes. "I was addicted to performing—had to be in front of a crowd. And I love to dance. The addiction is gone now, but the dance part is still there. I miss it."

She nodded. "This could fill that niche for you. Do you have routines worked out?"

I laughed. "Routines I worked up for exotic dancing. But that won't work for this."

"Why not? All you have to do is tweak them a bit. Kids love routines, fancy footwork, twirling, doing the splits and all of that."

"Kids?"

"Well, yes. Most of my clients are between the ages of eight and twenty-five."

"I thought it would be older people—thirties?"

"You can shape it however you want. It's a blank canvas. All I'm saying is there are kids who like it here and enjoy the classes I teach."

"I'll need a couple of days to think about it. Will you let me know if anyone else is interested in buying the business? I'd hate to miss out."

Sylvia smiled. "Take as long as you need. I'm in the first stages of dissolving it—classes are still in session until November."

"What about the building? Do you own it?"

"Oh, no dear. I rent it from the company who owns this strip of stores. It's a pretty good deal. When you come back we can discuss the finances, okay?"

I drove my recently repaired truck back to the ranch, my mind on how I could make this all work out. I felt giddy with the possibilities.

⁓⁓⁓

"You want to buy a business?" Tim looked surprised.

"It could solve my need to dance, Tim. It could be the perfect solution."

Tim glanced out the window, watching the swirling leaves. Clouds were massing and it looked like a storm was coming in. "I know Sylvia's place. It's popular." He turned to me. "But it might not be with someone new running it."

"Are you trying to dissuade me?"

Tim shook his head. "Just playing devil's advocate. Do you want to be on a schedule?"

"I'm not sure yet—still mulling it over."

"It would take some discipline."

"I managed it when I worked. Don't you think I'm capable of it?"

Tim smiled. "I think you're capable of just about anything you put your mind to."

When I went back a week later Sylvia welcomed me inside. She had a sheaf of papers in her hand. "Ready to go over the financial part?"

"I think so." I glanced at the studio, visualizing myself in front of a group. "You know I just figured out that being a teacher is a little bit like performing."

"Of course it is—teachers are notoriously vain—didn't you know?" She let out a chuckle.

I laughed. "Is it vanity or something else? Maybe the need to be seen?"

Sylvia nodded. "Absolutely." She held out the papers. "If you want to go ahead I think we should nail a few things down."

"Would you be willing to teach for a while?" I asked, grabbing hold of the papers. "You could maybe come in once a week? I know nothing about ballet, or…"

"The little kids are the only ballet students I have. The older ones are more interested in jazz. I have a yoga teacher who rents the space on Tuesday and Thursday mornings for an hour. She pays me monthly."

I glanced at the spreadsheet on the top. "Do I need a lawyer?"

"You should have an accountant look it over, Collie. Just so you understand what you're getting into. As far as how you structure things here—make it your own. If you lose some students then so be it. The yoga can stay the same, which will bring money in until your new style takes off. I have a friend in marketing who can you help set things up—you'll need an ad campaign at the beginning."

I was suddenly overwhelmed, realizing what this venture would entail. She must have noticed my expression.

"If you like you can start a class before the business changes hands. That way you'll have some students on board once I leave."

"Really? You'd do that?"

"Of course. Have you done any teaching?"

"Just my friend Sandra who now works at Bighorn Bar."

"You'll do just fine. With the proper marketing you could draw in women who want to learn exotic dancing—it could be touted as an exercise class. Pole dancing has become very popular, you know."

I nodded, thinking about a few removable poles I could install. "That sounds perfect. I only saw your name on the door. Does the business have a name?"

"You didn't see it? It's on the building in gold letters."

I opened the door and gazed upward. **Dream Dancer**. I had a moment of shock as I registered how appropriate it was.

It was late October when I signed the contract and deposited the first down payment into Sylvia's account. By that time I'd begun my first class, advertising it as 'exotic dance exercise class'. I had ten students that first day, ranging from around twenty to fifty years old. I stood in front of them and demonstrated while Van Morrison's Wild Night blared from the speakers. After that I led them through each simple sequence. At the end they thanked me and told me how fun it was. The second week I had twenty women, even a few with gray hair.

Once I saw Sylvia again she praised me. "I think you're doing great. There's obviously a call for this kind of dancing here—people don't want to be bothered with serious stuff like ballet anymore. They want to have fun."

We shook hands. I was officially the proud owner of Dream Dancer Studio.

When I got to the ranch Tim was in the kitchen making a sandwich, his back to me.

"I did it."

He turned, his eyebrows rising. "You bought it?"

"I did."

He came toward me and pulled me into his arms. "Congratulations."

EPILOGUE

Winter arrived and snow pillowed over all the rough spots, leaving a pristine blue-white blanket. The trees shook their branches from time to time, getting rid of the heavier stuff. The horses stayed in the barn, many of the sheep too. They were due to lamb soon and Tim didn't want to take any chances. With the colder nights I'd coaxed Tim into letting Scat stay in the house. He now slept on our bed at night, and ate his meals in the kitchen. Tim scolded me from time to time, saying it wasn't good for a working dog to be so pampered, but I knew he enjoyed him as much as I did.

I gazed at my open computer, noting that I was more interested in my sequel than working on edits. May was moving on in her life just as I was. Through the foggy glass of the closed window I noticed snowflakes gathering on the sill. In the shadowy dusk they looked like the feathers of some exotic bird. It was growing dark. I thought of the fire we'd have later, picturing the two of us curled up on the couch together reading.

Dean was in jail and would be for many years. He'd been charged with first-degree murder. We were finally divorced. Mary had divorced Bill and was reaching out to me, even talking about coming for a visit. I was still skeptical, but willing to give her a chance. Sandra was my friend again and brought me news of Bighorn Bar—she even occasionally came to my classes. It seemed there was another guy on the horizon.

Tim was out every morning before dawn. He'd found another man to replace Jorge, but he still missed his friend. We shared the cooking and took walks together when the sun came out. We no longer had the dreams, our full life together replacing the need to meet in some other reality.

I glanced down at the bump of my belly, moving my hands to cup my growing girth. I couldn't believe it, hadn't believed it until Tim mentioned the obvious changes. He was sure I conceived the first magical night I spent here, saying he knew the moment it happened. I was pretty sure he was right, considering the date I got when I went to the doctor. I remembered I'd run out of pills that night, telling myself that the protection would be in place until I could order more. Normally it took months, sometimes even years, for fertility to come back after being on the pill—but not for us. I figured with Kuruk's vision this one was destined to be here.

We'd already picked out names: Adain, if a girl, and if a boy he would be Kuruk, after the man who'd seen our future. I thought of him often, wondering if he watched over us.

My book would be published in April, around the same time as the birth. That is if I finished the edits they'd asked for and got it back to them. I'd gone with Mountain Publishing partly because of Karen, and partly because Putney Publishing hadn't offered me money up front. The edits were already paid for, and although the advance wasn't much, it was enough to give Sylvia as a down payment for the studio.

Tim was very protective, cautioning when I spent too many hours in front of my computer, and herding me outside at night to look at the sky. It was immense, the stars so close I felt like I could reach out and touch them. We wrapped up in blankets and sat together on the porch while he pointed out constellations, his explanations bringing them to life.

I rarely worried anymore, chalking it up to the hormones coursing through my body, but occasionally some horrible memory from my past would rear up, stripping away my peace. Tim always knew, saying that my energy had shifted. And just the knowledge that he was witness to it would send it scurrying back into the shadows where it belonged. If I needed more he was always there for me, his soft words calming my racing heart.

The studio was well attended, the word spreading. Some days Tim came by to watch me teach, occasionally joining in. I laughed when I saw him trying to bend and twist his inflexible body, attempting to follow along. I had the sense he wanted to keep an eye on me—afraid I might overdo it. I'd finally realized that dancing was a way for me to release the pain of the past. It was why I hadn't been able to give it up. When I danced in bars it was because I needed to be seen, to feel that I had control over the men watching me. It was a way to be validated. Now I only wanted to feel my body moving, any bad memories shaken out of me as I twirled and spun. I was no longer unlovable.

Sandra subbed for me when I couldn't make it in, assuring me she'd be there when I got too fat to do the moves. She even promised to fill in the gaps for the month or so I'd need after the birth. I fully intended to go back as soon as possible, already visualizing my baby sleeping in a basket while I directed the class.

Instead of needing to give up my dreams, I had all of them—the man I loved, a beautiful place to live, my writing *and* my dancing. And now a baby—a miracle I'd never expected could happen at my age. I was still in awe over it.

"Hey—you all right in there?"

I turned from the desk I'd set up in the bedroom to see Tim standing in the doorway. When Scat streaked by him and leapt on the bed I could see Tim struggling with whether to tell him to get off. The sky was dark now, the view from the window obscured.

I closed my computer and pushed myself up to standing. When I glanced at Tim he was smiling, as though he could read my mind. I smiled back at him. "I'm absolutely perfect."

To date Nikki has written 21 books, with several more in the pipeline.

To see her other books or sign up for her newsletter, visit
https://www.nikkibroadwellauthor.com/

And if you liked this book please leave a review!